D0344465

BREAKUP FROM HELL

BREAKUP FROM HELL

ANN DÁVILA CARDINAL

HARPER TEEN
An Imprint of HarperCollinsPublishers

HarperTeen is an imprint of HarperCollins Publishers.

Breakup from Hell
Copyright © 2023 by HarperCollins Publishers
All rights reserved. Printed in the United States of America.
No part of this book may be used or reproduced in any manner
whatsoever without written permission except in the case of brief quotations
embodied in critical articles and reviews. For information address
HarperCollins Children's Books, a division of HarperCollins Publishers,
195 Broadway, New York, NY 10007.
www.epicreads.com
Library of Congress Control Number: 2022946654
ISBN 978-0-06-304530-9
Typography by Jessie Gang
22 23 24 25 26 LBC 5 4 3 2 1

First Edition

For all my Michaelite sisters,
Saint Michael Academy, NYC, 1874–2010.
Our school might be gone, but we will never forget.
In holiness & justice.

I

In the beginning . . .

I'm going to crawl out of my skin. I glance over the sea of people in the pews around me, the face of each resident of my small, insignificant town so familiar they're like visual white noise. And the priest is droning on as usual in his monotone voice.

"You see, each day the Lord provides us with fresh powder. It is up to each of us to carve our own way down the mountain of life. Whether we choose a path through the twisting woods, or the security and predictability of the groomed trails—"

No.

Not a skiing parable. I just can't.

I start to rise, ready to quietly excuse myself, when I feel familiar, pincerlike fingers wrap around my arm.

My abuela hisses at me from beneath her black lace veil. "Miguela, where are you going?"

"I . . . just need some air," I whisper back.

Why can't I lie and say something more persuasive? Like, I need to go to the bathroom, or it's that time of the month, or I'm about to have a psychotic episode? My friend Barry finds it amusing that I am incapable of lying, particularly when my grandmother is giving me the searing look of death.

"I'll be right back, Abuela. Te lo prometo."

The Spanish does it. She releases me, and I scurry off as the adults on either side of the aisle flash disapproving looks my way.

When I get to the lobby, I step to the left, just out of view, and take a deep breath. The November day is unseasonably warm, so all the doors are open. I can see the last of the autumn leaves clinging to the bare branches of the small tree out front as if they're afraid to let go.

Relief floods my body in a wave. It's not that I don't have faith. It's just sometimes in our church and community, it feels like everyone is staring at me with all this . . . expectation; it feels oppressive. I pull my book from the backpack I stashed under the wooden bench and settle into the corner. Just a few pages, maybe a chapter or two; then I'll go back and sit next to my grandmother like a good girl.

I open the book and smile at my bookmark: my acceptance letter from UCLA. My grandmother is dead set on me going to Saint Michael's College here in Vermont, so I applied to my dream school in secret. I'll tell her about it soon, but for now I know it's safe tucked in my horror novel since there's no way in hell she'd look in there.

My phone buzzes with a message. The group text among me and my crew of three friends is so active we gave it its own name: "The Host."

Rage: Where'd you run off to?

Barry: Who cares? Run, Mica! Run away!

I smile, and type Shhh! I'm reading.

Rage: But you missed the second half of the parable!

Me: It's ok, I'm pretty sure Jesus didn't ski.

I run my hands over the book's pristine cover, feeling the glossy, embossed skull at the center, the black and red metallic ink glistening in the sunlight. Dante Vulgate. When a new book of his comes out, it's like Christmas, no matter the month. I open the pages to my bookmark, the new spine crackling like logs in a fireplace, and start where I left off at breakfast. I'm just getting into it, losing myself in the story, when a shadow moves into the doorway and blocks my light.

Someone is looking at me: I feel it on the top of my scalp, hot like the midsummer sun. I run my fingers through my hair as if I can brush the feeling away like a cobweb. I raise my head to see where it's coming from, and maybe give the light blocker a dirty look.

Standing in the doorway, silhouetted by the morning light behind, and lit golden by the gentle glow from the church, is a guy peering in from the threshold.

Christ on a whole wheat cracker, who the hell *is* that?

He's around my age, with a wave of jet-black hair framing his pale face, and eyelashes so dark they look like pirate guyliner. And he's wearing a suit! No one in Vermont wears a suit, like, ever. It makes him look sophisticated . . . worldly. Yeah, he's definitely not from around here.

Oh God, I'm staring. I look down at the book in my lap. But it's like a magnet is pulling my eyes up again, and I fight it as long as I can. When I can't resist any longer and glance back, I find he's staring at me.

Not just at me, into me.

And then the heat is not just on the top of my head; it's starting from my chest and spreading outward. You know in movies when the two lead characters' eyes meet and time slows around them while some cheesy-ass ballad swells up? It's like that, but instead of guitars there's only the distant drone of the priest and Johnny Pearson's perpetual snorting of snot from his usual spot in the back row. I'm having trouble remembering how to breathe, and my heart is slamming on the inside of my ribs—

Something grabs my upper arm, and I flinch.

"Miguela, what are you doing? Come back into the church this instant," my grandmother whispers in forceful Spanish beside me, pulling me to my feet with her bony fingers.

"God, Abuela, you scared me."

"We talked about you throwing the Lord's name around like it has no meaning." She notices the book in my hands. "¡Fo! I should have known. They should burn all that man's books. Now put it away and come inside." Then she peers toward the outside door. "And what were you looking at?"

The guy!

I look up, but he's gone. The huge doorway framing the pictur-esque Vermont morning in all its emptiness.

Damn.

After Mass, the congregation gathers on the grass in front of the church. My grandmother is talking to the neighbors about cas-seroles, the unusually warm weather, and other mind-numbingly dull things, when someone grabs me around the neck.

I'm about to flip whoever it is—can't deny my martial arts training—when I see Raguel's face grinning at me over my shoul-der, a wavy tumble of orange hair covering one of his blue eyes. He goes by Rage, which is ironic since he's the most diplomatic, friendly person I know.

"You're lucky I didn't flip you right here on the church lawn," I say calmly.

He puts his arm around my shoulders and winks. "Yeah, but we both know you wouldn't, even though you could."

"Gee, thanks, Sensei. Where's Barry?"

As if in answer, an off-key electronic version of—is that "Red Solo Cup"?—echoes down the street. Everyone turns as the larg-est, most ridiculous truck I've ever seen pulls up right in front of the church lawn. It's pearl white with mirror-shiny aluminum trim, and tires that look taller than I am. It has a flashing red light on top and way more racks on the roof than any one person would ever need. As we're gaping at it, the tinted driver's-side window rolls down and I see Barry's face, lit up with pride.

"That boy, he is always so subtle," I hear my grandmother say as she looks out over my shoulder.

"Yeah, Barry sure likes to make an entrance," Rage says, smiling. He and I walk to the truck.

"Barry!" I yell over the loud revving engine. "What's with the rig?"

He smiles. "Like her? She's new! I call her Pegasus." He pats the dashboard as if it were a dog.

I laugh. "Didn't picture you as the mythical creature type."

"Who doesn't like winged horses? Besides, I'm friends with you, aren't I?" He gives me a wink.

I have to say, the scale of Barry in the new truck is just right. He grew up on the farm and looks it. Forearms like tree trunks and a tan that ends where his T-shirt sleeves do, but with a smile like a five-year-old boy who just stole your last cookie. Rage looks lean and stylish in his Sunday best, but Barry? With his rolled-up sleeves and wrinkled tie, he looks . . . miscast dressed for church. I point behind the seats to Barry's mobile armory. "I see the gun rack has grown too. You expecting trouble after Mass?"

"No, but it *is* hunting season, missy! C'mon, Rage, the heathen's already got us a table."

I roll my eyes. "You know Zee hates when you call her that."

"Well, do you see her here on Sundays suffering through that Mass with the rest of us?"

Rage climbs into the passenger seat and looks back at me. "You coming with? McCarthy's? Red-white-and-blue pancakes?"

I kind of salivate at the thought. "I can't. I have to work."

My grandmother with her super-sharp old-lady hearing comes striding over to the truck. "You're not working on the Lord's Day again, are you, Miguela?"

Isn't it enough that I dress in these ridiculously girly clothes and sit in that airless church for an hour every week? Besides, what does she know about working? The woman volunteers all over town, but the humiliation of slaving for minimum wage? She knows nothing about it. I love my grandmother, but there's only so much I can bear. "Yes, Abuela. They need me."

She looks at me through narrowed eyes. "Even the Lord rested on the seventh day, m'ija."

Well then, he shouldn't have given Sarah the stomach flu. Good thing I didn't say that out loud, because that would bring a shit storm that no umbrella could save me from. "Sarah's sick, and I have to cover for her."

"Oh. Well, then that is the Christian thing to do." At that, she brushes the hair out of my face with brusque fingers.

Abuela approves of something I'm doing? That's like seeing a unicorn gallop down Main Street. Thankfully, she walks away and back to her gaggle of grown-ups.

"Did you start your paper on the Reformation?" Rage asks, leaning out the truck window.

I glare at him. "Wow. Not yet, *Dad*. Besides, it's still the weekend. Don't remind me about school."

Rage smiles that one-sided grin of his. "Oh, right, you don't really need to keep your grades up. Some of us didn't get early admission into our dream school!" His tone is kind of snippy. Rage has been weird around me since I got the acceptance letter from UCLA.

"Shh!" I hiss, and look back at my grandmother to make sure she—or anyone else, for that matter—didn't hear. In a small town, secrets rarely stay secret.

Then Rage reaches out the window and yanks the book from my backpack like we're still six. "Maybe you'd have it done if you didn't spend all your time reading this dark-ass shit," he says as he fans through the pages of the Vulgate novel.

I can already see the dust jacket curling and creasing in his hands. I yank it back and punch him on the arm, hard.

Barry leans over and asks, "You coming to the fair tonight, M?"

"No, I'm afraid my social calendar is too full."

Barry snorts. "Sure, it is. We'll pick you up at seven."

"In this monster? No way. If I go, I'll ride with Zee." I'm not going to go, but if I say that outright, I'll just get shit for it.

Barry shrugs, looking slightly hurt that I called his new truck a monster. "Suit yourself."

I give Rage a fist bump, wave goodbye to my grandmother, and walk off in the direction of the bookstore. The day is sunny and warm, but I can also sense a slight chill waiting for nightfall. I love early November in Vermont. The hordes of leaf-peeping tourists have petered out, and it's too early for skiers. Before I've gone a block, I've said hello to half a dozen people. Everyone knows everyone else in Stowe. If you hear a siren during the day, by six o'clock you know what the emergency was and where.

It's busy at the bookstore when I arrive. There are lots of locals looking for reading material to hunker down with before the snow starts to fall. I'm grateful when the late-afternoon lull hits so I can straighten up the store. I like putting books back into their rightful places, all clean and neat. I prefer it to dealing with actual people. So why do I work in a store where my entire job is literally customer service? Two words: Staff. Discount.

I'm reorganizing the biography section: some entitled rich white dude from Connecticut wreaked havoc on it earlier while trying to find a book about another entitled rich white dude.

As I turn toward the next bookcase, I jump a bit to see someone standing in front of the fantasy-and-horror section. I could have sworn I was the only one in the store. Then I look closer.

Oh. My. God.

The hot guy from church!

He's changed into dark jeans, crisp and fitted, and a light sweater that hugs his chest and shoulders. His hair is more tousled, like he runs his hand through it often, and he's wearing Australian Blundstone boots.

I love guys in Blunnies.

I have to talk to him, but how? I'm not the smoothest rock in the river. Not to mention that I've had a grand total of three boyfriends, and I'd known them all my life, no introductions needed.

I pretend to see something that needs sorting in the history section right next to him, and though I keep looking at the shelves, I can feel the heat of his gaze again, almost immediately.

"Excuse me, do you work here?"

Oh shit. He's speaking to me. My stomach starts to flutter. I turn around slowly, clutching a copy of *Vermont: A Haunted History* to my chest as if it were armor. "Yes?"

It comes out like a question, as if I'm asking *him* if I work here. But then I look at him and forget every stupid thing I've ever said.

His eyes are huge, and up close the brown seems to swirl as if just stirred. And his skin, it's so perfect, it damn near glows. He is literally the best-looking human I've ever seen in real life, and in that moment, I have no idea what to do with my hands, how to stand, how to even breathe, so I just rock back and forth a bit. Suddenly a cold shiver of fear runs down my spine; then it slowly changes to warmth, like a dry branch that catches a flame.

"Do you guys have the latest Dante Vulgate novel, *The Last Descent*?"

The horror geek in me brightens. "I just started it! Vulgate's my favorite author."

He smiles. "I love everything he writes. But I'd have to say my favorite is *The Mortal Comedy*."

"Mine too! I even sent him an email once telling him how much I related to the Maria character in that book. He never wrote back." I shrug casually, though my fangirl heart was crushed at the time. "Do you follow the listserv?"

"I checked it out once or twice. Too many trolls on there for me."

I nod. "True that."

He's still smiling at me. Why?

"So . . . do you have the book?"

"Oh! Right!" My face heats up. "Sorry, but we sold out the same day they came in. It's on order, though."

Truthfully, the one I was reading in church was the last copy, but damned if I'm going to tell him that. Don't care how hot he is, I've been waiting for that book for a year, and I'm only a quarter of the way through. "Should be getting more in next week, if you're still going to be in town?" Subtle, Mica, subtle.

"Damn. I was hoping to start it tonight. I only brought three books, and I've already finished them."

I laugh. "I have to bring about six books for each week when I'm on vacation."

He raises his hand. "Same here. My friends never understand why I don't just read e-books and then I'd never run out."

"Ugh! E-books are just—"

"Not the same," we say in unison, and then smile at each other.

He keeps looking into my eyes, and my palms are sweating all over the book in my hands. I discreetly wipe it on my shirt and shelve it with a neat *thunk*. Then I just stare at the spine.

"Did I see you at the church this morning?" I blurt.

"Yes. And I saw you." That smile. It's just a small lift on either side of his full lips, but these dimples appear that make my heart beat faster.

"I haven't seen you around."

"I'm renting a house up on Cottage Club Road for a couple weeks. I'm here on vacation—"

"Oh . . ." I sound disappointed. Do I sound disappointed? God. I'm humiliating myself. Luckily, he doesn't seem to notice.

"I've seen that church in all the pictures of Stowe, and I just wondered what it looked like inside. My family isn't exactly the churchgoing type."

I laugh. "You're lucky. I get dragged there by my abuela every Sunday."

He cocks his head a bit to the side like a bird. A very handsome bird. "'Abuela'?"

"Sorry, it's Spanish for 'grandmother': I was born in Puerto Rico."

"And you moved to Vermont? Bit of a change in climate, huh?"

"I know. I can't figure out why my grandmother would want to leave the island to come to this freezing place."

"Did you move here because of your parents?"

"No. My mom's dead, and I didn't know my father." Well, it's the truth, but there's nothing like dragging down a gorgeous stranger with your sad orphan story. I really need to work on my flirting technique.

"I'm sorry."

And he looks it. Sorry, I mean. His face softens, and his eyes look glassy. Then all I want to do is cheer him up. An idea pops into my head, and I walk across the store and behind the register. "You can borrow my copy of the book." Not sure where that came from, but it works: he's smiling again. I reach down beneath the counter where I'd tucked my backpack and hear him step up to the other side.

"Look, that's really nice of you, but I can't take your personal copy."

He's leaning over the worn wood counter, and as I straighten up, we're face-to-face. Close. Like, noses-almost-touching close. I breathe deep and take in his warm smell of coffee, sandalwood, and something underneath . . . like the smell right after you light a match. I've always loved that smell.

"No, I want you to, really." And I mean it, though I never loan out my books. Ever.

He looks down at the proffered hardcover and grins as he takes it from me. "Okay, then. But I'm only doing this because it means I get to see you again when I bring it back."

What do you say to a comment like that? "Thanks"? "You betcha"? "Marry me"? Instead, I ask, "What's your name?"

"Sam."

"Sam . . ." I repeat it like it's a sacred word. "Nice to meet you, Sam." Everything around us is out of focus; the sounds, the kids yelling as they walk by out front, the traffic, everything. It's just me and Sam . . .

He keeps smiling. What's he waiting for?

Oh! He wants my name. Duh. "I'm Mica."

"Like the mineral?"

"No, it's short for Michaela, or actually Miguela, in—"

"In Spanish." He finishes with a nod. "Nice to meet you too, Mica."

Then he shakes my hand, his skin surprisingly soft. He holds on for just a second longer than I expect, all the while looking in my eyes. After letting go, he turns around and walks toward the exit. I shiver, like he's pulling that warm out-of-control feeling along after him.

I stare at his back as he glides out the front door and onto the street, my book tucked carefully under his arm.

Lord, how I envy that book.

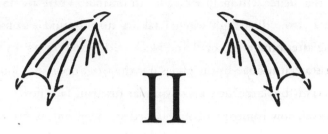

II

His face was like the sun shining in all its brilliance.
—Revelation 1:16

After work, I change into sweats and head out for a long run. Since it's part of my tae kwon do training, Abuela doesn't give me a hard time about going out alone. Rage used to run with me but never wanted to go as far as I did. The last time we went together, he was holding his side and bent over at the waist. "I think you'd go all the way to Los Angeles if you were given the room to run."

He's probably right. But it's been the weirdest Sunday ever, and it's the best way to clear my head.

Living right in town has its challenges, but our little one-story bungalow is running distance from two trails, and for that I'm grateful. I head across Main and down to the quiet path that follows the river.

I love the feeling of the dirt trail under my pounding sneakers, the clean smell of the long red pine needles that carpet the ground.

And the silence. I'm mainly here for the silence. There are no dog walkers around, though when I take a turn around a copse of trees, I see something small and black with stand-up pointy ears scuttle away into the brush.

I can't help but think about Sam at first, his face hovering in my mind like someone photoshopped it there, but as my muscles warm, I focus on the movement of my limbs and the rhythm of my breathing. By the time I get back home and jump in the shower, he's fading into the background. After dinner, I'm lying on my bed reading another book when I hear voices in the living room, the cooing sounds of my grandmother fussing over someone. Curious, I open my bedroom door and see Abuela forcing cookies on Zee.

"Miguela, lovely Zerachiel here has come to give you a ride to the fair, isn't that thoughtful of her?" The woman is positively beaming. She's always adored Zee. From her long blond hair to her flouncy "feminine" skirts, not to mention her sweet nature, I think my grandmother loves our friendship 'cause she's hoping she'll rub off on me.

I drop next to Zee on the couch. "It would be if I hadn't texted her that I wasn't going ten times already," I say with a groan.

"But then you turned off your phone and I thought you changed your mind!" Zee bats her eyelashes at me with that little lie.

I notice the golden salt-shaped crystals dangling from her ears, and I reach up and feel their rocky surface. "You've been wearing these a lot lately. What does this rock do?"

"They're citrine. It brings joy and enthusiasm."

"It isn't working on me," I whisper.

She ignores me. "I mean, as I was just telling your grandmother, the Autumn Fair is *such* a celebration of Vermont, I just couldn't let you miss it."

Abuela turns to me. "That is true, Miguela. Such a beautiful place we live. You should go, amor." This from the woman who never lets me go out at night when I actually *want* to.

Zee is beaming at me, and for just a second, I consider shoving her off the couch. I wouldn't really do it. Probably not, anyway, but she's been on this "don't you just love Vermont?" campaign since I told her I got into UCLA. I better just go along before she says something that gets Abuela curious. I roll my eyes and get up from the couch. "Fine. But I'm not staying long." I grab my hoodie and phone from my room.

Abuela comes over with a brush—does she have them stashed all over the house so she can torture me? "Home by nine thirty. It is a school night, niñas." She finishes dragging the brush through the front of my hair (doing the whole head would involve an hour and an act of God) and zippers up my hoodie, though it's almost sixty outside. (Which is mighty weird when you think about it.)

My grandmother walks us to the door, plants kisses on both our cheeks, and waves with a "Have fun, you two!"

It's a conspiracy, I swear. The minute we're out of hearing distance, I hiss, "That was totally not playing fair, Zee!" She puts her arm around my neck and pulls me closer with a huge grin. I catch her crisp scent of lemongrass and orange and immediately feel my heart rate slow. Don't know if it's her essential oils or just her manner, but the girl is emotional Xanax.

"Don't be mad, Mica. It's not healthy to lock yourself in your room and read about zombies all the time."

I open the passenger door. "I don't read about zombies! That's so 2019."

She gets behind the wheel and starts the car. "I remember you were into that *Running Dead* show—"

"*Walking Dead*!" I yell, but she's smiling. "You're just mocking me now."

"Whatever. Before you run off and abandon us, I just want you to consider what you're leaving behind."

"I know what I'm leaving behind, Zee, and I'll miss you all, but I need something different for a change, to see somewhere new. I feel . . . stifled here, like I can't really move or spread my wings."

She raises her eyebrows. "Wings? You have wings and you never told me?"

I ignore her. "Besides, I went with you to Oktoberfest, and apple picking"—I'm counting on my fingers now—"*and* the corn maze. We're acting like freaking tourists."

We pull into the fair parking lot, and when she shuts off the engine, she turns to me. "Look, Mica. I'm sorry if I'm coming on too strong. I just . . . don't want you to go."

Okay, she looks so damn sincere that I feel bad. "I know, Zee, but I just wish you could be more supportive of what *I* want to do."

She sighs. "You're right. I'll try. If *you'll* try to have some fun tonight."

I groan. "No promises." I have to slam the door to get it to close. Zee's parents offered to buy her whatever car she wanted, and she chose to get a twenty-year-old crappy station wagon with her own money. I love that about her.

As we walk through the gate, someone jumps me from behind. I whip around, ready to fight—I'm always ready to fight—until I realize it's just Barry.

"Jesus, B! Why do you guys feel the need to freak me out all the time?"

"We like to keep you on your toes." He musses my hair. "I see your grandmother attacked you with a brush, again."

Rage appears between me and Zee and puts an arm around both of us. "So, Mica. Zee make you an offer you couldn't refuse to get you here?"

"Yeah, she showed up at my house and enlisted Abuela."

Barry hisses through his teeth. "Ooh! She's playing hardball now."

And Zee gives me that smile. "Anything for our Mica." To the rest of the world, she looks so gentle, her face porcelain and heart-shaped, her blue eyes huge and full of wonder, but then you walk away and realize she's convinced you to do the very thing you didn't want to do.

As we walk, we get pulled into the sea of people moving between the white tents, and though I'd rather be home, I start to breathe easier, enjoying the thrum of music, carnival games, and voices. We pass by a group of girls from the public high school, and I see several of them checking out Rage as we walk by. He looks good tonight in his dark green sweater and Carhartt jeans. Of course, he's oblivious to the attention. Always has been.

"Ooh! Candy apples!" Zee squeals, skipping over to a booth with garlands of pink and blue cotton candy and fire-engine-red sugar-glazed apples. She's a vegan, only eats food that's locally sourced and ethically farmed, but girlfriend has a sweet tooth when it comes to fair time. She's already taking a big crunchy bite as she walks back to rejoin us.

Rage and Barry get distracted by a ridiculous strongman sledgehammer game, boasting that they're each going to win, while Zee looks through a rack of dangly earrings, and I'm left standing there, watching them.

Classic.

I'm considering sneaking away and walking home when I hear a voice right next to me.

"There you are."

I start a bit. I swear no one was nearby. But I look over to see Sam standing right next to me.

"I've been looking all over for you."

I resist the urge to look to see if he's talking to someone behind me. "You were? Wait . . ." I grin at him. "Are you following me?" Part of me is horrified at the idea; the other part is kind of hoping he was.

"Nope, I was just hoping to run into you since this appears to be the happening place to be."

I'm suddenly conscious of my oversized *Pet Sematary* T-shirt and third-day jeans, and for the first time in, well, forever, I wish I'd put some effort into my look.

"Want to walk for a bit?" He gestures off into the empty field where the fireworks are going to be.

I start to nod, then remember my friends. I turn around to see Barry and Rage have moved on to another carny game, and when I look over at Zee, she's grinning and making this "go on" gesture with the hand not holding the candy apple.

I turn back to Sam, shrug, and say, "Sure," as if this were something all the hot guys ask me to do.

Sam flashes that big, glorious smile and offers me his arm, and I take it. I look at him out of the corner of my eye as we walk, and everything and everyone around us begins to fade into a faint blur.

We head toward the paved recreation path that runs alongside the field. The warmth of his body makes me feel like I'm standing near a campfire.

Sam gestures back toward the festivities. "So, this is fun. Are there fairs like this every weekend here?"

"Nah, just this one. And Fourth of July. Wait, Antique Car Show Weekend. The British Invasion. Oh! Oktoberfest!"

He smiles. "In other words, every weekend."

I laugh. "I guess so. Never thought of it that way. It's just a bit . . . quaint for my taste."

"Well, it is. But this is Vermont, right? Isn't it the capital of quaint?"

"Yes, but it's so Norman Rockwell, postcardish." He's looking at me like these are all good things. I sigh. "It's boring, okay? I wouldn't mind going somewhere more exciting for a change." I picture the palm-tree-lined streets of LA when I say this.

"Yeah, 'exciting' places are not as much fun as they sound." He looks up at the stars overhead and sighs. "Staying put is under-rated."

As we walk, the sun does its final settling beyond the mountains, and even though I can't wait to leave for college, I see Stowe through Sam's eyes and can appreciate the natural beauty of the place. The farther we get from the fair, the quieter it becomes, and I hear the far-off honking of a flock of geese overhead heading south. It's one of my favorite sounds, because—

"Does anything say fall more than that sound?" Sam says in a whisper.

I look over at him in the darkening field; he's lit from the side by the lights strung from pole to pole for the fair, and I admire how it accentuates his strong jaw, the deep set of his eyes. His face isn't perfect; there's a bend in his nose as if it's been broken in the past and there's a slash across his eyebrow on one side, but the flaws only make him hotter. Also somehow . . . familiar. I just met him, but I feel like I've always known him.

A flood of texts come in from the Host, Rage wanting to know where I went, Barry asking who the guy is, and Zee telling them to leave me alone. I ignore them and put the phone back in my pocket.

Sam's about to say something when shouts rise from behind us. We look over and see two women running across the empty part of the field, screaming. Wait, I know them from church—Sandra and Elaine. I look in the direction they're heading. The fireworks are being set up on the other side of the bright orange event fencing. I see a low hole in the plastic fence material and then spot their toddlers slipping through the torn edges to the other side of the fence, heading toward the line of fireworks.

Jesus.

"The operator will see them, won't he?" I say to Sam.

"I'm not so sure." Then he looks over at me with a glint in his eye. "Let's go."

We start running, and as we get closer, I see a tall man behind the large wooden crates, massive sound-canceling headphones snug on his head.

"He's not going to be able to hear them yelling," Sam says.

Shit! We're all yelling now, trying to get the kids' attention over the blasting music coming to a crescendo as an intro for the fireworks.

I speed up; maybe I can get there before the mothers, and I see Sam's right at my side. I go full out, the grass whooshing underneath my sneakers, and Sam's keeping up with me. My body is moving faster than I ever thought it could. As we approach the fence, I look at the hole the kids went through.

"No way we're going to make it through that!" I yell.

"We're going to have to jump it!" Sam shouts over, and smiles at me.

Jump? I'm about to point out that the fence is over five feet tall, when he speeds up, lifts his legs, and leaves the ground, bounding over.

What?!

But as the fence is coming closer, my body doesn't slow down either. I pull my legs up and sail over the fence, landing on the other side with a clean thump right next to Sam. My heart is bashing on the inside of my chest. I don't know how I did that, but it sure was a rush.

The kids are almost to the fireworks, and I see the operator, his hands poised to flip the line of switches one by one and let loose the first series of pyrotechnics. The kids are just arriving at the boxes, their hands reaching up to the top of the wooden stands that hold the explosives.

The two mothers get to the fence, a crowd of people following behind. The screaming rises to a fevered pitch, while in a flash, Sam grabs the girl and hands her to me, and tucks the boy under his arm.

We run back, leaping the fence once more, but this time with kids in our arms just as the fireworks begin behind us, lighting up the people on the other side. We land on our feet, and as we place the two children on the ground, a swell of cheers rises around us.

Sandra gets there first and gathers the girl into her arms. She looks up at me, eyes wide. "Thank you, Mica. But . . . I don't understand how you did that."

I have no idea how I did that either. It was as if there were an electrical source in the center of my body that had never been switched on before, and when it was rushing through my veins, I felt I could do anything. I'm smiling at Sandra when I notice her pulling her daughter away, just a little. Did I see fear as she looked at me?

Sam hands the boy over to his mother, who is outright sobbing and just saying "God bless you" over and over as she clasps the toddler to her chest.

I look around and see that everyone is gaping at us and not the fireworks, and a chorus of whispers comes into focus. I start to feel like my skin is too tight for my body. I grab Sam's hand and pull him along until we break free of the crowd. Once I'm sure no one can hear, I whisper, "What just happened?"

He laughs. "We saved those two kids, or did you miss that part?"

"No." I stop and turn to face him. "I mean, I've never run that fast or jumped that high before. It was really weird and kind of scary, but it also felt . . . amazing! Like I could do anything."

He flashes *the* smile. "I have a feeling, Miguela, that's only the beginning of what we could do together."

III

He must remain for only a little while.
—Revelation 17:10

Standing next to Sam, that feeling, whatever that was when we ran and jumped the fence, lingers in my body, and I want it to last forever. It's so fitting that the fireworks are going off above us, mirroring the explosive energy running through my veins. I know I should absolutely be freaked out—it was beyond bizarre—but I'm just too damn . . . happy. I don't even care that people in the now-large crowd are still staring at us from across the field, whispering behind their hands.

Sam looks over at them too, and I hear him grumble "Shit" between a volley of red chrysanthemum bursts in the sky.

"What's wrong?"

"I promised my father I'd keep a low profile. Only in town twenty-four hours and it seems I've already blown that." He rubs the back of his neck.

"Are you some kind of celebrity?"

He laughs. "No."

We stand and watch the fireworks for a bit, and I focus on the warmth of his arm against mine, his spicy, clean scent. Did he even sweat after all the acrobatics we just did? I'm looking up, but I don't think I see any of the show as the volume increases for the finale. The electrical sensation in my body is slowly fading, but being with Sam is its own high.

I notice my friends standing off to the side, under the string lights. Their faces tilted up, the fireworks lighting them green and blue.

"Hey, wanna meet my friends?" I ask Sam.

He looks over to where I'm pointing, then actually pulls at the neck of his sweater as if he's nervous. "Sure."

We start walking over, and I realize I'm still holding his hand. I consider dropping it, knowing the buzz it will cause, but then we're standing in front of them and it's too late and I don't care. Zee looks at us with a smile that threatens to split her face, Barry like we're a science experiment he's puzzling out (if he actually paid attention in science), and Rage is . . . kind of glaring, actually. I clear my throat. "Sam, this is Barry, Zee, and Rage."

Sam gives a small wave. "Nice to meet you."

Barry steps forward while staring him in the eye. "Sup, dude?"

Zee skips over and gives Sam a hug. "We heard what you guys did, and it's so amazing! You were, like, superheroes!"

Even in the low light, I see a flush come to Sam's face as he looks slightly uncomfortable, but then he hugs her back with a growing smile.

Rage is the only one who hasn't said anything. He's just standing there, gnawing his lip, as if Sam were a fish he is considering throwing back.

Okay, well, this is awkward. I clap my hands together. "Should we go see more of the fair?"

The group parts, and Sam and I walk through like it's a gauntlet. I'm so conscious of the lack of talking, I jump when Barry appears on Sam's other side.

"I only caught the tail end, but that was pretty cool when you guys saved those kids. I've always known Mica is a badass, but you were booking it, man. You play football in . . . college, or something?"

Barry trying to establish Sam's age, and not too subtly, I might add.

Sam chuckles. "No, though I'm not terrible at lacrosse."

"Uri used to play lacrosse. That's Uri . . . my boyfriend. . . ."

And there's Barry trying to gauge if he's homophobic. But Sam doesn't miss a beat.

"Oh, you guys got a good team here?"

I just remembered: *this* is the reason I don't mix guys I like and my friends.

"Hold up!"

We look back and see Rage standing in front of a booth, tossing a baseball up and down. "Care to play?" he says to Sam. He points to the stack of milk bottles at the back of the booth. The difference between a Vermont carnival and others is that those bottles probably held milk until recently.

This is clearly a dick-measuring move on Rage's part. "Look, I—I don't—" I sputter.

But Sam's already walking over. Apparently confident he'll measure up. "Sure."

Rage's grin spreads. "I have to warn you, three years varsity baseball." He tosses the ball up once more, catches it with a snap, winds up, and hurls it. The top bottle flies off. He smiles, takes the second ball, and knocks off half the pyramid. With his third and final one, he knocks down all but one bottle, which stands there wobbling back and forth as if drunk. He turns around and grins at Sam.

Oh, this is some rom-com bullshit right here. Barry is always distrustful, but what is up with Rage?

Sam grins, takes a ball from the table, and wings it, but it misses the bottles by a hair.

Rage looks like he just swallowed the massive stuffed Tweety Bird that is hanging just overhead.

Sam throws the second; it misses.

Rage is beaming now. "It's okay, Sam. I bet they don't have baseball in the city you're from—"

And then there's the sound of exploding glass, and though I didn't see Sam throw the third ball, I look over and the entire stack of bottles is shattered, glass shards piercing the back of the tent.

We all stare at Sam, who shrugs.

Rage turns to the guy behind the booth, who looks shocked he's still alive. "Why would you use glass bottles?"

The booth guy is gawking at Sam. "No one's ever done that

before." He moves to the farthest corner of the tent, points up at the string of sad stuffed animals, and swallows. "Winner's choice." He never takes his eyes from Sam.

Rage is just standing there, staring at the empty table and shards of glass embedded in the tent.

"Mica? You pick," Sam offers, grandly gesturing at the prizes.

I point up at the badly sewn, brightly colored fabric faces leering at me from their nooses. "Oh, hell no! I'm not bringing one of those things into my house! I *know* they will kill me in my sleep."

Sam nods as if that's the most logical thing. "Like in *The Conjuring*?"

"I was thinking *Frozen Charlotte*, actually."

"When I read that book, I swore I could feel dolls running across my blanket."

"Yes! I can't believe you read that."

"Have you read her other book in that series? It's about a haunted Cornish inn—"

"Ahem," Barry says loudly.

I feel my face flush. "Oh, sorry."

"Wait, what about a goldfish? I don't think he could survive out of water long enough to kill you." Sam points to a bright orange fish swimming alone in a round glass container.

"And he couldn't hold a knife in his fins," I offer. We both laugh as he accepts the fish from the still-dazed booth guy and hands it to me.

"Sam!" a sharp voice calls from the edge of the fairway. We look over to see a group of people, all stylish and sleek, dressed in dark, rich colors and black leather. A tall girl separates from the group and walks toward us on high-heeled boots that are surely sinking into the grass. She has long fire-red hair and heavily lined eyes.

"We've been looking for you for over an hour." She glances at me, her gaze slowly sweeping from the top of my tangled head to my muddy Nikes.

I hold back a shudder. Is this Sam's girlfriend? I swallow.

A feline smile spreads across her face.

Sam is still looking at me when he answers sharply, "I don't have to tell you everywhere I go, Rona."

"Sam, aren't you going to introduce us?" She theatrically circles around me, arms folded across her chest.

Sam lets out a long, defeated-sounding breath. "Mica, this is Rona. My sister."

His *sister*. My heart starts beating again. "Hi."

She unfolds her arms and reaches her hand out, smiling. "Nice to meet you."

I hand the fishbowl to Zee and get ready to shake Rona's hand, but Sam grabs her arm before she can touch me. Rona looks pissed, but Sam pushes her off a bit, takes a deep breath, and a strained smile emerges as he turns to me. "Sorry, Mica, but I have to go. See you around?"

"O-Okay." What the hell was that?

"Rona, let's go," he barks at his sister, and turns around, hands shoved deep into his pockets.

His sister and I watch him walk away, but when he's a few yards from us, she turns back to me and reaches her hand out again with a grin. "Hope to see you again soon, Mica."

I extend my arm and put my hand in hers. The second our skin touches, my hand starts to heat up, like it's being held over an open flame. I try to pull it back, but I find I can't move it. I can't move anything. A scream builds in my chest, but I'm unable to gather the breath to let it out as the burning spreads up my wrist, into my arm, tears pouring down my face. The pain is unbearable, and I can hear the crackle of my own skin. Panicked and paralyzed, I look down at my arm and watch the skin bubble and blacken, the pain searing white-hot all over my body, my eyes losing focus. I struggle to take a breath, coughing from the smoke, the smell of burning flesh. I think I'm about to let out a scream—

"Ronova!" Sam's deep voice pulls me back into my body as his sister yanks her hand from mine, and I gasp. The breath returns to my lungs in one whoosh as I regain control of my body, coughing, hacking, my eyes darting around like a hunted animal. Sam is off in the distance glaring at Rona. "You coming, or what?"

I look at my arm, but the skin is whole, unburned.

Rage's face appears in front of mine. I can't hear him, but I see his lips move, asking if I'm all right. I spin around, trying to get my bearings.

I hold my arm up to him, and he looks at it with concern. "D-Did you s-s-see that? Is my arm okay?"

He gently takes my arm in his hands and examines it, pulling the sleeve up to look at the skin. "It looks fine. What did she do to you, Mica?" His eyes snap over to Rona.

She has a snakelike smile still on her face. "You're lucky. I was barely even trying," she whispers, then turns on her red-soled boots and stalks off, catching up with Sam and the others in the group.

Someone puts their arm around my shoulders, and I flinch. I look over and see Zee.

"Mica, are you okay?" she whispers.

I just shake my head, my eyes tearing up. I almost feel like I've been drugged.

Barry comes up beside me. "Is this guy for real?"

My voice is shaky. "I think so. But what his sister is, I don't know."

Zee's driving, but I can feel her gaze dart my way.

"Mica, remember when I told you about how empaths can take on another person's energy?"

I know she's only trying to help, but I can't connect with my chakras right now. I think they're broken anyway. I take a breath so my words don't come out too snarky. "Zee, I'm not an empath. And this was more than just feelings."

"No, I'm talking about me. I didn't even have to touch Rona to feel what she was giving off. And I'm talking about way more than the negative energy from the cranky old man behind me on the supermarket line." She shakes her head. "It came off her in waves."

I wait for her to say more, but she's looking ahead at the road as if she's gone somewhere else. "Wait, waves of what?"

Zee brings the car to a stop in front of my house and turns to face me. "Evil."

A part of me wants to tell Zee about the hallucination—that had to be what it was, right? Zee is really open-minded. She'd believe me. But I'm not sure I'm ready to admit that something straight out of a Dante Vulgate novel just happened to me in real life.

"Let's hope we never have to see her again," I whisper.

"Amen to that."

I lean over and give Zee a halfway hug with the non-fishbowl-holding arm. "Thank you," I whisper.

When we separate, she sits back and gives me a sad smile. "See you tomorrow at school?" I can hear her trying to force a normal tone into her voice, but there's been nothing normal about tonight.

"Do I have a choice? About the school part, not the seeing-you part." I smile and climb out.

I stay there waving until she drives away, but instead of going right in, I drop onto the front steps. I sit cradling my fishbowl prize against my stomach. I need to stop my brain from pinwheeling, so I take a long, slow breath. I notice the cold sandpaper feeling of the cement beneath me, the earthy smell of decaying jack-o'-lanterns from the porch across the street. It helps to focus on these things; they ground me. It was like I was teetering on the edge of reality all day.

My phone buzzes in my back pocket, and I switch the bowl to one arm while I pull it out. Of course, it's a flurry of Host texts talking about the fair, the rescue, Sam. I'm about to respond when one comes in from a number I don't recognize.

Did you make it home ok?

My breath catches. I type: who's this? The only other people who text me I've known for my entire life. Actually, when I think about it, that's kind of sad. Is it Sam? But how could he have gotten my number?

The guy who's holding your book hostage.

I smile. More Host texts come in, so I silence group notifications. I type Hostage? Really. What r your ransom demands?

The answer comes almost immediately.

Have dinner with me Friday.

Oh. My. God.

My heart starts beating so hard and fast I think it's going to explode and the shreds of it will be floating in the fishbowl. Wait, his sister wouldn't be there, right? Of course not. I type: Sure. What the hell. Acting all casual, as if I'm not completely freaking out sitting in front of my house. In the dark. Holding a fishbowl.

I'll pick you up at seven.

Oh no, Abuela won't like that. Meet me outside of Black Cap Café downtown, I type, then notice the time on the top of the screen. Shit! I'm a half hour late for curfew.

I slide the phone back into my pocket and get to my feet. I open the front door quietly, cringing at the slight squeal of the hinges. I slide it closed, relieved by the silence, and am tiptoeing across the living room, trying not to slosh water out of the fishbowl, when the lamp next to my grandmother's chair switches on with a loud click.

I jolt and put my hand over my heart. "Abuela! You scared the sh—beejeepers out of me!"

Her arms are across her chest, and she's glaring at me.

"Do you know what time it is?"

"Lo siento, Abuela, I was just . . . out having fun."

"Fun? Is being too tired to learn at school tomorrow fun? Is worrying your elderly abuela fun? I work very hard to support you, to prepare you for life, Miguela, and I expect you to take it seriously, especially your studies."

Oh Lord. I've been sent on this particular guilt trip about three thousand times in my life. "I'm sorry for worrying you, if you'd only let me text you, I could let you know when—"

"Ay, no, don't start with that. You know how I feel about those e-phones."

I stifle a laugh and don't correct her (neither would help my cause). I got her a smartphone last Christmas, but she only uses it to look up recipes. "Abuela, it's the twenty-first century. You should try to keep up."

She glares at me and says nothing.

"Well, again, sorry, but I'll be fine if I just go to bed—" I start making my escape toward my room.

"Oh no, you're not leaving yet, Miguela."

I freeze at the icy power of her voice. She's four foot eleven, about one hundred pounds soaking wet, yet she can stop me short with one sentence.

"M'ija, you have to be more careful."

The use of the affectionate "my daughter" relaxes me a bit, but I'm still not out of the woods. I try humor. "But you wanted me to go! And besides, what could happen? We live in the middle of nowhere!"

"No place is completely safe. I moved you here to protect you after your mother passed. Please, let us not tempt the devil."

I'm so tired of hearing the spiel that she moved me here to protect me. How freaking dangerous can a gated complex in Puerto Rico be? Besides, when does "staying safe" become "not really living your life"? But there's no use saying these things to her. She'd just shut me down. "I'm sorry I'm late, Abuela, but I'll never do it again, and really, I'm fine."

She's looking at me with her shiny eyes, like I'm squeezing tears from her body and she's fighting to keep them in. Then she walks over and puts one hand on my shoulder and nudges my chin so I'm forced to look at her. She seems to see something. "You look different. Did something happen tonight, Miguela?"

The question has a tinge of panic, so I rush to reassure her. "No! No, I'm fine, Abuela." But I look back into her hazel eyes and wonder, *How did she know?*

"Hmm." She stares at me for a bit longer; then her shoulders drop a bit. "I just want you to know, querida, that if you needed to, you could talk to me."

Yeah. Sure. But that's a one-way street. The woman never talks to *me* about what *I* want to talk about. Like about my parents; I don't even know how my mother died. Or why my father left.

She always changes the subject when I used to ask about our lives before Vermont. So, I just . . . stopped asking. The path of least resistance is my route of choice with her. "I know, Abuela."

She glances down. "What is with this fish?"

I don't know, something about the way she says it makes me laugh. Loudly. She seems a bit startled by the sound, then chuckles and shakes her head like she can't figure me out. Which, by the way, she can't.

"Okay, off to bed, Miguelita." She kisses me on the forehead and spins me toward my room.

I grab the doorknob with my free hand and turn around. She's switched off her lamp and is shuffling toward her room. "Abuela?"

"¿Sí, niña?"

Her voice is tired and thin, like the fabric on her chair that's slowly wearing away. I always wonder if that's what I do to her. "Te quiero."

I can see her smile in the light borrowed from the streetlamps out front. It's weary, like her voice. "Yo también, m'ija."

I hesitate, feeling like I should say more, but then I open my door and she yells from down the hall.

"You're grounded for a week for being late!"

Jesus Christ. And I thought we'd had a moment back there. I slam my door, lean against it, and slowly sink down.

"Why is she so freaking strict with me?" I whisper to the fish swimming in his bowl. I'm glad he's the only one who can see me cry. Why is anything good that happens to me always followed by something bad?

I meet a hot guy who seems into me.

But his sister is a sadistic ginger biatch.

Said hot guy actually asks me on a date.

My buzzkill-but-also-kind-of-sadistic-in-her-own-way grandmother grounds me.

My phone buzzes in my pocket. I dig it out and look at the screen.

It's Sam.

Actually, Friday night is WAY too far away.

My heart lifts with the message, then quickly falls with the weight of reality. I should just face it. My grandmother will never allow me to go out with him, a boy I barely know. I'm going to have to tell him I can't see him. I type with a shaking thumb: I can't go. I just got grounded and there's no way my abuela will let me.

I watch the bubbles indicating that he's typing. Then they stop.

I throw the phone onto my bed. "Damn her anyway," I say to my fish friend.

A new message buzzes. I get to my feet, put the bowl on the desk, and walk back to the bed to pick up the phone.

Zee said we were superheroes tonight. Superheroes don't need to do what their grandmothers tell them. It's one of the perks.

I snort, but it quickly turns into a sob-like sound. I'm about to type *I can't* but stop.

Why *can't* I?

At the thought of defying Abuela to see Sam, a thrill passes through me like a current. Kind of like when we were jumping over that fence. The woman controls so much of my life already. Going out with Sam is the first thing *I've* wanted in a long time.

I need that feeling again.

I look back at the screen and type.

Then I guess I better bring my cape.

IV

The sun will not beat down on them, nor any scorching heat.
—Revelation 7:16

My eyelids start to droop in calculus—because, calculus—but maybe I *am* a little tired after last night. I sit up straighter and force my eyes to stay open. But after just a minute or two of listening to Mr. Leach's droning voice, my head starts to drop and it's like I'm being pulled underwater.

Except, it's not water but fire that greets me. I jolt upright and feel searing pain in my right arm, like all my nerve endings are being thrown in a deep fryer. I look down and see long orange flames licking up my wrist, the skin crackling and snapping. The flames catch my sleeve as the fabric melts on my skin. I struggle to open my mouth, open it and—

"Ms. Angeles? Are you all right?" Mr. Leach is staring into my face, his eyes wide and panicked.

"What? What happened?"

"Dude, you just screamed in the middle of calculus," Marena Young helpfully explains from her nearby desk.

"Maybe you should go see the nur—" He doesn't get to finish as the bell rings for lunch.

Saved by the bell, literally.

I grab my books and mumble, "I'll be fine," and scurry out the door. When I get into the hallway, my brow is dripping with sweat. I hold my books to my chest, go right past the cafeteria (yeah, no interest in food at the moment), and retreat to the only place on school grounds where I feel comfortable.

Whenever I can sneak out of class or when I just need to be alone, I go to the small in-school chapel near the front entrance. Not to pray, or anything formal like that, there's just something about the dramatic wood-trimmed room that draws me in and calms me down. The quiet in here is like no other; it's as though the hush of a thousand prayers hangs in the air beneath the ceiling. I step inside the room, the dark wooden pews empty and waiting for tomorrow's morning service.

I walk to the front and stand, staring at the ornate altar. I'm fascinated by its carvings of Saint Michael and his host of archangels flying above an evil army, swords drawn. Abuela thinks it's unnecessarily violent, particularly for a "house of God," but it's action-packed and horror-filled, just how I like it.

I look back to the door to make sure I'm alone and step up on the platform that holds the altar. I switch my books to one arm and tentatively reach out with my fingers to run them over the carvings. I used to do this when I was in middle school and hiding out in here. Back then, I would imagine myself as a warrior. I could almost hear the clang of swords and feel the wind of the mountaintop in my hair.

But this time, the moment my fingertips graze the wood, it comes.

Another fiery hallucination—or is it different, like a vision? I don't feel afraid or panicked like I did at the fair, but whatever it is comes in flashes, like lightning. I'm running through flaming halls with tall ceilings, heading toward a doorway of sunlight, until I burst into a courtyard filled with smoke. I look down and see a boy in my arms, coughing, eyes half closed. I turn around and see I'm standing in front of a huge, institutional building that's entirely engulfed in flames. All around me are children, screaming as they run, their faces contorted in abject terror. Nuns in black habits are herding them away from the crumbling building. There are palm trees all around the grounds, and the sky is a shocking shade of blue, a contrast to the billowing black smoke that is spreading, darkening even the sun. A firefighter runs up and takes the boy from me, rushing away in his yellow jacket.

It's then I notice the blood on my sleeves, but I don't think it's mine. And my right arm, it's tired and vibrating, like I've been fighting. . . .

"Miguela?"

I jerk my hand back, stumble, and almost fall backward off the platform. I whip around and see Father Murphy, the middle school history teacher, standing in the doorway. Seeing me stumble, he starts to move forward to help, but I step to the floor and wave at him that I'm all right even if I'm unable to talk. I take off running down the aisle, feeling the brush of his cassock as I pass him on my way to the door.

Just as he appears in the hallway, calling my name, the bell rings again, and the hall floods with students. Relieved, I lose myself in the river of people. I wish he hadn't interrupted me; it was like the altar was . . . talking to me. I know how crazy that sounds, but it really did feel like it was giving me a message, or a warning, or something.

Of course, as soon as the next class starts, I get called to the guidance counselor's office. One incident wouldn't have been as noticeable, but two? I convince her I'd had a bad dream in class, and she lets me rest on the leather sofa for the balance of the afternoon. I don't lie, but I can be convincing when I want to, particularly with adults other than my grandmother.

After the final bell, I gratefully break free of the building and see Zee waiting in her car right out front. Thank God. On the days Rage has baseball practice, Zee gives me a ride home so I can avoid the humiliation of being the only senior on the bus. The school is only about two miles and five minutes away from downtown, but when you're on a bus with twenty fourteen-year-olds? It's an eternity.

I drop into the passenger seat and let out a huge, dramatic sigh.

Zee stares at me, a slight smile on her face. "You okay?"

I don't answer. I notice that today's earrings are midnight black and opaque. When I touch them, they're smooth like glass. "Damn, the light sucking stones can't be good."

"Obsidian for protection from negativity."

"I think I need some of those."

"Mica, what's going on with you?"

I rub my hands over my face. "I don't know. I really don't know, Zee. I think I might be losing my mind."

"Yeah, I don't think so."

I look at her for a breath. "Well, it sure ain't normal."

She scoffs, "You haven't spent time in *my* head." Then her voice gets gentle again, like she's talking to one of the patients she works with when she does her volunteer hospital shifts. "I heard you screamed in calculus."

"Lord, word travels fast in this place."

"You're having bad dreams?"

"Honestly, I don't know that they're dreams; they're more . . ." I stop, afraid to sound completely wack, but when I look at Zee, I just start talking. "They're more three-dimensional; detailed. It's like I'm really there; like memories of things that never happened to me? Oh, I don't know, it sounds so crazy." But she's not laughing. In fact, any remnant of a smile bleeds from her face as she just stares at me.

"What? Why are you looking at me that way?"

She ignores the question. "What happens in these visions?"

I tell her what happened during class, and the vision I had when I touched the altar. The color drains from her face as I talk, and she starts playing with her earrings, running her fingers over the crystals. "Zee, what's wrong? Why do you look like you're going to puke?"

"It's just that . . . I've been having visions too. They started this weekend."

My heart skips a beat. "About the same thing?"

She shakes her head. "No, but just as dark. Mine take place here, in Stowe. Pits of fire and people I care about, dying. . . ." She trails off and stares into the distance.

"Why didn't you say anything to me?"

She shrugs. "Same reason you didn't want to tell me. But I can feel a lot of things. And I sense you're freaked out right now, but I know we're not crazy, okay?"

Zee takes my hand and gives it a squeeze. Instantly, it makes me feel better. At least I'm not experiencing this weird shit alone.

The moment is broken by the sound of a loud crack, then a cacophony of voices hooting and hollering.

We look over to the baseball practice going on in the field next to the parking lot and see familiar red hair sticking out of a batting helmet. Rage takes off around the bases, while the rest of us watch the baseball fly up, out of the field, over Route 100, and land somewhere in the farm across the road. When he arrives at home base, I see the coach holding up the other half of the cracked baseball bat, looking at Rage with shock. After touching home base with his cleats, Rage says something to the coach, tosses his helmet off to the side, and jogs toward the school, still holding the ragged handle. I'm staring at him in disbelief as he notices Zee's car and takes a detour, glancing back at the team still standing around, mouths open.

"What the hell was that?" I ask as soon as he sticks his head in my window.

His pale freckled face flushes, and he shrugs. "I got a good piece of the ball, that's all."

"No. Uh-uh. 'A good piece of the ball' is one that lands outside the playing field, not in the next county."

Zee's phone rings, and she takes the call from her mom.

Rage puts a hand on my shoulder. For some reason, I get goose bumps. "I heard you had an 'incident' in calculus. Why didn't you come get me?"

"And interrupt your favorite class? Nidor!" I say as he smiles at me. "What, that means 'never,' right?"

"Actually, it's means 'odor,' or 'smell.'"

I shrug. "I didn't say Latin's *my* favorite class."

"I'm serious, Mica. Between that and last night, I'm worried about you."

"I'm not going to lie, Rager. It's been a strange twenty-four hours."

"I hear that."

"You too?"

He pushes back his hair. "Well, I'm a good batter, but I've sure never hit a ball *that* far." He points toward the field across the road. "Plus, it's like the air just feels . . . weird today, you know?"

I nod. I do know.

"Mica, if anything like that happens in class again, just text me and I'll be there in a split second."

"A split second, huh?"

He gives me his one-sided grin. "Or less."

"What's less than a split? Like, a nanosecond?"

"Or maybe"—he lifts the splintered wooden handle he's still holding—"a *bat* of an eye?"

"Ugh!" But I laugh. Truth is, he would be right there for me, and just knowing that makes me feel calmer.

Zee says goodbye to her mom, and Rage's name is being shouted from the field.

"I guess I better go get some more bats. This is the third one I've broken this afternoon."

"Seriously, what is going on with that?" Zee asks, but Rage is already heading toward the school's front door, jogging backward.

Just as he gets to the doors, he yells, "You two going to McCarthy's later? Lattes on me."

I shake my head. "Nah, grounded remember?"

Zee says, "I've got a volunteer shift at the hospital."

He looks disappointed; then a new chorus of his name rises from the field. "Gotta go. See you tomorrow, then."

Zee shakes her head as she starts the car. "Something is going on, Mica. Something serious."

I sit back and stare out the window. There *is* something going on, and the timing of it coincides with Sam and Rona showing up in Stowe. This is not lost on me, but I don't share that thought with Zee just yet. Not because it sounds insane—this week has redefined that term after all—but because I'm certain she'll tell me to stay away from Sam, which is the opposite of what I'm planning to do.

If this hunch of mine is right, I've got to find out where Sam and Rona came from—and why they're really here. And for that, I need to spend more time with the guy.

It's a tough job, but somebody's gotta do it.

V

But in your mouth it will be as sweet as honey.
—Revelation 10:9

Friday has never seemed further away, and the week goes by at a slow crawl. It's all the worse since I'm grounded and imprisoned in the house every day after school, but thankfully I haven't had another vision. In fact, it's almost as if things are back to normal and what happened a few days ago in the chapel never happened at all. But that doesn't sway me from my quest to get to the bottom of it. Tonight, I'm pretending to write a research paper on my laptop and doing some research into Sam and his family. While watching TV with Abuela, I start digging on social media.

I click the search icon on Instagram but freeze with my fingers hovering over the touchpad when I realize I don't know his last name. Why didn't I ask? *'Cause that would be weird, Mica.* I type in "Sam" and about fifty million Sams come up. Of course they do.

Wait!

Rona. The creepy sister. That name's unique enough. I enter it, but every Ronald in the world comes up. Then I remember Sam called her something else when he was mad at her, something longer.

Ronova.

I type that in. The small circular photo of the first account loads, and I see distinctive fiery hair. I click on the name, and as the profile pic enlarges, I feel a queasy stirring in the bottom of my belly.

Yep, that's her.

She has three hundred thousand followers? WTF? Of course, she's only following fourteen people, so that makes my quest easier. I click on them, and right away I see a Sam Sheol and recognize the handsome face. I hate to admit it, but my heart does a skip thing when I see his dimples. Then I notice the little black padlock symbol.

Private?

The account is private. Shit. Well, we *do* have a date Friday, so he'd probably approve my follow. But that would be admitting I was Instastalking him. Yeah, no. I scroll down Rona's page, looking for a photo that includes Sam. She's listed as an "influencer," and when I review her photos, I understand why.

Rows and rows of beautiful photographs of her and her gorgeous friends taken all over the world. Endless tattoo and bikini shots with a background of azure-blue water, zip-lining in Costa Rica, partying in Singapore. Envy starts to build in my chest: I didn't think I could hate her any more. I catch sight of the first image of Sam and click.

It's the same group from the fairgrounds at Coachella.

Eww. Coachella.

Sam is at the center standing next to a reality television star, her implanted boobs bursting out of her crop top like rising bread dough. I'm about to move on and scope out the rest of Rona's account, when I notice the photo changing. Is it a video? A Boomerang? Sam and his friends' faces begin to darken, their smiles turn grotesque, their lower lips pierced by sharp canine teeth. What the hell? Sam is particularly alarming, his handsomeness a parody of itself, like that spider that has a fake face on its back to distract its prey while it strikes from its real one.

But it's the celebrity and the people from the crowd that are most disturbing. The skin on their faces is melting, exposing raw red muscle, glistening fat, and, finally, bright white bone. Their flesh is dissolving onto their brightly colored designer clothing, their mouths frozen open in screams, their perfectly coiffed hair now flaming manes. I can't stop staring at their eyes, wide with terror, before the eyeballs themselves burst then melt, pooling in the empty sockets of their skulls.

I give a weird, strangled scream and shove the computer off my lap and onto the living room floor.

"Miguela? ¿Qué pasó?"

My head snaps up, and I see Abuela with her knitting in her lap, staring at me with concern. I'd forgotten she was there.

I giggle nervously. "Nothing!" I cough. "I mean, nothing, Abuela. I was just—" I look up at the television. "I was just anxious . . . about . . . what Agent Gibbs might find at the crime scene." I'm totally winging it, but she's subjected me to this freaking show my entire life, and I'm confident that comment would fit every single episode.

She narrows her eyes, then peers at the laptop on the floor. "And that necessitated throwing an expensive computer across the room? You know we are on a fixed income, Miguela. I cannot afford to replace—"

"Sorry." I smile wide until she shakes her head, starts knitting again, and glances back at the television screen.

I let out a long breath, pick up the laptop, and stare at the photo. But it looks fine now. No melting faces, no popping eyeballs. I click the image again, but nothing changes. Could it be a special effects app or the scariest filter I've ever seen? Highly doubt it.

Looks like I'm going to have to add this to my list of things to grill Sam about during our date tomorrow night. Maybe this damn show will come in handy after all.

Come Friday, when I get home, I head straight to my room under the pretense of a headache. When Abuela calls me to dinner, I tell her through my closed bedroom door that I'm not hungry, that I'm going to bed early. Not lying, just avoiding. After forcing Tylenol on me and feeling my forehead, she finally leaves me alone. I hear her wash the dinner dishes, then settle into her armchair to watch her telenovelas, the ridiculous Spanish soap operas that she was so delighted to discover when we got "the Netfleeks" as she calls it.

As usual, in less than an hour, I hear her snores rising in waves over the sound of the television. If I'm home and she doesn't have to incessantly worry about my safety (her favorite pastime), she doesn't even make it through one episode. It's like digital melatonin. I quietly raise my bedroom window, then stop and listen again. Still snoring. I push out the screen, careful to grab it before it falls, and place it on the ground. I hike one leg over the windowsill and drop to the grass.

I run between our house and the neighbor's, down the block, and around the corner to find Sam waiting in front of the coffee shop where I'd asked to meet. It's closed, of course—the streets of Stowe roll up wicked early—and he's on the porch, leaning against the supporting column. He doesn't see me yet, so I take a moment to watch him, his lean body dressed all in black, his posture relaxed, his angular and perfect face looking up at the moon rising over the hardware store across the street with a small smile, as if he's thinking of something nice.

He sees me, and the smile blooms. Stay focused, Mica. You're in detective mode, remember? But a tingling feeling stretches across my skin, and I can't help but answer with a huge grin of my own. He saunters down the steps and stands directly in front of me. I look up into his eyes.

"This week was way too long." Even though we're not touching, I swear I can feel the sound of his voice vibrating in my chest.

"You're telling me? I had to go to school *and* work . . . and feed Sharknado, of course."

He tilts his head. "Sharknado?"

"The goldfish you won for me."

He grins. "Ah. The name fits."

He takes my hand in his and turns toward the lone vehicle sitting in the spaces in front of the coffee shop.

A sleek black convertible crouches there like a cat about to pounce.

Apparently, he senses I'm not impressed. "Too much? I'm trying too hard, aren't I? It's not even mine."

"Wait, did you steal it?"

"No!"

He seems so taken aback, I laugh. "I'm just kidding." *Kind of.*

His shoulders visibly drop, and I'm relieved I'm not the only one who's nervous. "It's a rental."

"A rental? You can't rent a car until you're twenty-five. Wait . . ." I look at him through narrowed eyes. "How old *are* you?"

He laughs. "Not *that* old! I'm nineteen. And . . . my father kind of owns the rental car company. Or, actually, the corporation that owns the company." He rubs the back of his neck again and looks embarrassed.

It's not like wealth surprises me. I mean, I do live in Stowe.

He's looking from me to the car. "You hate it."

"No, no, it's—" I look over at him and wince a little. "Yeah, I kind of do."

"Ouch!"

I shrug. "Sorry. I have this thing about not lying."

"No, I respect that. I just wanted to impress you. Most people would kill for a car like this." He gestures to it like we're on a game show and he's showing me what I could win.

I shrug. "It's just . . . kind of a gas guzzler, no?"

He looks at me and does the bird tilt of his head. "You're different."

I bristle a bit. Been hearing the d-word my whole life. "Different how?" I ask cautiously.

"Well . . ." I can see him thinking before he speaks. Don't know many people our age who do that. "The girls I know are impressed by things like fast cars, designer labels, and black cards."

"Sounds like you need to widen your social circle."

"Now *that's* the truth."

He opens the passenger door for me, and I slide in. He basically bounces behind the wheel like he's excited, then peels backward out of the parking space and onto Main Street. As he puts it in drive and we take off in the direction of Mountain Road, I ask, "Where are we going?"

He indicates toward the back with a nod of his chin. "You'll see."

I peer behind my seat and see an old-school wicker picnic basket with a frosty bottle sticking out of it. "A picnic? I love picnics!" I clap like I'm five, but I kind of feel like I am.

"Well, this one is going to have a view."

Then it hits me that I'm in a car alone with a guy I just met whose sister made my hand feel like it's burning. Yeah, not my smartest move, but I *am* a black belt and, truth be told, I don't regret it at *all*. Still, I fire off a quick, direct text to Zee, letting her know where I am.

As we drive up Mountain Road, the wind lifts my hair around me, and I close my eyes.

"You good?"

"Mmm . . . So, *this* is why people like convertibles!"

He smiles. "They have their advantages."

"Normally it's way too cold to have the top down this time of year." Seriously, the evening is warm and springlike. It's November. Come to think of it, the weather has been different since he got here too. I look over at him. His short black hair is blowing back, and his eyes are glassy from the wind. I remember being at the beach in Puerto Rico at night once, and the moon glinted off the surface of the water like diamonds. His eyes are like that. I find myself getting lost in them, and that feels . . . awesome.

His phone rings and it's paired with the car, so I see the name "Rona" and a photo of his sister fills the screen. I stifle a shudder.

"Ugh," he says, and presses decline call.

My feelings exactly. Still, I don't want to be rude. "You could have taken the call. I wouldn't mind." Which is the truth. You learn a lot about people from eavesdropping on their phone calls. Not that *I* would know.

He shakes his head. "Nah, I don't want her to know where I am."

"Okay . . ."

He sighs. "She's . . . challenging, but I'm kind of stuck with her, you know?"

"I don't. I don't have any siblings. Sometimes I wish I did, but then people who do have told me their horror stories."

"Yeah, siblings sound better on paper."

We continue winding up Mountain Road, and I realize we're heading for the ski resort. He pulls into the empty parking lot on the left, the gondola and ski lifts asleep at the bottom, waiting for winter. I look over at him. "You know the resort isn't open yet, right?"

He parks in front of the darkened building, gets out, and comes around to my side of the car. I'm still confused and not overly trustful, but when he opens the door and holds out his hand, I take it.

"It's too beautiful a night to spend inside." And he nods toward the ski trails and the silent lifts as he picks up the picnic basket from the back seat.

As we start walking toward the base of the mountain, I see something out of the corner of my eye. Something small and black, like a moving shadow. I stop. There's a rustling sound in the brush next to the building. What was that?

"Anything wrong?"

"No, I just . . ." I catch sight of a head, pointed ears like the ones I saw near the running trail, and glowing orange eyes. "Sam, do you see that?" I whisper, pointing to the creature just as it turns and a pointed tail *fwap*s around before disappearing.

"What?" But by the time he looks, there's no trace.

"Weird. I thought I saw . . ." I look around, but I don't see it anymore. I start walking again. "Must have been a cat or something." Or something.

When we get to the base of the lift, I look up the familiar mountain and back at him. "You do *not* expect me to climb that mountain? I mean, I like hiking, but not at night without a headlamp."

"Of course not."

I gasp when the ski lift starts humming, the lights coming on one by one up the mountain, the engines roaring to life.

He walks over to the chair that's waiting at the bottom and raises the safety bar. "Our ride is here." And he grandly gestures to the padded seat.

I look around with a nervous grin. "I don't think we're supposed to be here."

He turns toward me, and his eyes are glittering from the lights of the chair lift. I feel the ground shift beneath me, just a bit. He is so damn gorgeous.

"If you're not comfortable, Mica, we can totally head back to town, catch a movie or something." He points toward the car sitting there, waiting in the empty lot like a faithful dog.

But he misunderstood me: I don't care if this is illegal or against the rules. I should care. Normally I would care. But nothing is penetrating this happy bubble I'm in right now.

I smile and take a seat. Sam sits next to me, placing the picnic basket on his other side, and pulls the bar down in front of us. As the chair starts to move with a jerk, I'm thrown closer to him, and he puts his arm around me. He's as warm as freshly baked bread.

My heart should be racing. Any minute, staff or even police could come running across the parking lot and charge us with trespassing. Instead I'm calm enough to settle back and feel the warmth of his arm on the skin of my neck. I breathe deep. The air smells of pine trees and freshly mown grass.

When we arrive at the top of the lift, I get ready to leap off, but the chair just stops. I look down at the ground, which is still alarmingly far away. "It doesn't usually do that; it usually goes around and then back down the mountain."

"I have a feeling we've both had enough of what's 'usual,'" he says as he easily jumps and lands.

Oh, he has no idea.

The lift is high off the ground; without the snow, it's way farther away, and my short legs are dangling. Sam reaches up to help me off with the hand not holding the picnic basket, but I leap off with my arms spread as if I'm flying, until my feet hit the packed dirt with a muffled thump yards from the lift. When I turn around, I see him smiling at me.

"What?"

"You're a total badass, Mica Angeles."

"Why, yes, yes, I am." I can't stop smiling as I take his hand.

We arrive at the flat area at the very top of the trail, and Sam pulls a blanket from the picnic basket and lays it out on the grass. I look around and see the entire town spread out below us like a dark green carpet. And the stars. From this vantage point, I can see the entire sky full of them. Vermont might be small, rural, and boring as hell, but even I have to admit it can be magical.

"Beautiful, isn't it?" Sam's voice is a whisper. I can feel it run across the surface of my skin like static electricity.

"I was just thinking the same thing."

"Are you hungry?"

I nod and sit down on the red plaid blanket, which is soft and warm. He opens the basket, and the smell reaches me before he pulls the container free.

"Chicken wings?" I laugh. "I love chicken wings! They're my favorite."

"Mine too."

I reach for a wing. "I'm surprised—I thought you'd be a fancier picnicker."

"Me? What gave you that idea?"

"I don't know—the sports car, the champagne . . ." I point to a frosty, dark green bottle nestled in the basket.

He reaches for it. "This? It's sparking grape juice. As an athlete, I didn't imagine you were a drinker, so I thought this was a better choice."

"How do you know I'm an athlete?"

"Well, that leap over the fence might have been a hint. And—" His gaze darts down to my legs for just an instant. He goes back to studiously opening the bottle as if embarrassed.

Now it's my turn to flush. *C'mon, Mica. Focus.* "Speaking of athletics . . . so, that night at the fair. I'm a fast runner, but I've never been able to run like that."

He laughs. "You looked like you've been doing it all your life."

"It felt that way."

"Maybe, if you gave yourself enough room to run, you could feel that way all the time."

Rage says this kind of thing to me a lot, that I'm holding back. I feel weird thinking about Rage while I'm with Sam, kind of disloyal. No. Focus. It's time to ask *him* some questions. That's what I'm here for. I take the wet wipes he offers, and as I'm cleaning the wing sauce off my hands, I casually inquire, "What about you, Sam? Why can you run like that?"

He produces a pair of glass champagne flutes from the basket and fills them with sparkling juice. "All superheroes can. Don't you get the newsletters?" Sam hands me the drink with a sly smile and holds his up to mine. "To mountainside first dates."

I look at him. "Is this?"

"Is this what?"

"A date?"

"God, I hope so."

I try to think of something clever to say, but he's looking into my eyes. I mean, really looking, like he wants to memorize every cell.

And I look back.

I don't know how long we sit there, staring at each other, but for the first time in . . . well, maybe forever, I wouldn't want to be anywhere else.

No.

Wait. I need to figure out what's going on. I pull back a bit, but it's hard, as if fighting a magnet. *Stay focused, Mica.*

"Everything okay?" Sam asks, but as he straightens up, there's a rustling sound from inside his jacket. "Oh! I almost forgot." He reaches in, takes out a folded paper, and hands it to me. "This was in your book."

My acceptance letter! "Shit, I need to be more careful with that."

"Congratulations, by the way."

I look at him.

"It fell out when I opened the book, and I couldn't help but see."

"Oh. Thanks."

"Are you going to frame it? That why you want to be careful with it?"

I shake my head. "Nah. My grandmother doesn't know I applied. She insists I go to Saint Michael's College here in Vermont."

He nods. "In-state tuition is much more affordable."

"No, it's not that." I swallow, hard. "She's always so worried about keeping me safe. She doesn't want me out of her sight."

"From where I sit, seems you can handle yourself just fine."

I look at him. "Thank you. I think I can too."

"I'm sure it's just because she cares about you, even if she's wrong."

I smile.

"But your friends are supportive, right?"

At this I feel a weight on my chest, and the smile disappears. I want so badly to say yes. We've been so close our whole lives. *Yes, they support me in everything.* But I can't. I stare at the plaid pattern on the blanket. "Not really. They also want to keep me in Vermont. It's like, this path has been built for me, all set in stone. But I had nothing to do with the design or any say in where it leads."

"Then why not step off?"

I look up at him. "What do you mean?"

"Off the path. Isn't that why you applied to UCLA?"

"I don't understand."

"It's not my business, really. It's just . . ." He starts gesturing with his hands as he speaks. "My father is always questioning what I do and how I do it, always telling me how I *should* be doing it. I swear, I can never do anything right in his eyes."

That sure sounds familiar. I sit up on my knees as I listen.

"He's laid out my future as if I don't have my own plans, my own dreams."

"Exactly!"

"It's like he's holding me on a leash and all I want to do is run."

"Yes!" I almost yell.

He shakes his fist at the sky. "Vexilla regis prodeunt—" He stops himself, looks at me, like he'd forgotten where he was.

"Wait, what does that mean?"

Instead of answering, he rubs his hand over his face and takes a deep breath. "Sorry, I get a little emotional talking about my father." He looks at me. "I just wanted you to know that I totally get it."

"Get what?"

He takes my cold hand in his warm one, the letter clutched between us. "Mica, you need to make your own path. Don't let anyone tell you differently."

These are things I've wanted to hear *my whole life*. My heart is galloping in my chest, like it was finally given enough room to run, and without thinking, I lean forward and press my lips to his. His lips are soft, and I catch the sweet scent of grapes on his breath. I can feel his breathing quicken, and all I want to do is make it go faster. I've never been drunk or high, but I imagine it feels something like this. The entire mountain is spinning as we kiss, his hands caressing the sides of my face to keep me close to him. There's this warmth starting from my mouth and spreading throughout my body in a shudder.

I could kiss Sam like this forever, but I slowly pull away. He gasps a bit, and I resist the urge to kiss him again. I feel like I need to catch my breath and regain control over my body. We stay like this, faces centimeters from each other, for a few heartbeats.

"Does that mean you also think it's a date?" he asks.

"God, I hope so." I'm starting to lean in to kiss him again when I stop. I had important things to ask him, didn't I? I realize something and pull away. "Wait. You're not, like, a prince or something . . . are you?"

He laughs, low and sexy. "Why would you ask that?"

"My abuela, she makes me watch hours and hours of Hallmark movies at Christmas. I mean, talk about horror! Anyway, in almost every one, there's a guy from out of town who meets a local girl, and he turns out to be prince of some small European country where they magically speak English. At first, they don't get along, but they slowly fall—"

"You talk too much, Miguela." And his lips are locked with mine again.

When Sam drives me home, I forget to tell him to drop me back at the coffee shop so I can walk the rest of the way and sneak back in. My head is so fuzzy, my lips deliciously swollen from the best kissing I've ever experienced. Actually, I no longer consider what I did before kissing. This is an entirely different category, like when I asked Abuela to get me Oreos and she brought home some knockoff garbage called Crème-O's because they were fifty cents cheaper. We pull up in front of my house—when did I tell him where I live?—but I'm really on another planet and have zero interest in returning to earth. I look in at the dark windows and sigh.

"Everything all right?"

"I'm sure Abuela has figured out I'm gone and is nuclear pissed at this point. I'm surprised she hasn't called out the National Guard."

He takes a lock of my hair between his fingers, not trying to control it like Abuela, he seems to be . . . admiring it. He brings it to his face and breathes deep. Heat flushes through my body.

"Don't worry." He looks over at the house. "I'm sure your grandmother is sound asleep in her bed."

I snort. "You don't know my abuela. She sits in her chair in the living room like some kind of sentry."

"No, I don't know her. But I'd like to."

I stare at him, not sure I heard right.

He continues. "I mean, I'll have to meet her soon. If I'm going to date her granddaughter, it's only proper."

"*Are* we dating?"

"I thought we established that earlier? On the mountain?" He points back toward Mount Mansfield, as if I haven't burned each glorious moment into my mind.

"Yeah, but the noun 'date' is different from the verb 'dating.' Are we verb dating?"

He smiles. "Verb, noun, adjective, preposition. We are whatever part of speech means I get to see you again."

Something stirs inside me, reminding me about Rona. I look over at him, willing myself to ask him about her, but when I see his face, and the dreamy way he's looking at me, I just press my lips gently to his for one last kiss. As I close the passenger door, he grins at me in the light of the dashboard, and I have to force my legs to move.

I practically float up the walkway and give one last wave. When Sam's car disappears, a weakness comes over me. It starts in my knees and travels up my spine. It's almost as though I was tied up for days and finally released. As I reach for the doorknob to steady myself, the door creaks open, just a bit.

She knows.

I take a deep breath and open the door to face the wrath of Abuela.

I look around the darkened living room. The lamp doesn't snap on. I silently close the door behind me and take a few tentative steps, my body recalibrating.

Her chair is empty.

I tiptoe over to her room and gently open the door. There she is, tucked into her bed sound asleep, just as Sam predicted. I look closely: yep, she's still breathing. In fact, she even has a smile on her face.

"Huh." I close the door and stop. I can't help but feel suspicious. Like Sam had something to do with this. It's way more likely that Abuela thought I was asleep; she probably didn't check and just went to bed. But there's no denying that Sam has this magnetic energy that pulls me toward him, to the point where I can barely think about anything else when I'm with him. It makes me think of what Zee said a few days ago, about us not being crazy. But I kind of feel crazy—like my feelings aren't exactly mine.

I peel off my hoodie and jeans and drop onto my bed, suddenly exhausted. As I close my eyes, I remember Sam saying something, in Latin I think. Vex something, reguss . . . prudent? Rage is president of the Latin club, but there's no way I'm going to ask him. I grab my phone and search. It takes a minute to get the spelling right, but I find it.

Vexilla regis prodeunt. Translates to "The royal banner forward goes." Wikipedia says it's a hymn.

Why would Sam quote a hymn?

The bed is so warm, my limbs are aching.

Tomorrow. I'll figure it all out . . . tomorrow . . .

I awake with a jolt and find myself standing in the center of town with Zee, Barry, and Rage. People are pouring down Mountain Road, screaming, their faces shadowed with terror. I look up to see where they're coming from, and there's a flood of glowing lava rushing down the ski trails, down the road, heading for the village. I watch it pick up a woman running with her baby in her arms, and they disappear into the molten mass. I turn around to look at my friends and find their faces are melting like in the Coachella Instagram photo. I grab Rage—I have to save him! I feel blazing heat growing at my back as I pull him behind me running up Main Street. In front of the church, I turn around and see I'm dragging a skeleton, its empty eyes staring up at me.

I wake up silently screaming, my mouth open, my vocal cords frozen. I look around the room, panicked, trying to get my bearings, and for a second, just a second, I see a figure in the corner. I switch on the lamp on my night table and see that there's nothing; it was just the dream bleeding into real life, and my pulse begins to slow, my eyelids heavy again . . .

Tomorrow, I'll figure this out tomorrow . . .

VI

You have forsaken the love you had at first.
—Revelation 2:4

————————

I'm dreaming of earthquakes. No. Someone is shaking me. I open my eyes, and as they come into focus, I see Rage sitting on the side of my bed.

"Rage? What are you doing here?" I wipe my face, trying to clear a fog of sleep.

"I could ask you the same thing." His words are slightly clipped.

"I live here?" I sit up, I'm awake now and getting kind of pissed. I realize I'm only wearing a tank top, so I cover my chest with my arms. "Why are you in my room?" Did I see someone in here last night? I glance over to the corner. Things were so fuzzy after I got home.

"Your grandmother let me in."

Huh?

He misinterprets my look because he adds, "She insisted I leave the door open."

I do a "turn around" move with my finger, and once he's facing the wall, I throw the sheet aside and pull on a proper shirt and jeans. "You still haven't told me what you're doing here."

"Tae kwon do? We go every Saturday? Ring any bells?"

"Class isn't until eleven! What is it, eight-thirty? Nine?"

"It's ten-forty-five."

"No." I grab my phone and look at the time. He's right. This makes no sense. I'm an early riser; all my friends are. It's a Vermonter thing. I snatch my gym bag and sniff my dobok uniform. Ugh. It'll have to do. I cram it in, then dig for sneakers at the bottom of my closet.

"When I got no answer to my texts last night *or* this morning, I figured I better make sure you were still alive."

"What texts? I turned the notifications back on after . . ." I didn't finish that sentence. "I didn't get any—" I pull up my phone again, and when the screen lights up, there are eight texts on the Host. "That's so weird. I always hear texts come in." The first few were from last night, around the time I was sitting out front with Sam, the last one five minutes ago from Rage. I pull on some old sneakers, then rush up to the dresser and run a brush through my hair. I see him staring at me in the mirror, doing that nervous gnawing-on-his-lip thing. "What?"

"Nothing." He shakes his head, as if doing a reset. "This is just . . . weird for you."

"What's weird?"

"Sleeping in, forgetting class . . . brushing your hair."

He actually had me feeling bad until the last one. I throw my brush at him, and he ducks just in time. "I didn't forget class. Now, let's go or we'll miss it." I grab my bag and push by him. As we hurry through the living room, I yell into the kitchen, "Going to class, Abuela!"

I jump into the passenger seat of his car, shoving the fast-food containers to the side so I can fit my feet in the footwell. Ugh, I love Rage, but he's a complete slob.

As we maneuver through weekend tourist traffic, he keeps looking over at me. I'm not going to ask why.

"We missed you at Barry's last night." Pause. When I don't say anything, he continues. "Sucks you were grounded. Did you end up watching telenovelas with Abuela or something?"

So, Zee kept the text with my whereabouts to herself. I owe her one. Every Friday night, we gather in Barry's oversized garage and hang out while they drink hard lemonade out of warm bottles. These parties are silly and hickish, but still fun. This is the first I've missed since I had mono in sophomore year.

"Yep. And then I went to bed early." The words slide out so easily, which is strange since I've never lied to Rage before. Ever.

He's silent as we turn onto Route 100. Part of me wants to fess up, to tell him all about how I snuck out of the house for the first time, rode the ski lift after-hours, kissed a boy under the stars.

Had the most romantic night of my life.

I flush at the realization. With all these strange things happening to me—which all began when Sam and I met—I still feel my head spin at the thought of him.

How in the hell would I ever explain that to Rage? I don't even understand it myself.

When we pull into the dojang parking lot, we both rush out of the car, bags in hand. We go to our respective locker rooms, and I'm glad there's no time for further talk. I run out just as class is starting and take my place in the front row with Rage and the other black belts. The whole sleeping-late-and-almost-missing-class thing is still weighing on me. But as we begin the opening exercises, I ease into the familiar movements, and my brain gradually shuts off. That is, until halfway through class, when the sabom turns to us.

"Rage and Mica, will you demonstrate a spinning hook kick for the class? Rage, grab the pads. I want Mica to kick."

I groan. "Can't someone else do it?"

The instructor stares at me. "What's the rule about talking back, class?" he calls out without taking his eyes from me.

"Never talk back to your sabom!" They yell in unison, including Rage from behind me.

Traitor.

Thing is, I never have. Until today. I'm not in the mood to fight Rage. I just lied to him for the first time, kicking him now would be the definition of injury to insult. I hang my head a little and stand in front of Rage, reluctantly assuming a fighting stance.

Rage takes the kick pads, holds them out, and faces me. Our eyes meet. He has that intense, focused look he always gets in class, but there's something else there. I saw it earlier when I woke up and found him in my room acting all mad. I spin and execute the kick, hitting the pad with a neat *thunk*. Rage absorbs it easily, and I settle back into fighting stance.

"This is what I wanted to go over this week, class. That was perfectly executed in a technical sense, but just because you do the moves precisely doesn't mean you do them right. Try that again, Mica, but put more energy into it."

Energy? I feel the heat of embarrassment rise behind my face and set up again for another kick. This time my foot hits the leather pad harder and Rage's hand jolts back a bit.

"Better, better. But, Mica, this time, do it with intention."

What does that even mean? I breathe deep and do it again, but as I'm spinning back around, I can see the instructor isn't happy with this one either.

"Good effort, Mica. Class, let's move on."

Rage starts to lower the pads, shaking his head. "You're holding back, Mica."

And then the flame catches.

Before I know I'm moving, I spin around so fast the room blurs, my leg snapping out like a snake. The sound of my foot hitting the leather is a rifle shot, and Rage flies across the room, eventually smacking into the padded wall behind him and sliding to the floor.

I rock back in perfect fighting stance, my breath ragged. I glance around, confused. I hear Travis, a middle schooler, say to his friend, "Did you see that? She spun so quick I didn't even see her move!" His friend just nods and gapes at me with her mouth open.

I look over at Rage, who is trying to get to his feet. He leans against the padded wall but stumbles a bit. My hands rush to my mouth. "Oh my God!" I rush over, grab him under the armpits, and help him up.

He holds up the pads. They are destroyed, the leather hanging off in strips of skin, the inside padding spilling out like entrails.

"Rage! I'm so sorry! I don't know how that happened." I take his face in my hands, gently, and turn him to look at me. "Are you okay?"

He smiles and my whole body sinks with relief.

"I'm fine, M. But are *you* okay?"

We gaze at each other, and I notice how the sun from the sky-light makes his blue eyes look like they're lit from behind. He still has the spray of light freckles across his nose, and the skin beneath is as pale as a pearl. I can see my childhood friend in there, but sometime in the last few months, the edges of his features got sharper, the scale of him larger, stronger.

I hear Travis behind me. "Eww. Are you gonna kiss now?"

I sit up and realize everyone is staring at us. I glance back at Rage, and there's a softness to his expression I've never seen before.

Oh no.

"Mica?"

My eyes lock on the pads again and panic swells inside my chest. My limbs go numb, my pulse races.

I hear Rage call my name again, but everything sounds muffled. I head toward the side of the room, grab my bag from the bench, and take off out the front door, only breathing again when the fresh air hits my sweaty face. I don't even bother putting on my shoes. I start walking fast, following the road on the grassy shoulder.

I'm going north, not even in the direction of home, and the ground on my bare feet is cold, but I don't care. A storm of thoughts surface in my head. They're just a tangled mass of lightning. I start taking deep breaths, and my mind begins to clear. Two questions rise above all other thoughts. One: What is happening to me? I first felt that surge of power with Sam at the fair, and I loved it. But kicking Rage felt almost out of my control, like there was somebody else working my body.

I hate to admit this, but I'm scared. Really scared.

Two: What's going on with Rage? When I thought I'd hurt him, there was a feeling I'd never had before. A feeling that I can't explain. What startles me most is the realization that when I'm with Sam, it's like there's a tunnel and everything blurs so all I can see is him. But in that moment with Rage, nothing faded away, but the only person I wanted to see was him.

I've known Rage for pretty much my entire life. Our friendship is the one solid thing I could always stand on when everything felt unsteady. I don't want to screw that up.

Right?

I hear an engine start, then gravel spitting from beneath tires. As the car slows next to me, I stop but don't look over right away.

"Mica?"

The sound of Rage's voice instantly calms me.

Damn it.

I get in the car silently, and as he does a U-turn, I blurt out, "Look, Rage, I'm sor—"

"Do not apologize! That could not have been more badass!" A grin stretches across his face.

I smile back at him. Can't help it. He's too cute. "It *was* pretty badass, huh?"

"With that devastating kick, you could compete in states! Hell, maybe even nationals!"

I feel a rush of pride. "Really? You think I could win?"

"What? Of course you could!"

Then the excitement deflates a bit. "Abuela would never let me compete."

"Why? She's the one who made you take the class in the first place."

"I know. Ironic, huh? But you know, 'Pride goes before destruction, a haughty spirit before a fall,' Proverbs—'"

"'Sixteen, verse eighteen'. Yeah, my parents quote that one too."

"What, do they compare notes, or something?"

We laugh. Then an awkward silence settles.

"Why did you run off, Mica?" Rage asks. "There was a second when I thought . . . I don't know. You just seemed terrified all of a sudden."

"Well, you saw those kick pads. I have no idea how I did that, and it scared me."

"Why?"

"It's like you breaking bats this week at practice." I look over at him. "I think something is changing with both our bodies."

I see red spread across his pale face as he avoids looking at me.

I stammer to clarify. "I—I mean, we're getting stronger. Like, *really* strong. And it all started . . . suddenly."

"Mica, we've been training for ten years. And hiking in the summer, mountain biking, cross-country skiing. It's not sudden at all."

"No. Something else is going on, some . . . unseen energy."

He laughs. "Now you're sounding like Zee."

"Maybe we should be listening to Zee more often."

He glances over at me as he drives. "You're serious."

"Yes, I'm serious! Can't you sense it too?"

"Sense what?"

"That we might be in danger."

He turns onto my street. "Is that why you're going to LA?"

I slump in my seat. He pulls in front of the house and turns to me.

"Be honest. . . ." He puts his hand over mine, and I feel a tingling across my skin. "I'm worried about you. Are you running away from something?" He swallows hard. "Or someone?"

I give him a small, sad smile. "No, I'm not running from any-thing."

Maybe that's the second lie I've told him today.

VII

Here I am! I stand at the door and knock. If anyone hears my voice and opens the door, I will come in. . . . —Revelation 3:20

I get out of the car and wave goodbye to Rage. As soon as he pulls away and turns the corner, I hear my grandmother call out from the flower garden.

"Can I help you, young man?" Her voice is insistent, drill sergeant wrapped in a deceiving little-old-lady package.

I spin around and see Sam, standing there holding a book in his hand. "Hello, ma'am. I'm just look—" When he catches a glimpse of me, he smiles with relief. "Oh, hi."

Abuela stands up over the orange daylilies and wipes her hands on her dress. "Who is this, Miguela?"

I blurt out, "A friend," then grab his wrist and pull him toward the door.

"Where are you taking me?" he whispers.

"Inside. Come on."

He stops at the threshold. "You sure?"

"Yes! Come in."

I shut the door behind us with a release of breath.

He's standing there, inches from me, holding my horror novel like a bouquet of flowers. "So I've been demoted from verb dating to just a friend, huh?"

I was going to grill him for showing up unannounced, but his grin is infectious and the words leave me.

He dips his head and leans in, then stops. "We better not, right?" he whispers.

"I feel my grandmother's eyes on me."

"Through the brick wall?"

"You don't know her: I bet she has laser vision."

He grins. "So, you get the superhero gene from that side of the family, huh?"

There's something different about how I feel with Sam right now. Still wonderful, but more . . . normal. My emotions don't feel as intense, and the tunnel-vision thing has all but disappeared.

Then I remember that I'm still in my gym clothes, and now I wish that *I* could disappear. "So, what are you doing here?"

"I wanted to return this." He hands me the Dante Vulgate novel. "And I was hoping to see your bookshelves."

Okay, that's the sexiest thing that anyone's ever said to me.

"Sorry I surprised you. I was just in the neighborhood," he says. Then Sam notices the pictures on the mantel behind me.

He walks over and picks up one of my mother, the only one we have, really. It's posed, high school graduation, and she's wearing a white button-down shirt, cascades of wavy dark hair spilling over her shoulders, and a smile on her lips that looks like she's keeping a secret.

Or many of them: she was an Angeles after all.

"Is this your mom?"

"Yeah. She died when I was really young." I have this powerful urge to yank the picture out of his hands and put it back where it belongs. A part of me really doesn't want him touching it.

"I don't have any pictures of my mother. After she died, she left me this." He pushes up his sleeve and points to a wristwatch with a leather band and mother-of-pearl face. It looks like an antique.

"What did she leave Rona?"

Hopefully nothing.

"We don't have the same mom," he replies. "Do you have anything of your mother's to remember her by? Like an heirloom?"

"You're holding it."

"This is it? A framed picture?"

I nod, afraid my voice will break if I speak.

He focuses on the photograph again. "You look like her, you know?"

"You think so?" I glance at the photo, the haze of Latin glamour, the poised and confident tilt of her head. I used to pray that I would grow up and resemble her, that when I looked in the mirror, I would see part of her gazing back, like she was still kind of here.

I finally take the frame from him. "I don't see it," I say as I set it back on the mantel.

"What happened to her, Mica?"

Even though I should be the one asking him questions right now, I feel my heart soften. I want to talk about my mom. Talking about my mother makes her feel more like a memory and less like a dream.

"I don't know. I was almost two, and we were living in Puerto Rico. Something happened, an accident, I guess. But it must have been bad 'cause Abuela never wants to talk about it."

"Is that when your dad left?"

I just nod, feeling old tears rising to the surface.

"I'm sorry. I didn't mean to make you feel sad." He takes my hands in his.

"It's okay. I'm over it," I say, though we both know that is about as far from the truth as it gets.

He lifts my chin up. "I just want to know more about you."

Here it is. The perfect moment to probe him—with some questions, obviously. "Sam, strange things have been happening around here since you and Rona came to town."

He takes a step closer. "Really? Like what?"

Suddenly the room feels warm, as if the fireplace were lit. He takes another step. Now our bodies are inches apart.

I start to lose my train of thought but manage to say: "Where did you come from?"

"Down south," he says, tilting his head, just a tiny bit, and—

Three sharp raps sound on the front window.

I jump back and look over to see Abuela, her hands on either side of her face, trying to peer in.

"I guess I better go," Sam says, as if it is the last thing he wants to do.

The heat pulls away with him, and a cool breeze replaces it. Damn, if his temperature is that much higher than mine, you would think he'd look sweaty, but he always looks as cool as a cucumber.

I get a slight chill and rub my arms as I follow him out the door. The second I step onto the stone landing, my grandmother is ready to pounce.

"So? Who is this new 'friend'?"

I clear my throat. "Abuela, this is my friend Sam. Sam, this is my grandmother."

"It's an honor to meet you, Doña," he says.

She examines him as she does wilted vegetables she's about to throw in the compost: with equal parts distrust and annoyance.

She finally shifts her gaze from Sam to me. "Miguela, I need your help with the ladder." Abuela points to the side of the house.

"Oh, let me help, Señora." Sam starts walking toward her.

"No."

Sam freezes. She used a tone that could make a clock stop in fear and intimidation.

"Miguela and I can manage just fine. Thank you."

The last two words are less an expression of gratitude than a dismissal, and he takes the hint.

"Well, it was nice to meet you, Señora Angeles."

Abuela just nods, then pulls on her gardening gloves.

Sam walks quickly over to me, and I accompany him down the walkway. "Sorry. She's . . . having an off day."

I hear Abuela clear her throat. When I glance over, she's on the top of the ladder, grabbing a fistful of wet leaves and throwing them to the ground with a look of disgust.

Sam shakes it off, though.

"Don't worry about it. Hey, I almost forgot to ask you, are you still grounded?"

"No, why?"

"Great! Are you free at eleven tomorrow morning?"

Another clump of wet leaves hits the ground with a moist thud. Abuela calls out, "Miguela, we have our monthly trip to Costco in the afternoon. We must leave by two o'clock to make it home before dark."

"I'll have her back before two, Doña Angeles, I promise," Sam says, but he gets a huff in response from my grandmother.

"Ignore her," I say. There's something about her rudeness that makes me defensive of Sam, even though I'm also suspicious of him. I'm being pulled into two completely different directions at once, and it truly sucks. The only thing I can think of to do is take the opportunity to learn more about him. "So, what's happening tomorrow at eleven?"

"It's a surprise. Are you in?"

"Yes. I'm in."

"Great, I'll come pick you up—and text you beforehand."

"Cool."

I watch him walk away, and after I admire how his jeans dreamily hug his perfect butt, I vow that tomorrow I'll find out everything there is to know about Sam, even if I have to lie, cheat, and steal to do it.

"Miguela. Come here."

But first I must face Grandma Killjoy.

I turn around and head toward Abuela, who is still perched on her ladder. Leaves are scattered across the lawn in clumps like a plague of frogs.

When I get near, she looks at me and says, "You must be more careful."

I let out an exasperated breath. "I can take care of myself, okay?"

She pulls another handful of leaves, flinging it to the ground. Another. The rhythm of it is kind of hypnotizing. The musky smell of decaying leaves wafts up as they hit the grass.

"This is how it starts."

"How what starts?"

"You let down your guard, and then it's too late. Look at your parents!"

Her voice gets high at the end, and I know the last sentence was a slip. She never intentionally brings them up. "I'd like to, Abuela, but how can I? You never tell me anything about them!"

She sighs and I can see she feels bad, but I'm not letting her off the hook.

"How do I not repeat their mistakes when I have no idea who

they were? What they did? Why they left?"

"Your mother never would have left intentionally. You know that."

"Do I?"

Her head snaps in my direction, and she points a knobby, arthritic finger at me. "Never doubt your mother's love. She gave her life to protect you!"

Wait. "What?" She didn't die while giving birth to me. How could she have died *for* me? "What does that even mean?"

Abuela waves me off like I'm a mosquito. "It does not matter. I can't trust you to do the right thing anymore."

She holds on to the ladder with one hand, reaches into her housedress pocket with the other, and pulls out a crumpled and all-too-familiar letter. "I found this when I was doing laundry."

"I told you, I'd do my own laundry!" I whine, panic growing in my chest.

"Do not change the subject! You defied me, Miguela. We agreed you'd go to college here in Vermont, and then you apply to this school in California behind my back?"

"That's bullshit. We didn't agree. *You* decided. Like you always do."

A gasp. "Miguela Luisa Angeles. You do not talk to me like that, do you understand?"

Something in my chest pops, gives way, and anger floods in. "No, I don't understand, Abuela. I want to get out of here and build my *own* life! One that you can't try to control."

"I'm not trying to control your life. I'm trying to protect you."

"From what? Tell me what you're so scared of."

"You can't leave before—" She catches herself before she finishes.

"Before what? Abuela!" I'm yelling now, and I don't care.

But she seems to have gathered herself. "No. Now is not the time to talk about this." She reaches up for another fist of leaves, but I can see her hand shaking.

"Well, I'm going to LA, and you can't stop me. I don't need your protection; I can handle myself. Just because you couldn't save your daughter doesn't mean you get to ruin my life too!" Then I slam my hands against the side rails of the ladder and stalk off toward the front door.

As I grab the knob, I hear a loud metallic scraping sound. I whip around and see the ladder sliding across the gutter, heading for the ground with my abuela clinging to the top, a bunch of wet leaves still clutched in her fingers. I leap, and in one bound I'm there, lifting the ladder with her on it and righting it against the house until the metal feet are solidly on the ground once more.

My stomach lurches, but at the same time I feel an electric jolt rushing through my limbs and fingers. It's as though I could leap over the entire house. I stare at the long, heavy ladder and do a quick calculation of weight. I probably just moved two hundred pounds like it was nothing.

Holding it steady, I look up at Abuela and see that she's staring down at me, hand to her mouth. Then she does the sign of the cross.

She climbs down, her legs shaking, as I stand holding the ladder, ready to catch her. I feel a weight on my chest, and I wish I could take back everything I said.

When she reaches the bottom, I pull her into a hug, and I'm surprised that she hugs me back. "I'm so sorry! I shouldn't have said those things."

"Shh, shh," she whispers into my hair. "It is not your fault, m'ija. I'm fine." But I can feel her whole body quivering.

"Let's get you inside," I say, putting my arm around her shoulders.

She smiles, but I see tightness at the corners of her lips, and I wonder if she might be hurt. I get her inside and settle Abuela into her chair.

"I'll go make you a café con leche." I turn around to head to the kitchen, when I feel her take my arm.

"How did you do that, Miguela?" she whispers.

"I don't know," I say.

But tomorrow I intend to find out.

VIII

Blessed is the one who reads . . . —Revelation 1:3

The next morning, I rush home right after early Mass, change my clothes in a flurry, and am waiting outside the house in record time.

Breathe, Mica. Breathe.

At precisely eleven a.m., a car turns the corner and my heart speeds up. Wait, no, it's a silver Tesla. Not Sam. But it pulls in front of the house, and as the driver's side door opens, Sam climbs out and walks around the front of the car with a big dimpled smile. He's wearing a wool jacket that fits his body like it was sewn there, and a black T-shirt.

I stand up and point at the car. "What happened to your ride?"

Sam smiles. "Well, you called it a 'gas guzzler,' so I called the rental company and traded it in for something more environmentally responsible."

I grin; I can't help it. "I'm impressed."

"Oh, I'm just getting started," Sam replies with a wink.

I climb in the car, and he shuts the door after me.

When he gets behind the wheel, he pulls out his phone and starts typing, like he's firing off a text. He immediately gets multiple notifications, but then he silences the phone, like he's hiding something. He puts the car into drive, and all I can think of is sneaking a peek at his messages.

"So where are we going?" I ask him. Sam reaches over to massage my knee. "I told you, it's a surprise."

"Well, Vermont isn't full of many surprises, so you might as well give it up," I say.

"Nope. My lips are sealed. For now," he says.

Okay, that's kind of hot. But still, I better get started on this interrogation. I'm about to grill him when he lets out a wistful sigh. "You're lucky to have grown up here, hidden from the world," he says softly.

I can tell there's a lot to unpack in that sentence, but I try easing into a comfortable conversation in the hopes he'll share something useful. "I mean, I guess so? It's pretty and all, but it gets boring after a while. The same faces, the same streets, same mountains. It's like being trapped in a snow globe."

That makes him chuckle. "You seem really tight with your friends. Tell me about them," he asks as we leave the town proper and pick up a little speed.

I hear his phone vibrating against the console between us. It's blowing up with notifications, but he's just ignoring it. I wish I could see who is texting him, but if I don't want him to figure out that I'm plotting to snoop, then I better act normal.

"Well, for the most part, Stowe is made up of the haves and have-nots. The rich people who live on the side of the mountain and the locals who work at the restaurants and hotels. My friend Barry is a little of both. His family owns several farms and acres and acres of property, so he's a local boy but with money. He's a hunter with a full gun rack, but he worships Taylor Swift. A boy of many contrasts."

"How so?"

I shrug. "He calls himself a queer redneck. To top it off, he has a black skier boyfriend. Between them they've blown about a dozen New England stereotypes."

"Cool. What about the one with the bohemian vibe?"

I smile at the thought of her. "Zee? Her family is actually pretty conservative, so I have no idea where *she* came from. She's vegan, plans her life by astrological charts, dresses in flowery clothes, and is a fiddler in a bluegrass band."

"She's what I pictured when I thought of Vermonters before visiting. You know, the four Bs: Birkenstocks, Bernie Sanders, Ben & Jerry's, and Burton Snowboards."

I laugh out loud. "Yeah, that pretty much sums up Zee. But she's also the gentlest, kindest human I know. She feels everything very deeply."

Wait. Why is he so interested in my friends? What is he up to?

"The redheaded dude. What's up with him?" Sam shoots me a

sharp glare as we pull off at the Montpelier exit. "I think his name is Raguel? Looks like a gym rat."

I flinch at his comment. Is that an insult? I don't let anyone talk smack about Rage.

He picks up on my irritation. "I just mean he's got some guns. And I don't mean the real kind like Barry's." He points to his not-so-shabby biceps.

So, it was a compliment. But still. When he started talking about Rage, his voice changed. And that look he gave me was beyond chilling.

"He's pretty much my best friend," I say.

"Oh, I think he wants to be more than that."

I feel heat rise to my face, and I give him the side-eye. Yeah, that's quite enough of that. "What about your friends? The ones I saw you with at the fair?"

He pauses a bit, but then he answers. "I've known them forever. We go a lot of places and do a lot of things together."

Yeah, saw that on Instagram.

"Tonight, some of us are flying to Boston for a party."

"Wait, you're leaving? Tonight?"

He smiles at me. "I'll be back tomorrow, don't you worry." The smile fades a bit. "But really, I think they only hang out with me because of who my father is."

Damn. "That's kind of sad."

He nods distractedly as he navigates the side streets of the city.

"Who *is* your father, Sam?"

He sighs. "Well, I guess they'd say he's someone really, really important."

"And what would you say?"

"He's the only person I care about impressing, and the one person who's always completely disappointed in me."

That hits me in the chest like a punch. Probably because I feel the exact same way about Abuela. I try to shake it off and come up with some kind of diversion that would help me access his phone. Should I lie and say I lost mine and need to make a call? But then I notice that we're pulling onto the campus of Vermont College of Fine Arts, and I get distracted.

I narrow my eyes. "Wait . . . what are we doing here?"

"You're just going to have to trust me."

"Yeah, that's not something I do easily . . . or often."

"I know."

He enters the crowded lot next to Alumnx Hall but finds a space right away, as if it were reserved for him. He grabs his phone and puts it in his pocket, so I'm shit out of luck for now. Then he takes my hand as he helps me out of the car. I notice that he doesn't lock it as we walk away—must be nice to be so rich, you don't care about things like your rental car being stolen—so I have another chance. I can make an excuse to come back to the car and see if there's anything interesting inside.

I'm committing a plan to memory as we walk up the marble steps in front. But when I see the sandwich board behind a column, I stop short.

"A lecture? With Dante Vulgate?" I read off the sign in a shrill voice. "Dante's *here*?" I want to jump up and down, I swear. But I restrain myself. "Why didn't I know about this? I'm on all the book event mailing lists."

"It's part of the MFA in writing residency, not open to the general public. But luckily, I have connections."

I'm so overwhelmed and touched that I jump up and throw my arms around his neck, hanging there while doing this pig squealing sound. "Thank you. This is amazing," I whisper in his ear.

He kisses my neck gently as hugs me back. "*You're* amazing, Mica."

I feel a pang of guilt near my ribs when we walk in—how can I spy on Sam when he's done something so unbelievably nice for me? I see a cavernous auditorium with wood floors and brick walls. There's a stage set up along the side, surrounded by hundreds of folding chairs, and they all appear taken.

Then I see a poster of the event that's about to start: "Guest Lecture: Dante Vulgate on Trusting Your Instincts."

It's a literal sign. From the universe? Maybe. If I run out to the car now, I can get back in time to find out.

"Sam, I'm just going to the ladies' room real quick." I point to the lobby, where I noticed a handicapped bathroom. I mean, since I'm not going to actually use the bathroom, that's fine, right?

He nods. "I'll get us some seats."

I smile and rush toward the front of the auditorium. I look back to make sure he's not watching, slip out the front door, and head to the parking lot. As I reach for the car door handle, I feel a momentary panic that I'm wrong about it not being locked, and

I'll set off an alarm system, but it opens with no problem.

I drop down and start riffling through papers in the glove compartment, but it's only info on the rental, the car manual, nothing interesting. Then I peer under the seats. Nope, nothing in front. I switch to the back seat, but there's absolutely nothing. I pop the trunk. There's only a spare tire and a jack. I mean, it's a rental, so how much could there be? Wait! Tesla's have storage in the front. I find the lever to release the hood and am certain I'll find something there, but it's completely empty, and perfectly clean. Damn it! Yeah, I wouldn't make it ten minutes on *NCIS*.

I close up the car and rush back into the auditorium. I look over the heads and see Sam waving to me from the second row. As I make my way over, I notice the cascade of fire-red hair next to him.

Oh shit.

I slow down, but I can't turn around now. As I get closer, I see the angry set of Sam's lips as he mouths, *Sorry*, and moves over so I don't have to sit next to Rona. I drop to the seat, dazed, and she leans out over Sam.

She's dressed in a slinky, short black dress with bare legs and sky-high pumps. Very literary-event ho Barbie.

"Maga! So great to see you again." She puts her hand out to shake mine.

Oh, *hell* no.

"It's Mica," Sam and I say at the same time.

She pulls her hand back with a sneer and nudges Sam. "I didn't know you were bringing your little flavor of the month. How cute."

The president of the college climbs on the stage to introduce Dante, and Sam leans over and whispers in my ear, "I had no idea she'd be here."

"Did she follow us?"

Before Sam can answer, Dante Vulgate walks across the stage, all writerly disheveled and adjusting the oval-shaped glasses that are slipping down his nose. Everything fades to the background as the audience applauds. I sit up a little straighter, hoping he might be able to spot me in the crowd somehow. I'm fangirling, and I don't care who knows it.

But his lecture is a little uninspiring. Trusting your instincts boils down to generic writing tips that anyone could find online, and his voice is almost a monotone, like he's just going through the motions of this presentation. I must say, I'm pretty disappointed. But then he says something that floors me.

"In fiction, characters are left to the devices of authors, who are essentially gods, setting every single action into motion. But in reality, we are on our own, and the only things we can trust to guide us are the undeniable feelings burned into our DNA from those who went before us."

I let out a gasp. Rona snaps her head toward me and glares, but Sam just studies me curiously, like he was expecting my reaction.

"Now I'd like to read from a yet-unpublished short story called 'The Bargain.'"

Dante takes a deep yet shaky breath as he shuffles some papers at the podium, like he's trying to convince himself to carry on. Lucky for me, he does.

"'Melvin? Well, he was taught not to want much from this life. Good enough job. Faithful enough wife. Two point five kids, and a house with a goddamn picket fence. See, Melvin didn't know much, but if he knew one thing, it was that he wanted more. No, needed . . . more.'"

It feels like he's talking to me, reading it off my heart. I swallow and lean forward in my seat, waiting for the next sentence.

"'The only question was how far was he willing to go to get it?'"

The writing in the piece is more abrupt than his novels, the format a bit more experimental, but I love it as much as anything else he's ever written.

When he finishes, the audience wildly applauds, though Rona has her arms crossed in front of her, pissed off about something. Sam sneers at her, then whisper-shouts something into her ear. I lean over to try to hear, but the clapping and cheering around us is way too loud.

When it dies down, though, I can make out Sam saying, "Leave Mica alone. I mean it."

Then Rona stalks off, shoving some people out of her way.

Dante thanks everyone and says he will be signing books in the back. "Damn! I don't have my copy to get it signed," I say, but then I notice the scowl on Sam's face as we wait to exit the aisle.

"Are you okay?" I ask. "Where did Rona go?"

"Yes, I'm fine," he replies, though the tone of his voice says otherwise. "And Rona just took off like she always does. So. What did you think of Dante?"

I can barely contain myself. "That short story was *amazing*! I can't believe I got to hear something from his new collection that isn't out until next year." Sam is starting to smile. I guess my enthusiasm is infectious. "When he talked about his pain as 'a scab covering a still-unhealed wound'? I almost died it was so perfect. And in the end, I thought he'd save Melvin, but instead he leaves the hero isolated on an island with no hope of redemption for all eternity? So deep and dark!" I realize I'm geeking out, my voice *way* too loud, and that Sam has been leading us up to some red velvet ropes.

"We're not leaving?" I look over and see we've joined the line where they're selling *The Last Descent*. "Oh, did you want to get your own copy? Let me buy it for you. It's the least I can do—" I go to reach in my bag.

Sam puts a hand on mine before I can unzip the backpack. "Actually, I'm going to introduce you to him."

I freeze. "What?" I ask in a small voice, then grab his upper arm tightly.

He grins from ear to ear. "Yep," and he moves us forward with the line as I stare at him.

"Wait . . . you know him?"

"Yeah, my dad did some business with him a few years back."

"So, I take it you didn't actually *need* my copy of his book?"

"Nah. I just wanted to see you again."

I can't even react to that; I'm too freaked out and nervous. I clutch his jacket sleeve. "No, see, you don't understand. I can't! That would be like my abuela meeting Marc Anthony or something. Like, he's my Elvis."

"I was counting on that."

I hold on to his arm—I must be cutting off his circulation by now—and my heart beats faster as we slowly shuffle forward. I'm staring at Dante's salt-and-pepper hair, the easy way he talks with the writers while signing their books. This is the man who wrote my favorite stories of all time. Mere feet from me.

As if he'd heard my thoughts, Dante glances up and his eyes lock with mine. I must have some kind of panicked look on my face, because he gives a small laugh. Then his gaze lands on Sam.

It's like a switch has been thrown.

Dante's eyes widen, and he ignores everything else around him. I watch as his face tightens and goes completely pale. The person at the front of the line pushes their book at him, and he jumps a little, looking at them with surprise, like he'd forgotten where he was. His publicist whispers to him from behind, and he nods abruptly and scribbles into the pages of the book. With each book he signs, it becomes clearer that all charm and engagement have vanished. Like all the life has been sucked from him.

We inch closer and closer, and I watch him, trying to understand what's going on. He nervously glances at Sam every few minutes, as if to keep track of his whereabouts.

Then we're next. Dante watches us walk up.

"Sam," he says with a nervous laugh. "What are you doing here? Did your father send you?"

Sam waves his hand in dismissal. "No, no. I'm not here on business." He puts his arm around me. "My friend Mica is a huge fan, so I thought I'd bring her to meet you."

Dante doesn't even look at me, just nods and says, "Hi." But it sounds obligatory, like when Abuela used to make me greet new people at church. He looks back at Sam. "I did what you wanted. I was told my work was done."

Dante's forehead is breaking out in a sweat, while Sam seems completely at ease. What the hell is going on here?

Sam hands a credit card to the bookstore representative and pushes a copy of the book across the table at Dante. The author stares at it as if he's never seen it before.

"Her name is Mica. Sign it 'to Mica,'" Sam says, and Dante jolts a little, waking up, moving like a windup toy whose key has just been turned. He scribbles on the page his familiar illegible signature and pushes it back without looking at me.

Sam and Vulgate nod at each other, and we step away. I open the book and stare at the generic "To Mica."

"You hungry?"

I look up at Sam, surprised. He's smiling, as if that entire exchange wasn't as charged as a lightning storm. As if things like that happen all the time. I look back, and the bookstore clerk is rushing people along while the auditorium empties like an hourglass.

Sam takes me by the hand and walks me toward the exit. I

can't just let this go; I feel like this is what I'm here to discover, but my gut is telling me if I outright ask him what that was about, he'd find a way to evade my question. He's *really* good at that.

My brain is spinning, and an idea forms. When we get to the car, I open the book and exclaim, "Shit! I grabbed the wrong copy!" I look at Sam, who is already climbing into the driver's seat. "I'll be right back." I turn and dash back to the auditorium entrance.

I hug my correctly inscribed book to my chest and careen toward the table. Good, he's still there. I run up to him, almost breathless. "Mr. Vulgate?"

He glances up, sees that it's me, and nervously looks to either side. He takes a deep breath when he doesn't see Sam.

"I'm sorry, miss. I have to go," he says, practically jumping out of his seat.

"Mr. Vulgate, what kind of business did you do with Sam's father?" Not terribly subtle, but I don't know how long I have before Sam comes looking for me or, more likely, Vulgate bolts.

His eyes snap back to me. "That's between me and him, young lady." He starts to turn around but looks at me again. "Why do you want to know?"

It's the same face I've sighed at on the back of dozens of books. But it's also different. Darker, angrier, less handsome. "I just wondered what his father does . . . and why you looked so scared."

I didn't know I was going to say the last piece until it came out of my mouth, but I watch it land on the man's chest like a shove; then his face flushes with rage.

I just decided: I don't like this Dante Vulgate.

"You'll have to ask Sam that." He narrows his eyes at me. "Wait—Mica . . . is that short for Miguela?"

I nod and grasp the book tighter in my hands.

"You're the one who wrote me that email, about Maria in *The Mortal Comedy*." He points at me. "You're *her.*"

He remembers my email? He must get thousands of fan letters a day. "Yes. Why?"

The author looks at me for a beat, starts to say something, then stops when he notices Rona lingering by the exit, grinning, hands fisted at her sides.

His voice drops to a whisper. "A word of advice? Stay away from that family. They're evil. They're not even human. You'll be lucky if all they do is kill you." The minute he sees Rona approaching, he stops talking and grabs his leather bag.

Is he speaking metaphorically? "What does that mean?"

Dante turns to the bookseller. "Is there a back way out of this place?"

He gestures grandly toward an unmarked door.

"Wait! But what does that mean?" I call after him, but he takes off in an open run.

I stand there and watch him escape as Rona creeps up next to me.

"Gee, he left in a hurry. Wonder why," she says, admiring her bloodred manicure.

"He saw your face," I say. "Can't say that I blame him."

Rona steps in front of me, squaring off. "You think you're so badass, but you don't understand the shit you've stepped in."

"Oh, really? Why don't you enlighten me?"

Rona smirks. "You'll find out. When the time is right."

I feel some sweat rolling down my forehead and swipe it off. It's as if Rona's stare is burning a hole through me.

But I won't back down.

"Maybe I'll figure it out on my own," I say.

Rona throws her head back in a cackle. "Yeah. I highly doubt it."

I'm about to use my book as a weapon and clock her one, but she fishes out her phone and checks it, like she's reading a text.

Then she starts to back away and leaves without saying another word.

As I leave the building and step out into the cooling evening air, my head clears a bit, and I realize that whatever situation I'm in is *way* more interesting than any Dante Vulgate novel.

When I get to the car, Sam has a phone earpiece in, gestures for a minute as he smiles apologetically, then launches into a diatribe in French while pulling out of the parking lot.

As he drives, the conversation continues, getting heated at times. I find myself wishing so hard that I'd taken French instead of going for the easier grade in Spanish.

He doesn't get off the call until we reach Stowe.

"I'm so sorry, Mica. I hate when people do that to me, but I had to take that call."

He turns on to my street, and I can see Abuela standing by her car already. Shit! "What happened back there?"

Tilted bird-head gesture. "What do you mean?"

Um . . . where do I begin?!

"With Dante Vulgate. You guys were acting pretty weird. Then I ran into Rona and she was giving me crap. And that call just now sounded like it was a huge argument."

Sam waves his hand. "Vulgate's always been a head case." Pause. "Same goes for Rona. And the argument on the phone was with my father."

"Your father speaks French?"

Sam shrugs. "Well, he's in France at the moment, so . . ."

As if that explains it. "What were you fighting about?"

"He's getting impatient with some business he wants me to finish up. He won't stop texting me. It's so annoying."

We're pulling up to the house. Time is running out. "What business?"

He brings the car to a stop and runs his hand over his face, as if trying to wipe something away. "The kind I no longer want to do."

"Miguela!" Abuela barks from the driveway, and Sam and I look toward her, hands fisted on her hips, lips tight.

"Costco awaits," he says with a shrug.

Damn it.

IX

I will come like a thief, and you will not know at what time
I will come to you. —Revelation 3:3

The weekly trip to Costco is painful. Even more painful than usual because it cut my time with Sam short and I'm dying to talk to Zee about what I learned, but my phone died before I could finish the text. And heaven forbid Abuela should have a charging cord in her car. Actually, since it is basically run by hamsters on a wheel under the hood, it wouldn't have the juice to do it anyway. ("I know we can afford a new car, Miguela! But why would we need it? This one runs just fine, gracias a Dios.")

To top it off, when we're on the interstate, Abuela takes a breath like she's preparing to deep-sea dive and starts in. "We need to discuss that college in California that you applied to behind my back."

"UCLA."

"I know what it's called. Do not be patronizing to me."

There's a long silence, and then she breaks it with "You must withdraw your application."

"No! This is my choice. And I don't want to talk to you about it anymore!"

She glances over at me, then her eyes return to the road, her arthritic fingers grasping the wheel at ten and two with white knuckles. Then in a voice that is quieter, less sure, she says, "You've changed lately, Miguela. I fear for you."

I can't help but think she's referring to the ladder incident. I scared her. But the truth is, I'm scaring myself these days.

The rest of the drive is silent, and when we turn the corner onto Maple Street, we're greeted by a wall of flashing blue and red in the fading afternoon light.

"What's going on?" My voice is strung tight.

"Ay Dios, is it Mr. Pembly?" Abuela says while making the sign of the cross.

As we inch forward, I gasp. "No, it's our house!"

Abuela parks in front of our neighbor's home behind a line of cars with blazing lights on their roofs. I see Barry's truck up ahead and Rage standing next to it. I jump out as soon as the car comes to a stop and run over to him.

"Mica, we've been trying to reach you." He takes my shaking hands in his. "Why aren't you answering your phone?"

"My battery died while we were shopping. What happened?"

"Barry and I were driving through town when we heard it on

the scanner, a break-in. When they said the address, we rushed over."

Thank God Barry is on the rescue squad and has a police scanner at home and in his truck.

Abuela quietly steps up beside me. "Raguel? ¿Qué pasó?"

Rage puts an arm around each of us and walks us to the house. "Mr. Pembly noticed your front door was open. Since he knew it was Costco day and you weren't home, he called the police."

For the first time ever, I'm grateful for nosy neighbors.

We arrive at the front door, then step into a hive of activity. "It's kind of a mess, but the police need you to see if anything was taken," Rage says.

I glance around the living room, and my throat tightens. There are uniformed people standing around talking quietly, writing things down, examining our personal things. The furniture is turned over, the drawers of the desk pulled out, the shelves empty, and my precious books scattered across the floor. Even from a distance, I can see that my room is in the same state. A sick feeling settles in my stomach, and I wish I could just run out and not come back. I look over at Abuela standing next to me, and her face is pale, but I see a fire stoking in the way she's looking around. She's pissed.

A young police officer comes up to her. "Mrs. Angeles, I'm Officer McHugh, and I—"

"I know who you are, dear." She pats his hand distractedly. "I'm in the knitting group with your mother, remember?"

The policeman looks a little flustered, but he keeps going, as if he has a script he is following, "I know this must be hard for you; I just have a few questions. It appears whoever did this was looking for something. Any idea what that might be?"

"We don't have anything worth stealing," I reply.

That fact used to bother me. Now? Not so much.

However, I notice a distant look on Abuela's face, like she's secretly plotting something. She can't seem to make eye contact with me either. God, I'm an idiot. Here I've been so focused on unraveling the mystery of Sam and Rona when my grandmother has been hiding things from me my whole life—and now it seems to have caught up to her.

The flash of anger vanishes when I see her staring at her favorite devotional candles that are all smashed. What if this had happened before we went to Costco? When she'd been alone in the house?

Wait a second.

Sam. He showed up here yesterday. He was poking around, asking questions. He knew when we'd be out. He had that whisper fight with Rona, a fight that had something to do with me.

And then there was Dante Vulgate's warning.

You'll be lucky if all they do is kill you. Is it possible? That there's a link between Sam and Rona and the past that Abuela has been hiding from me?

"Let me walk you through the house so we can figure out what might have been taken," the officer says in a gentle voice. Abuela nods again as she takes in the mess, head held high, but purse clasped tightly against her stomach.

I go to the kitchen and plug my phone in the outlet, then return to Abuela's side while the phone charges. We walk about the living room and take in all the damage. It's one of the most painful things I've ever done.

"Oh, my Lladró figures!" Abuela exclaims with a trembling voice. She bends down and picks up the robin's-egg-blue figure of Don Quixote that is lying headless on the floor. My grandmother is not a sentimental person, but she loves those silly Spanish porcelain figurines.

I feel like I might cry as she clucks her tongue and looks around for the knight-errant's head. Rage finds it in the far corner and brings it back to her. "I can fix it. Some superglue, and it will be fine."

He's smiling at her, holding the two pieces together as if he can make it all right with sheer will, but I can see the sadness in his smile.

She absently pats his cheek, then her hand goes to the saint medal under her sweater. For not the first time, I wonder what's on that medal since I've only caught glimpses of it. Why does she never wear it outside her clothes?

As they're moving into Abuela's bedroom, I notice the photo of my mother is facedown on the mantel. I pick it up and rub my sleeve all over it, trying to wipe off any trace of invasion, but it just doesn't feel clean. Something breaks inside of me, and I start sobbing.

"You okay, Mica?"

I see Barry standing in front of me, and I stumble forward, hug him tight, and bury my snotty face in his flannel-covered chest.

He rubs my hair and holds me tight. "We're going to find out who did this."

I might already know.

"Mica?" Rage calls as they move into my room. "They need you to look around in here."

Barry gently wipes the tears from my cheeks with his calloused farm hands, and I've never felt so much love for the big lug. I gently put Mom's photo back on the mantel and take a deep breath. "Coming."

My room is torn apart, but I don't see anything that's obviously missing. More of my beloved books all over the floor, my laptop is open but still there and working. The whole room smells different, like leaking batteries and soil. The walls feel like they're moving in closer and closer, so I excuse myself and check on my phone in the kitchen.

I enter my password with shaking fingers. There's a missed text from Sam with a photo of him in his roomy first-class plane seat.

Miss you already!

The time stamp of the text is right while we were at Costco, so it seems like he had nothing to do with all this.

So, that leaves Rona. I should tell Officer McHugh about her. But what am I going to say? That she's mean and made me hallucinate? If I told him that, he would probably send me to the hospital to get my head examined. Besides, this is personal, and I'm going to handle my business, even if I have to take off my earrings and throw down with that redheaded biatch.

✗ ✗ ✗

Fifteen minutes later, we're all sitting in the living room, drinking coffee and fielding questions while Officer McHugh writes our answers in his little book. My eyes are starting to cross when Zee appears in the front doorway, still dressed in the uniform from her hospital shift. The minute I see her silhouette and the colorful tote bag on her shoulder, I burst into tears all over again.

"I came as soon as I could!" she says, hugging me.

For the rest of the questions, Rage sits on one side of me, and Zee on the other, holding my hand in both of hers, while Abuela and the policeman sit like sentries in the two armchairs.

When they're all done, Barry sees the last of the police crew out—he knows them all by first name—and closes the door behind them. He turns to us and claps his hands together. "Okay, Mrs. A, put us to work."

Zee reaches into her bag and holds up a bundle of herbs wrapped in string and a pink spray bottle. "I brought some natural disinfectant spray and some sage to smudge the hell out of this place." She flushes as she realizes Abuela is standing nearby. "If that's all right with your grandmother, I mean."

Abuela leans over. "Why wouldn't it be, m'ija?"

Zee shrugs. "I don't know, some devout Catholics consider burning sage . . . too magicky?"

Abuela dismisses this with a wave. "Not Puerto Rican Catholics, my dear. Our roots are African and Indigenous, so we are not so—how should I say it?—closed-minded in our beliefs. And who couldn't do with some spiritual cleansing, ay?" She winks at Zee and goes back to bossing Barry about.

Zee smiles, waits until Abuela is across the room, and reaches into her bag one more time to produce a pile of deeply colored fabric. She whispers, "I also stole some of my mother's two-hundred-thread-count Peruvian cotton sheets so you can sleep comfortably and luxuriously tonight."

I start to cry again, but she just places the sheets in one of my hands and takes the other, gently leading me into my bedroom.

With all the extra hands, the work goes quickly. Zee helps me put things back together, and make my room feel less . . . violated. I love the woodsy smell of the burning sage, and Barry and Rage help restore order to the rest of the house with Abuela supervising.

"No, no, Barry dear, that end table goes on the other side." She's standing straight, hands on her hips, voice loud and strong. My grandmother appears revived by being able to boss people around.

Zee is still buzzing about, adjusting things, probably considering the feng shui of each placement. She notices my mother's photo, which I had clumsily placed before my crying spree. She picks it up to adjust it, but when she touches the silver frame, she jolts as if it gave her an electrical shock.

I watch her quickly place it on the mantel and shake out her hands.

"Zee? What's wrong?" I ask her.

She forces a smile as she looks at me with fear at the edges of her eyes. "Nothing. I was just . . . admiring how beautiful your mother was."

Yeah, not buying it, but I don't push. I can't handle any more bad news tonight.

When all is returned to relative order, we walk Barry and Zee to the door, Abuela pouring gratitude and God's blessings all over them. Zee gives me one last hug and whispers, "You call me anytime, day or night, and I'll be here."

When I close the door, I lean my head on it, grateful for my friends. I turn around, and Rage is settling onto the couch.

"I'm not going anywhere, Mica, so don't even bother trying to kick me out," Rage says, grabbing the remote and making himself at home. "No way I'm leaving you guys here alone tonight. You're *way* too important to me." He says it while looking at me but then looks over at my grandmother. "Both of you are."

I'm about to argue but find I don't want to.

Abuela just rubs her hands together. "Well then, I will start on dinner, yes? I will make your favorite, Raguel, grilled cheddar sandwiches and tomatoes. It will be just like old times." She shuffles off to the kitchen with renewed energy.

I walk over and whisper, "Aren't you lactose intolerant now?"

"Shh! I don't have the heart to tell her. She looks so happy."

My heart warms in my chest. She does, and she needs it after this afternoon. We all do.

Rage eats that sandwich with gusto as we sit around our small kitchen table, though by the end his stomach is already rumbling. Abuela takes it as a sign he's still hungry. As I watch him convince her that she doesn't need to make him another sandwich, I feel as though my heart is literally swelling in my chest. How many times has he eaten with us at this very table? How many times has he been there for me?

After cleaning up, the three of us move to the living room to watch a movie. Rage builds a fire, and it takes a while for me to find something light enough after the dark end to the day, but we settle on something Pixar. Before the end credits roll, Abuela is nodding off.

"Well, niños. I'm going to bed. This was too much excitement for an old lady."

Rage starts to get up from his seat on the rug. "Can I get you anything, Mrs. Angeles? Let me help you."

"Don't be silly, Raguel. I'm fine." She hustles to the hall closet, comes back with a soft hunter-green blanket, and gives it to him with a warm smile. "Thank you, joven. For everything." She leans down, kisses him on the forehead, then me, and begins to shuffle toward her room.

I feel our argument from the car haunting the both of us now that the shock of the break-in has waned. "Abuela?"

She slowly turns around. "Yes, mi cielo?"

On impulse, I jump up, run around the couch, and yank her into a fierce hug.

She's surprised at first but then gives a warm chuckle and hugs me back.

I whisper into her hair, the clean, woodsy smell of her hairspray so familiar, "I'm sorry I've changed." And in the moment, I am. I want everything to go back to where it was, before the break-in, before I met Sam, before everything.

She takes my face in her hands and puts her nose right up to mine. "Never be sorry for change, m'ija. It is hard, but always necessary." She kisses my forehead again, gives me a smile, then heads to her room.

I go back to the couch and settle into my usual corner.

Rage stretches, his long arms reaching up as he yawns. "You gonna turn in too, M?"

I shake my head and then slide down from the couch and onto the floor next to him. "Rage, I'm not going to lie; I'm freaking out."

He puts his arm around me and pulls me close. I drop my head onto his shoulder and close my eyes.

When he speaks, I feel the vibration against my cheek. "I think you might be right. Something *is* going on. My parents, they're acting all kinds of weird."

"Really?"

"Yeah. They, like, whisper-shout at each other and then stop the moment I walk into a room," he explained. "Have you noticed anything strange with your grandmother? I mean, other than today?"

"Abuela is always nervous. She's like a human chihuahua, always fiercely barking at shadows."

We sit there in silence for a while, tucked together on the floor of the living room. A memory bobs to the surface. "Remember that sleepover in middle school when you stayed with us 'cause your parents went to Europe and I insisted we watch *Blade*?"

I feel a chuckle rumble in his chest. "How can I forget?" He points to the floor in front of the fire. "We were right there, in sleeping bags. And you were so scared that you wouldn't calm down until you grabbed the two largest knives from the kitchen. I zipped our two bags together and swore that I'd help you fight the vampires."

I nod. "I wore one of my grandmother's rosaries around my neck for a week."

"I remember all the garlic pizza you ate. The smell started to come out of your pores!"

We both laugh, then settle back into comfortable silence. The only sound is the crackling of the logs in the fireplace and the ticking of the mantel clock.

I'm just nodding off when he says my name, then gently tugs my face up by my chin.

"Do you have any idea how much you mean to me, Mica Angeles?"

I gaze at him; I know the angles of his face better than my own.

"I swear, I would do anything to protect you and your abuela. Anything."

I feel a wave of gratitude rush through me. For him being here for us today. For his staying. For always, *always* being there for us.

I glance at his soft lips and lean forward. The feel of his skin, his smell of detergent and woodsmoke, spread like warmth in my chest as we kiss. Our lips part and our tongues find each other's, and the warmth starts to spread all over my body. I open my eyes a little and instead of seeing my best friend's face, I see Sam's—the same grotesque image that I saw on Rona's IG page.

I jolt backward, my stomach churning. Then I'm on my feet, my breath ragged, before he even knows what's happening.

"Mica? What's wrong?"

His voice is groggy, and he sounds disoriented, like someone who's drunk.

"I . . . I gotta go to bed. Thanks, Rage. For staying."

I sprint to my room, not looking back at what I imagine is a hurt look on his face. When I close the door behind me, Rage's question is ringing in my ears.

What's wrong?

Everything.

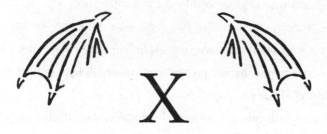

X

Whoever has ears, let them hear. —*Revelation 13:9*

The next morning, Rage is gone, the pillows returned to their usual place on the couch, the blanket neatly folded, no sign of him anywhere. I'm disappointed and relieved all at once, heat rising to my face with the memory of our kiss.

I shuffle to the kitchen and find my grandmother already fully dressed and scurrying about.

"You okay, Abuela?"

"Yes, of course," she mutters, then looks over at me. "Miguela, why aren't you dressed?"

"For what?"

"School!" She looks at her watch. "Get your uniform on. Zee will be here to pick you up in twelve minutes!"

My mouth hangs open. "Our house was broken into yesterday!

I figured I'd stay home and help clean some more."

"I've been cleaning for two hours; it's all done. Besides, life doesn't stop because of some ruffians." She doesn't even pause in her fussing, fluffing of cushions, returning Rage's blanket to its closet nest.

I'm still staring at her when she notices, then stops.

"M'ija, you must go to school. We cannot allow the sins of others to slow us down. Your education is more important than a little dust or dirt." Then she turns me around and smacks my bottom gently. "Now go!"

I can't believe this. To say I don't feel like going to school is the biggest understatement of the century. I throw on my uniform with robot-like movements and let her push me out of the house.

Why is she so eager to get rid of me?

Zee's late, so I walk up the street to keep an eye out for her.

I stop at the corner so I can see in both directions in case she comes the other way, but when I glance back down the street, I see Rage's mom getting out of her car in front of my house.

That's weird.

Then Barry's father pulls up behind in his giant mud-covered truck.

Wait, is that Zee's mom's Mercedes parked in the driveway?

"Good morning!" I hear Zee's cheery voice coming from the idling car at the curb.

I climb into the passenger seat, still staring down the street.

"You sure you feel up to going to school today? I couldn't believe it when my mom told me to pick you up. I thought Abuela would at least give you a day to recover." She pauses. "What are you looking at?"

Without turning my head, I point down the block. "Zee, why are everyone's parents at my house?"

"What? No, my mom said she was going to a library board meeting."

I shake my head. "Her car's parked in our driveway. Look."

Zee lifts up her sunglasses and squints. "Huh, that's weird. And is that my dad's car? He's supposed to be at work."

"I'm telling you, something's going on. I'm texting the guys."

Me: Guys, all our parents are having a secret meeting at my house RIGHT NOW

Barry: Nah, my dad was at the feed store first thing.

Me: I'm telling you, he's at my house, along with your mom, both of Zee's parents, and both of your parents, Rage.

Rage: WTF?

Me: I know! We need to figure out what's going on. Come quick so we can check it out.

Rage: Don't you have class in two minutes?

Me: Um, what aren't you getting about SECRET MEETING?

Rage: I'd love to, M, but if I miss another homeroom, the coach will pull me from tonight's game.

Barry: Yeah, I'm skating on thin ice too. Can we meet after school?

Me: I can't go to class. I'm too hyped up.

Barry: Then c u later, you truant!

Rage: Be careful.

I unbuckle my seat belt.

"Wait, where are you going?" Zee's pulling out her phone, trying to catch up on the Host conversation.

"Go ahead to school if you need to, Zee. I have other things to do."

"Wait." She does a quick U-turn.

"What are you doing?"

"Friends don't let friends ditch alone." She parks down behind the church, near the rec path, where her car can't be seen from Main Street. "Besides, there's some next-level shit going on around here, and we need to figure out what."

I smile wide. "You're the best, do you know that?"

"Yep!" she says as she slams her car door.

We make our way up the hill and across the street, but Zee stops at the corner. "We can't just waltz in there and demand to know what's going on. They'll just join forces and stonewall us."

"Yeah, I wasn't planning to go in through the front door. C'mon!" I lead her behind the row of houses, careful to stay close to the buildings so we're not spotted. "I never locked my bedroom window after sneaking out Friday night."

We cross the Pearsons' big yard, ducking behind the forgotten and rusty swing set as Zee whispers, "Did you tell your grandmother about the UCLA acceptance?"

I glance back at her. "Really, Zee? Now?"

She shrugs, stepping over a rake. "I was just wondering if that might be what this is all about."

"No way. Why would your family care? Abuela found the letter when she was doing laundry anyway."

Zee stops. "She did? Why didn't you tell me?"

I really, really don't want to talk about this now, so I don't answer and keep moving.

"I'm just saying, maybe you should think about what your grandmother says. Maybe she's right and you should stay and go to school in Vermont."

I stop short and whip around to face her. "Seriously? You're going to side with her over me?"

"Mica! There aren't any sides. We're all on your side, don't you know that by now?"

"Oh, so now it's 'we'? Jesus, Zee, I thought you'd back me on this. I thought you understood."

The air between us is thicker than it's ever been, and it's almost hard to breathe. I wait a beat, then start moving again, and after a short pause, I hear her following behind me. We cut through the Clarks' backyard, jump a hedge, and tiptoe up toward my house.

I gently slide open my window and listen. There are voices coming from the living room.

"I hear them, but I can't make out what they're saying."

"Well? Are we going to break and enter, or what?" Zee gestures impatiently at the window.

I slide it open all the way, pull my body up onto the ledge, and rather ungracefully dump myself into the room and onto the floor, my uniform skirt up around my waist. Good thing I'm not worried about being "ladylike," as Abuela puts it. Zee follows but lands much more gracefully.

Zee's clearly done this before, but I'm too distracted to tease her about it.

We pad over to the door, and I ever-so-quietly turn the knob and open it, just a crack. We both lean as close as we can, and strain to listen.

"No, I *know* they were looking for it," Abuela's saying.

Rage's mother responds first. "Well, thank God it's not here! If they'd gotten it, there'd be no reason to keep you two alive."

Zee and I gape at each other.

"But our first priority is protecting the children," Zee's mom says.

I assume "the children" is the four of us, but safe from what?

"Do they know about the others, or just Miguela?" Rage's mother asks.

Abuela shakes her head. "Just Miguela, as far as I can tell."

The others? Zee mouths.

I hear Zee's dad's voice cut in, even more firm and alpha than it normally is. "Well, I think it's clear: we have to take the kids and run in different directions. That way they're spread out."

Zee's eyes get big and glassy.

Barry's dad scoffs, "Easy for you to say! My family's been here for generations. Nobody's gonna make me leave my land."

"No, no, Justin, you will not have to run." Abuela pats Zee's father's hand. "We brought them here so they could be safe. Out in the country, surrounded by mountains. This county was determined to be the safest place to avoid natural disasters in the nation, for heaven's sake! It was the best option."

"But we have to face that it might not be the best option moving forward!" Zee's dad's voice is getting louder with each word.

Zee's mom puts her hand on her husband's shoulder. "Wait a minute, honey. We don't even know if they've inherited the legacy. For all we know, they could just be four normal teenagers. So why would they be in danger?"

Legacy? Zee mouths.

Normal? I respond.

Rage's mom pipes in. "No, I think Justin's right. The safest option is to split them up and run. I have three other children to worry about, not just Raguel. For years, this group has had to focus on our firstborns, but I need to think about *all* of my family."

Then everyone's talking at once, until Abuela's declaration breaks through.

"No. Miguela and I will take it and leave. She's the one they know about, no need to uproot all the other children."

Excuse me?

Zee takes my hand. I squeeze it tight. My heart is beating so loudly, I'm worried they'll hear it.

Silence. Hold on, does that mean they all agree? They'd let us go so easily?

"When will you go?" Barry's father asks.

My throat tightens.

Abuela sighs. "I need a couple days to make proper arrangements. Forty-eight hours?" Her voice is tired but resigned.

Whispered words of regret, appreciation, and goodbye follow, but it's all a meaningless hum to me. I ease my door shut as the front door closes, and Zee and I stand there, the sounds of Abuela shuffling into the kitchen and washing the coffee cups echoing through the house.

I'm having trouble breathing.

Zee puts her hand on my shoulder and points toward the window. I nod, we climb out, and I ease the window shut.

We walk back to the car in silence, shaken to our cores.

After we get into the car and slam the doors shut, Zee turns to me.

"Clearly our parents have some serious secrets."

"Ya think?"

"Your grandmother said they all brought us here to be safe, but I thought our families had come at different times. And as Barry's dad said, his family's been here for generations. Or have they?"

We sit in silence for a minute; then Zee jolts a bit, turns the key in the ignition, and starts backing the car out.

"Zee, where are you going?"

"You up for a road trip?" she asks. "We need to do some research, and I know just the place to do it."

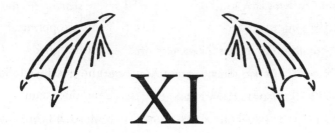

XI

Blessed is the one who reads aloud the words of this prophecy,
and blessed are those who hear it and take to heart what
is written in it, because the time is near. —Revelation 1:3

I unbuckle my seat belt and sink down so I can't be seen.

Zee looks over and chuckles. "What are you doing?"

I peer up at her from my spot, crammed in the passenger seat footwell. "Look, I'm new to this cutting school thing, all right?" With my arms and legs folded in, I fit surprisingly well, but the smell of warm vinyl and musty carpet is so overpowering, I keep my head up near the glove compartment.

"Yeah, but don't you think acting like a fugitive is a wee bit excessive?"

"Have you *met* my grandmother?"

She lets out a breath. "True."

I look up toward the windshield and see a clear purple stone hanging from the rearview mirror, glinting on and off as the sun hits it. "What's that kind of stone for?" I say, gesturing up toward the dangling rock.

"Amethyst; excellent for protection."

"Good." I'm not going to tease Zee about the crystals anymore. I'll take all the protection I can get.

Once we're safely out of downtown, I climb back into my seat. "So, are we going to process whatever that was we just heard?"

She smiles at me. "Aw, Mica! Processing? I'm rubbing off on you!"

"Yeah, yeah." I wave her off, but I'm secretly pleased she noticed. "They said all four of us are in some kind of danger when they were talking about the break-in, and that *they* didn't find *it*."

"Well, the obvious questions are: What kind of danger? And *who* didn't find *what*?"

"Exactly."

Zee glances over at me. "Should we talk about Sam and his possible connection to all this? You didn't seem to want to go there before."

I look out the window, comforted by the expanse of just-shorn cornfields. "I admit it. There was a part of me that didn't want to face it."

She put her hand on my arm. "I get that. I felt his pull just meeting him once."

My head whips at that. "You did?"

"Sure. In that short time we were with you guys at the fair, and especially when I hugged him."

So, she feels it too. I tell her about what happened at the book signing, and Dante's warning. "What do you think? Are Sam and Rona some kind of witches or demons or something?"

She's quiet for a moment. Then a sigh. "I'm not sure. But there's good in his heart; I felt it."

That brings me more comfort than she knows. "Zee, what did you feel when you held my mother's photo last night?"

A shadow passes over her eyes as she stares ahead. "It was just an echo, really. Like the people who broke in left residual energy. It was everywhere before we smudged but strongest on the photo, like . . . fingerprints."

"Whose fingerprints?"

She shakes her head. "I'm not sure. But the picture held some power, some significance to the person who held it. Like they couldn't handle your mother watching them."

I think of Sam holding the photo, of my overwhelming need to take it from him. His question about a memento.

Zee asks, as if my thoughts were somehow part of our conversation, "What was that about a memento? Could it be something of your mom's Sam's looking for?"

I stare at her. "How do you do that?"

"Do what?"

"Zee, can you read minds now?"

"Not really read. It's more like I can feel particular thoughts, emotions." She glances over at me. "And it's gotten stronger over the past week or so. Like, it's hard to concentrate on anything else. Forget paying attention in school, all those raging hormones? It's chaos."

Guess Rage and I aren't the only ones who are experiencing changes. We sit with that for a minute; then finally I answer her question. "Thing is, Sam couldn't have broken into my house." I tell her about the photo from the plane.

"I mean, it's not exactly iron clad, but it sounds like it wasn't him."

"Now, his sister on the other hand . . ."

Zee shudders. "Just being six feet away from her I felt my skin crawl."

My phone buzzes. "Great, it's Abuela. The school must have ratted me out." I decline the call.

As if on cue, Zee's ringer goes off. "Yep. Let's text them that we're safe, then shut our phones off."

"Good idea." The sound of both phones powering down brings me comfort. "Speaking of parental units and grandmothers, let's try to figure out what's going on with them."

"Especially since they were talking about *our* lives."

"Did you get the feeling our families have been meeting in secret for years?"

Zee's eyes widen. "Yes! That makes total sense. Remember those 'parties' when we were all playing and they locked themselves in our den?"

I chuckle. "Yeah, we always wondered if all adult parties were so boring."

"When your grandmother mentioned them bringing us here, I figured we could look into the families' histories; see what the true story is. Hence the road trip. Saint Michael's College has a record of all Catholics families who moved into the state. We should be able to find info on Barry's family, anyway."

"Excellent!" I say it like I'm excited because I am. It's so good to be able to *do* something.

"Mica?"

"Hmm?"

Zee keeps looking forward; it doesn't seem like she's really seeing the road ahead.

"The visions are getting worse. Flames and darkness, melting faces—"

Melting faces. I swallow.

"—and so much screaming, and . . . creatures."

"Creatures?"

She nods. "A being, with big black wings and flames for hair . . ." She stops herself for a moment, then goes on. "It's like there's another world flashing in and out over ours; like that world is slowly going to overtake this one."

"It sounds a lot like how Rona made me feel. And by the way, her hair is pretty damn flame-like. Did you see the creature's face?"

She shakes her head like she's trying to block out the memory. "No, but I can't help but think it's related to whatever our parents were talking about."

We're both silent then for a time, trying to piece together all this information. I start to feel like I can't breathe. "Zee, mind if I open the windows? It's hotter than Hades in here."

"No, let's." The windows stutter open, and we both sigh as a warm breeze blows through. "The weather report says it'll be over seventy degrees today."

"In November."

"Yep."

"Huh." Finally, I ask what's on both our minds, the question I know neither of us has an answer to: "What does this all mean?"

Zee shrugs, such an ordinary gesture about a situation that is anything but ordinary. "I don't know, but I think we might as well find a priest while we're there too."

The campus is hopping when we pass through the front gates of Saint Michael's College in Colchester, and as I watch a group of students cut across the parking lot, I try to picture myself among them, walking to class in the sun, books in hand. But right now, there's too much darkness in the way to imagine anything in the future. Even sunny LA is obscured in my thoughts. When we pull into the library parking lot, we easily find a space and head into the imposing brick building. The college offers all Catholic high schools in Vermont access to their resources, so luckily our school IDs get us in.

I point to the severe-looking nun behind the circulation desk. "Let's do this old-school. I don't think we should leave a digital trail until we know what we're dealing with. Or have I been watching too much *NCIS* with Abuela?"

"Girl, whatever is going on, they already have access to our heads, so I'm not sure we need to worry about internet searches.

But I happen to like old-school." We make our way over.

"Excuse me, Sister? We're hoping you can direct us to the Vermont Catholic Church Records?" Zee puts her school ID on the counter, heading off the first question.

The nun looks up with dark ferret eyes and peers at us, taking in our uniforms, our obligatory smiles. "You girls know all this is available online now, right? It is the twenty-first century after all."

Just what I need, to get schooled on digital resources by a four-hundred-year-old nun.

But Zee just turns her charm to eleven. "Oh, we know, but our teacher wants us to do this the traditional way. She's taught us all about card catalogs and the Dewey decimal system. It's fascinating, really. I think we've lost some . . . depth from the research process without those tools, don't you?"

And the woman's face shifts, the lines soften, a smile threatens. "Oh, young lady. You have no idea. You children will never know the joy of flipping through a drawer stuffed with cards listing all the knowledge in the world, of walking down a long row of musty tomes, following the letters and numbers until you arrive at your book as if led there by divine providence." She sighs, and I know we have her.

She stands up and comes around the desk. "Follow me, girls."

I smile at Zee and whisper, "You're *way* too good at that."

She shrugs. "What can I say? It's a gift."

And it *is* a gift. Zee's always been able to talk her way out of things, sense change in the air, sometimes even know what's going to happen before it does. It's like her superpower.

The librarian nun leads us into a small room with rows and rows of black binders; the physical copies of all that was digitized, and though it's overwhelming, I'm also excited. One of these books could hold answers, something I've had very little of in my seventeen years.

"What years are you looking for, young ladies?"

I say, "The last fifty to a hundred?"

She leads us to a corner bookcase and indicates a row of black binders on the bottom shelf. She turns to Zee and pats her arm. "I'll be at the front desk if you need anything, dear."

No wonder Abuela is so taken with Zee. She's a Boomer whisperer.

Zee throws her bag on the floor and starts examining the spines. "Let's start with Barry's family. They've been in Vermont the longest."

We settle in and get to work.

Time loses all meaning in that room of information, and the next time we look up, over an hour has gone by.

I slam the most recent book closed in front of me. "We know they've been here since the very beginning. And though his ancestors included some influential people, lawyers, judges, doctors, they kept a pretty low profile."

Zee is in the last pages of hers. "A *very* low profile. Interesting, Barry didn't inherit that trait."

I snort.

She discovers binders of newspaper articles, finds the ones related to Stowe, and starts flipping through as I slog through the Catholic records from the early eighteen hundreds.

After about twenty minutes of reading, Zee lets out a small gasp. "Mica. Look at this."

I walk around the table to look over Zee's shoulder. It's a 2007 article from the *Stowe Reporter*. "Wait . . . Barry's family funded the building of our school? And your family too?"

"Apparently, not only did they 'bring us here,' they built us a freaking school!"

"Yeah, but why didn't we ever know this? I mean, we go there every day!"

"And it says the chapel altar houses a religious relic and was shipped in from . . ."

She stops reading, and I look down at the page. As the words come into focus, my breath catches. "Puerto Rico?" I stare at her, both of us remembering my vision when I touched the altar, the fire, the feeling of searching.

"We need to find out what's in there."

We do some frantic digging in the papers, hoping to learn what the relic could be. We find several more articles about the school, but no more details about the altar or its contents. We need more information. I head back to the circulation desk to find an old priest sitting there. His chin is on his chest, and I swear to God his skin is the same color as the paper he's holding in his lap.

He's dead. Has to be.

"Can I help you?" the corpse says with a creaky voice, and I hold back a scream.

"Um, yes. We're trying to find information on a religious relic that was brought to Vermont?"

He squints at me, and I can't help but focus on his white eyebrows. They're, like, four inches long and loom over his eyes like white spider legs. I have an overwhelming desire to grab the scissors from the desk and trim them. "Which one? You must be more specific, young lady, if you hope to get anywhere in this world."

Ugh. Maybe I'll cut his eyebrows completely off. "The one in the altar in the chapel at Sacred Line Academy."

He springs up like a freaking jack-in-the-box, and I almost scream again. He comes out from behind the desk and walks at a speed I thought impossible for someone of his advanced age. As we buzz by the room we were in, I call out, "Zee! Follow us!" She runs out to follow, but even she can barely keep up.

He stops in front of a particular bookcase, lowers the glasses that were perched on the top of his head, and examines the titles, until he arrives at one in particular, and pulls it down with a skinny, gnarled finger. He looks at the table of contents, opens to a particular page, and slams it on the nearest table. Then taps at the book like it killed his dog. "There."

We glance at the drawing, and there it is, the altar I visit every day I'm able. The one that I think is trying to talk to me.

"It looks so new," Zee remarks.

The old priest scoffs. "Hardly! That altar is hundreds and hundreds of years old."

Like you, I think but don't say. "And it was shipped from Puerto Rico? From where?"

He peers at the small text again. "It says right here, 'It was miraculously untouched after the fire at Academia de San Miguel in Santurce, Puerto Rico.'"

San Miguel's? "When was the fire?" I ask as a cold feeling spreads through my chest.

He looks. "Two thousand and six."

The year I turned one.

"September twenty-ninth, to be exact."

The day my mother died.

"It burned down on the feast day of Saint Michael. Tragic."

Zee continues with the interrogation as I try to regain the ability to breathe. "So, it has a relic inside it?"

"Yes."

"What is it?"

"No one knows. Could be anything. I used to teach at Mother Cabrini High School in New York, and her body was in the glass altar."

I swallow. "Her body?"

"Well, minus the head, heart, and an arm. Those were sent to different places."

Jesus. And Abuela judges my love of horror?

Zee brings him back on track. "Are there any theories about this particular relic?"

"Oh, sure, there are theories. It's thought to be a relic of Saint Michael."

"*The* Saint Michael?" Does that large wooden box I touch all the time contain an archangel's body parts? Um, that would be kind of lit.

"Is there any other? But those are just theories, you understand. Reality is usually way less interesting than imagination."

I think of something else. "Father, do you know of any myths about a redheaded woman and a fire?"

"There are any number of them." His voice starts to rise as he speaks. "Because red hair is fire stolen from the very depths of hell!" He's yelling now, and people are staring. "All red-haired people are evil! Evil, I tell you!"

A woman rushes out from a back room and puts her hand on the priest's shoulder. "Father, Human Resources talked to you about this, remember? You can't say that to people."

"Well, is it 'unconscious bias' when Judas himself was a redhead? I ask you!"

Okay . . .

He turns back to us, calmer now, though his face is still flushed. "Now, is that all? I have many other projects that need my attention."

"You've already been *so* helpful, Father. Thank you," Zee coos.

He grumbles and turns to walk away, when something pops into my head: that Latin phrase that Sam said on our first date. I had planned to research that further; why didn't I remember until now? "Wait, Father. The Latin saying 'Vexilla regis prodeunt;' it's from a hymn, right?"

He stops and turns, very slowly. "What do I look like, Google?"

He notices the crests on our jackets with a sneer. "The education at Sacred Line is clearly lacking." When we don't respond, he rolls his eyes. "Yes, it is a phrase often attributed to the Christian poet Venantius Fortunatus, but any decent scholar knows that it was actually written by Theodulph of Orleans, prelate, poet, and one of the leading theologians of the Frankish empire."

Oh, I'm *so* sorry I asked. "O-Okay, thanks, Padre." I wave Zee toward the door.

But the priest isn't done. "But that's not it's most famous use in modern times."

I turn slowly, kind of afraid. "No?" We were so close to escaping.

He smirks. "No. In Dante Alighieri's *The Divine Comedy*, specifically in 'Inferno,' he opens Canto 34 with the phrase 'Vexilla, regis prodeunt inferni,' which translates to 'The banners of the king of hell draw closer.'" He gives a self-satisfied look and walks away.

Dante. King of hell. Draw closer. I jump when Zee grabs my arm.

"Let's get out of here before he turns around to give us a full-blown lecture on the poetry of the medieval period."

I stumble through the door and am surprised by the sun as it hits my face. I follow Zee in a daze, my mind a rock tumbler. *Dante. King of hell. Draw closer.*

Zee is still chuckling as she walks, until she turns around and looks at me. "Mica, you all right?"

"I really don't know. I feel like I don't know anything anymore."

Zee shudders. "Let's go to Al's French Fries and talk about it. I need some fries and vinegar to handle all this."

I just nod as we near the car.

"Well, shit," I hear her say with a sigh.

I look down at her car and see a totally flat rear tire.

I shrug, par for the course of this weird-ass day. "Let's call Triple A."

She looks over at me. "The account is under my father's name. Then my parents and your abuela will know that we not only cut school but took off to Colchester."

I take off my uniform jacket and start to roll up my sleeves. "Good thing we've known how to change tires since we were, like, four. You got a jack?" Zee walks to the back, opens the trunk, and lifts the carpet, removing a sad spare tire.

"I think this was a jack . . . once." She holds up a rusty implement as she hands me an equally rusty lug wrench, and I start loosening the bolts. We work together, and once the car is up, Zee takes over getting the tire off and manages to get the spare on but drops one of the bolts under the car. "Oh no!"

And then several things happen at once.

Zee leans on the car as she reaches under, and a loud screech comes from the jack as it slips, releasing the car toward her head and shoulders.

For me, it's as if time slows down.

I see the car start to move with my friend's vulnerable head right there, and I lunge forward, put my fingers beneath the back bumper, and lift.

Zee pulls back from underneath the car with a jolt, runaway

bolt in hand, sees the jack on the ground, and her eyes land on me holding the car up. "Holy shit!"

I grit my teeth. "Just get the tire on, Zee." My mind is sputtering, and that rush of power is running through my veins, but I'm focused on the task at hand.

She drops to her knees and resumes screwing the bolts on the spare, looking up at me every few seconds.

As she's working, I notice something moving out of the corner of my eye and turn to see several small black shadows duck beneath a car, one pointed tail trailing behind for an instant. I'm about to ask Zee if she sees it, but I need her to get the tire on. And besides, there's nothing there now.

When she's finally done, she sits back and watches me lower the car.

I brush off my hands as she puts the tools and the flat tire into the trunk, and we both get in the car without a word. She goes to turn the key and stops.

"Mica, that was . . ."

"Next-level shit?"

Zee starts the car and nods. "Yeah, you could say that."

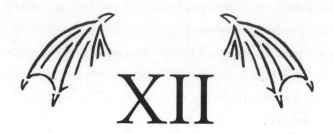

XII

They will be tormented day and night. . . .
—Revelation 20:10

By the time Zee drops me off at my house, it's getting dark. My hand is barely on the doorknob when I hear my name barked from the depths of the living room.

"Mica, the school called."

Shit. I step through the door and drop my backpack on the floor, saying nothing.

"Well? What do you have to say for yourself? What were you doing all day? Were you with that boy?"

"No."

"All these lies, Mica. You've never lied to me before, but this week you're lying and coming home late—"

I feel heat rush to my face. "*I'm* lying? What about the secret meetings you and my friends' parents are holding while we're at school?" I can see I surprised her with that one, but I keep going. I'm on a roll. "And what about the fact that Barry's and Zee's parents paid for the founding of our school? Did you contribute to that too?"

"We had to ensure you all had a proper Catholic education! You should be—"

"Why? What aren't you telling me?"

"Miguela." She says my name like it's a reprimand, a warning, and a curse, all wrapped up in seven letters. "We have done nothing but look out for your and your friends' best interests. How dare you question me about our actions."

She's trying to put me on the defensive, but it won't work. "What were you and the others talking about this morning? How are we in danger?"

She sighs, and I'm shocked by how tired she looks, how fragile. When did that start to happen? "None of that matters now. Tomorrow night you will pack up your things. We are leaving town for a while."

I take a deep breath and face her. "No."

She shoots me an icy glare. "Excuse me?"

"You heard me. I'm not going anywhere."

"When I tell you to stay, you say you want to go. When I tell you to go, you say you want to stay. Is that it?"

I watch her cheeks puff and deflate, all the while staring into my eyes. Finally, her shoulders slump and she shuffles to the door of her bedroom.

"Fine. I'm too tired to fight anymore."

I watch her pause, silhouetted in the light, hands on either side of the doorframe. She speaks to me without turning around.

"Everything I've ever done, Miguela, was to keep you safe." Then she goes in and closes her bedroom door.

I watch her retreat and realize that she really is just a little old lady. For my entire life, she's seemed huge, bigger than life, but tonight we both found out that she has no power over me . . . and something about that makes me so very sad.

My phone buzzes as I walk back to my room and close the door.

Hey beautiful.

Oh Lord. As if I need this right now.

But . . . I hadn't turned my phone back on yet.

I feel a chill pass across the back of my neck.

I can't stop thinking about you.

I don't want to hold the phone anymore; it feels . . . dark suddenly. I open my night table drawer, drop it in there, and slam it closed. I grab my laptop and lie down on my bed, balancing it on my belly. If I'm going to have to write about the Reformation, at least I can relax while doing it.

I get a couple of paragraphs down, a welcome distraction, but I must fall asleep. I don't know for how long, but it's as if my own voice suddenly yells from inside my head, *Wake up!* I jerk up and look around with half-lidded eyes, but all gravity is pulling me back toward unconsciousness. As I'm about to roll over, I see something again, a silhouette in the corner. Though it's dark in my bedroom, a figure stands in the shadowed corner staring at me with glowing orange eyes. I feel around with my hand behind me and switch on the desk lamp. In the millisecond when the bulb fires, I see Sam standing in the corner staring right at me. Then he's gone. Just . . . gone. I look around the room, in the closet, at the closed window. He's not there.

I get up and start to pace the room. What kind of sparkly vampire shit is this? I mean, does he watch me every night? I don't know how anyone can think something like this is romantic—if that *was* Sam, it's stalking, plain and simple.

I jump as the phone clatters in the drawer with texts, one after another. I peer into the drawer and am relieved to see it's messages from the Host. I look at the clock: midnight. Can't be good.

Rage: C'mon, guys! You're starting to freak me out.

Barry: Yeah, you tell us our parents have a clandestine meeting, then you ghost us?

Rage: "Clandestine"? Nice vocab, Barry!

Barry: Thanks, bro!

Zee: Sorry, my phone wouldn't charge, I don't know what's wrong with it.

Me: We need to call a meeting tomorrow, before school.

Zee: Yeah, we do.

Rage: You 2 okay?

We both pause. I type. Define okay . . .

Rage: Whatever it is, we're here for you.

Barry: I got work to do in the barn before but can meet at 6:30. McCarthy's?

I picture all those people sitting nearby. No, don't want it to be in public. Let's meet at the barn, and Zee and I will fill you in.

Barry: Good, I found something out too. C u then.

Zee and I get to Barry's a few minutes early. The sun is just rising behind the farm, and I stop to admire the orange that's slowly bleeding into the expanse of sky. The view from Barry's family farm is spectacular, the range of mountains above a sea of dark green pines. When I catch sight of the ski trails, though, a roiling grows in my belly as I remember the lava flowing down the trails from my dream. Will I ever be able to look at Mount Mansfield again without thinking about that?

"I'm going to go say hi to the girls," Zee says as she skips off into the barn. She calls the cows her "girls," and I'm beginning to wonder if they truly do understand each other when she talks to them. After all I've seen this past week, it wouldn't surprise me a bit.

I haven't seen Rage since the night of the break-in and our make-out session, so I'm nervous. I decide to look for Barry, and I find him behind the main barn near the pigsty. When I notice the smaller piglets scampering around in the mud, I clap excitedly. "The babies!" I rush over to where Barry's feeding the mother, who is just about the size of a Buick. At least by now I know not to jump into the pen, since he told me one of the most common injuries when raising pigs is getting your kneecaps bitten off by the full-grown ones if they feel threatened.

I stand next to Barry, who looks up with a grin. "Hey, M."

I point into the sty. "They've grown so much since July!"

"Most of them are around fifty pounds already."

"Seriously? Wait, where's the one you called 'The Donald'? The one with the blond tuft on his head who bullied all the other babies?"

"See that brown one there?"

"Yep."

"She ate him."

"Wait. One baby ate the other?"

"Well, just chewed his legs off while nursing. But there was no coming back from that for Donald."

"Jesus, Barry!" Truthfully, I'm horrified. And I have a *lot* to be horrified about these days.

He shrugs. "Nobody ever said farming was for the faint-hearted."

I watch the babies chase each other in circles, though it's hard to think of them the same way after that. The mother is busy munching in the corner. I point to her. "What's her name again?"

"The sow? Penelope."

"What happened to . . . ? Portia—that was it!"

He smiles wide. "She was delicious."

My mood dampens. Well, circle of life, I guess. Plus, I love bacon, so who am I to judge? "Well, the babies are still cute."

We hear the rumbling of Rage's car on the gravel out front, and we both head into the barn.

Rage is walking in, swiping a tumble of his curly hair, half his uniform shirt untucked, his dress shoes out of place on the straw floor of the barn. He looks distracted and worried. But also, kind of handsome.

He gives me a hug, but it's stiff, quick. Awkward. That's never happened with us before.

Barry puts down his bucket. "So? What's up? Did you find out what the meeting was about?"

Zee looks at me.

I take a deep breath. "Well, it seems our parents have been meeting like this for years, and that we're all in some kind of danger. The people who broke into my house were looking for something they didn't find, but our parents clearly know what it is, and Abuela told your parents that she would take me and leave so you all could be safe." I gasp, running out of air.

They're both just gaping at me for a beat; then Rage says, "Your abuela is making you leave?"

"Well, she wanted to, but I told her no."

Barry's eyebrows raise. "You? Told Abuela no?"

"Yep." I glance over at Zee, but she seems somewhere else. She looks so small and pale, especially next to Barry. I can see the blue of her veins beneath her temples. She reminds me of a woodland creature whose survival you worry about. Rage's eyes follow mine.

"You all right, Zee?" he asks.

Zee looks at me as she talks. "I've been having these visions."

"What kind of visions?" Barry asks.

Zee doesn't answer, so I say, "The fire-and-brimstone type."

Barry looks from me to her. "Really?"

Neither of the guys looks surprised. Why don't they look surprised?

"They've been getting worse, happening all times of the day and night." She wrings her hands in front of her. "Now we're in them"—she gestures to the four of us—"but it's like a different reality, a dark one. And . . . pretty much all hell is breaking loose."

Barry whistles, then asks, "Did you tell your parents? Is that why they're all acting so wack?"

"You mean the meeting at my house?" I ask.

"Partly. My dad had a new security system installed, and he's getting all freaked out if we come home late."

Rage adds, "Yeah, mine too." He looks over at me. "What about you, Mica? Other than the meeting, anything else been going on?"

A perfectly reasonable question, I know. But I'm guessing he's digging, and in truth, I'm having trouble talking.

Zee lifts her eyes to me.

"Ugh. Okay, fine." I tell them about the vision I had at the altar, the things we found out at the library, and the lifting of the car. I even tell them about seeing Sam in the corner last night.

When I'm done, Rage and Barry are just standing there, mouths open.

Finally, Barry speaks. "Dudes, I've seen this movie. It doesn't end well."

Zee gapes at him. "You believe us?"

"Hell yes, I believe you!" Then he leans forward and says in a whisper, glancing back toward the sty, "My pigs have been acting weird as shit! Yesterday, I swear to you, Penelope's eyes were glowing orange."

I realize Rage hasn't said anything. He's just standing there with a serious look on his face. I elbow him playfully. "You good?"

He doesn't look at me. "I'm fine."

I don't believe that for a minute, but I don't push it. I should never have kissed him. I'm an idiot.

"Wait, Barry, was that what you wanted to tell us?" Zee asks.

"Oh! No! God, I almost forgot." He turns to me. "Last night, I overheard my mom talking to the town clerk on the phone. The woman said that a redheaded girl in black leather had come into the town offices asking about local Catholic churches, and . . . about you." He pauses, then adds, "Two days before you met Sam."

I step back like I've been struck.

Rage stares at me. "Jesus, Mica. They came here looking for you."

Zee and I get to school at the same time as the guys, and when we separate to our respective classrooms, Rage just lifts his hand reluctantly and mumbles, "See ya."

I feel sick to my stomach. The idea that Sam and Rona were looking for me has freaked me out, I might have screwed up my friendship with Rage by necking with him, plus I'm fighting with Abuela.

When the lunch bell rings, I head to the chapel. I have no

interest in food, and given what I learned might be *in* the altar, I want to have another look. As I walk silently to the front, the hum of sounds from the cafeteria floats down the hall like the buzzing of a hive of bees. Laughter and secrets and talk. Normalcy. It's comforting to think that for the rest of the school, life is going on as it always has.

I hear a text buzz from the phone in my backpack, but I ignore it. I know it's Sam. I don't know how, but I do. It feels like my fault he's doing whatever he's doing. I should never have gone out with him, never invited him into our lives.

I stop in front of the altar. It looks different now that I know it contains something important, something . . . holy.

"I thought I'd find you in here."

I jump back and look toward the door. Rage steps into the light coming from the side wall sconces. I watch him walk up the aisle, his easy gait so familiar. He stops in front of me and gives a sad smile.

"Rage, I'm sorry about the other night. I—"

He puts his fingertips gently on my lips. "No, I'm sorry." He takes my hand. "I've been thinking about it all morning. You were vulnerable, hurting. I should have stopped it."

I didn't want you to stop it, I think but don't say aloud.

He continues holding my hand and turns us toward the altar. "So, there might be, like, the liver of an archangel in there, huh?"

"I doubt a liver. The soft tissue organs degrade really early on. Now, bones, they—"

He smiles at me.

"Sorry." I raise my hand. "Horror geek."

We go back to staring at the altar.

"You afraid to touch it after what happened last time?"

I snort. "Yeah, not something I want to experience again." But still, I gently drop Rage's hand and step closer. Tentatively, I touch my fingertips to the wood . . . and nothing happens. I hear Rage let out a breath behind me. I run my hand over the carvings, liking the touch of the wood against my skin. "It always feels slightly warm, like someone was leaning there and only just left."

Rage steps up next to me and puts his fingers against the wood, right next to mine. "Whoa. You're right!" He turns to smile at me, our faces centimeters apart, and I catch the slight scent of woodsmoke on his uniform jacket, feel the gentle breeze of his breath. My eyes brush down to look at his soft lips. With that small flick of my gaze, I feel Rage gasp a little, and I step closer, until our bodies are just up against each other, one of our hands still touching the altar. I'm thinking about pressing my lips to his when I feel a ripple of electricity pass along the front of my body.

"Do you feel that?" Rage whispers.

"You can feel it too?"

He nods, his face glowing. He sees me staring at him again and leans his face forward, the electricity catching in sparks that gently rise up our chests—

Rage's phone buzzes; he looks at the screen and gives a shrug. "What's up, Barry?"

"Where are you two?"

"In the chapel. Why?"

"Take cover." He ends the call, and Rage and I look at each other.

The alarm starts to sound throughout the school, the principal's voice booming on the speakers.

"Attention: SLA is in lockdown mode. All students, faculty, and staff are to shelter in place."

We look at each other for a beat, then duck around the far end of the altar. We're crouching down against the wood when a text from Barry comes in.

Barry: You guys good?

Rage: Yeah, hiding behind the altar. You have eyes on Zee?

Barry: Right next to me. She says hi.

That's so Zee. I chuckle. Quietly.

Rage: How did you know ahead of time?

Barry: Rescue squad call, got it on my phone. Tell M, they said it was a woman with red hair.

I curl my legs up to my chest. I swear I can feel the flames burning my arm.

Rage: What did she do?

Barry: Attacked Mr. Dubois.

"The maintenance guy?" I whisper. Rage nods.

Barry: When he wouldn't do what she asked, she picked him up, and dropped him from thirty feet up.

Rage: OMG is he ok?

Barry: Don't know, they just took him off in an ambulance.

Rage: Is she gone?

Barry: Seems to be. Lockdown should be over soon.

Rage: Wait, how could she do that?

Barry: Do what?

Rage: Drop him from thirty feet. Was she in a tree, or something?

Barry: Um . . . he was kinda out of it. Said she had wings.

Rage and I look at each other, mouths open.

Barry: That's not as crazy as it would have been a week ago though, is it?

Rage: Nope.

"Ask him to find out what she wanted him to do," I prompt as Rage types.

Barry: They won't tell me, but I'll find out eventually.

Rage: Thanks man.

We sit in silence for a few breaths, the school eerily quiet, the flashing red light bathing the chapel in a menacing red on and off over the warm wood room.

I can feel the carvings of the altar against my back, and I twist around to look at them. I need a distraction. "I've never been around this side."

Rage snorts. "Five years of altar-boy duty; I've walked by it a thousand times."

"The carvings feel different here." I turn around fully and pull out my phone to turn on the flashlight.

"You sure you should be doing that during a lockdown?"

I shrug. "Gonna have to face Rona sooner or later."

"True. Terrifying, but true. Do you think she really has wings?"

"At this point? Anything's possible." I lean closer to the wood.

Rage looks over my shoulder. "It's a list of names."

"Michael, Gadreel, Harut . . ." I skip down and see there are empty spaces at the bottom. But when I lift the flashlight up, I notice the last name on the list.

Alejandra.

I crawl back a bit and drop to my butt on the hard marble dais, staring at the nine letters carved into the wood in front of me.

"You okay, Mica?"

I point to the last name on the list. "My mother's name was Alejandra."

It's then that I understand what the altar was trying to tell me. "Rage, I think my mother was at that fire, the one that destroyed the school in Puerto Rico."

Just then, I hear a scuttling sound at the large stained-glass window and look over to see a shadow hovering, then rising up and disappearing out of sight.

Zee gives me a ride home after school. I tell her about finding my mother's name on the altar, and that I'm going to confront my grandmother. When I get home, I see a note from Abuela on the memo board that she went to the store, if that's even true. I don't know what or who to believe anymore.

I drop my coat and bag to the floor and go straight to the mantelpiece. I pick up the framed photo of my mother and stare into her one-dimensional eyes, urging her to talk to me. I don't know how long I stand there when I finally decide to rustle up something to eat, but when I go to put the frame on the mantel, the velvet back swings open. I sit down on the couch and turn the frame over. As I pull open the backing with its easel, I see handwriting on the back of the photo. In my grandmother's curly script, it says:

Alejandra
St. Michael's Academy
Santurce, P.R.
1999

Jesus.

Was that why her name was carved in the altar? Did she actually *die* in that fire?

I hear Abuela's car pull into the driveway, and I jump to my feet. I start to close up the frame but stop myself. *I'm* not doing anything wrong.

She struggles through the door, balancing four reusable bags full of groceries, puts them down, and closes the door behind her. I usually would jump up to help, but not today.

Abuela goes to lift the bags again and sees me out of the corner of her eye. She starts, her hand rushing to her chest.

"Madre de Dios, don't scare an old woman like that, Miguela." She's smiling, until she notices the open frame in my hands. She stalks over, pulls it out of my hand, and closes the back with shaky fingers. As she's placing it back on the mantel, she says, "That is all we have left of her. We must be careful with it."

"Is it?"

"Is it what?"

"All we have left of her?"

"Don't be ridiculous, Miguela, I don't have time for—"

"My mother went to Saint Michael Academy in Puerto Rico. Which burned to the ground." A statement more than a question.

She looks at me for a second, then says, "Yes." She starts back toward the groceries, and I follow.

"And the other parents built the new school and put the altar from that school in it. Did you have something to do with the founding of the school?"

She's very busy putting away cans of beans, bags of rice. She doesn't answer.

"Is that why her name is carved in the side of the altar?"

Her head snaps at that. "What were you doing sneaking around the altar?"

"Why do you care? What don't you want me to know?"

Her movements are jerky now. "Some things it is better you don't know."

I stand between her and the refrigerator as she holds a carton of milk. "I deserve to know who my mother was, Abuela."

She raises her gaze to me, her head shaking. "I will not be interrogated by you, Miguela."

I take a step toward her, and she suddenly looks frightened. She jolts, drops the milk, then scurries off to her bedroom.

I listen to the door close, and stare at the milk gurgling out to the edges of the faded linoleum.

She was afraid of me.

Did she really think I could ever harm her?

I'm pacing in my room again, my heart beating faster and faster until it feels as though it's going to burst from my chest. I've never felt so . . . helpless before, and I don't like it. I need to do something to figure out just what is going on.

I pick up my phone.

Me: What are you doing tonight? Like, late?

Zee: Not sleeping if tonight is like every other night this week. Why?

Me: I need to go see Sam. It's time to get some answers.

Zee: YESSS

XIII

Those who practice magic arts . . . —Revelation 22:15

I open my door and listen. I can hear Abuela snoring from her bedroom. I tiptoe toward the front door, then decide to make a detour and grab my black knit cap from the coat hook. As I'm tucking my mass of hair under the wool, I notice she's put a new quote on the board: 'Woe to the obstinate children,' declares the Lord. Isaiah 30:1

Subtle, Abuela. Subtle.

I slip out the front door and I'm glad I decided to ditch my hoodie at the last minute. It's warm as a midsummer night out here. I jog up toward the coffee shop, wishing I could go for a run instead, just do something normal. With all that's going on, I've been off my routine, and I can feel it in my tightened leg muscles. Not to mention my anxiety.

Zee's car is sitting in front of the shop, and I slide into the passenger seat to find her smiling at me.

"What's with the hat? We cat-burglaring him too while we're at it?"

I grin. "You never know."

Zee backs out and inches the car through town.

I look out the window at the shuttered storefronts, the empty sidewalks. Even the six-foot stuffed bear in front of Shaw's looks sleepy beneath his fishing hat.

We turn onto Mountain Road, and as we pass the first few hotels, it hits me how little Stowe has changed throughout my life. "Think about it, Zee: we know who owns each and every one of these businesses; we even went to school with half their kids."

"We do, and we did. Why does that matter?"

"It doesn't. Wait, no, it kind of *does* matter. I never thought about how safe and familiar this all is, you know?"

She looks at me, then back at the road. "Is this about UCLA, or about the next-level goings-on?"

I sigh. "A little of both, I think."

"Cottage Club Road, right?"

"Yeah."

We turn onto the road and pass the Alchemist Brewery, the yeasty smell of hops heavy in the air.

Zee glances at a house number across the street. "This one is number four hundred and two. What's the address?"

I grin at her. "Um, Cottage Club Road?"

"You don't know where he's staying?"

"He said he's renting a house here." She's staring at me, so I do a small shrug and look out the windows as we start going uphill. "I've never been so far on this road before."

As we drive, I begin to feel a slight pressing on my chest, like a shadow of fear is passing over my heart. I take a deep breath and try to center myself, like in tae kwon do. In my gut, I know Sam is the reason why my world is turned upside down, but a part of me is hoping that I'm wrong. I would never say this to anyone else, not even Zee, but in some ways, Sam has been good for me. But I feel guilty even thinking that.

The scenery thins out, and the businesses and bars are replaced by homes that get more lavish as we go up the hill, the yards sprouting tennis courts and man-made ponds as the altitude increases. As we round a corner, we come upon a long row of expensive vehicles with out-of-state plates parked up and down the side of the road.

"Maybe this is it. Could he be having a party with his douchey friends?"

Zee parks at the very end of the row, behind a Cadillac Escalade, and locks the car (though, if I was going to break into a car, it wouldn't be this one). She comes around and stands next to me at the base of the hill.

I look up and notice smoke rising above the trees ahead. "So what do we do? Just knock on the front door and ask if this is the house where Sam is staying?"

Zee looks around. "I think we should assess a bit first."

I smile. "You mean, like, reconnoiter?"

"Watching *NCIS* with your abuela is paying off." She points up the hill. "We might as well hoof it straight through the trees."

"Stealth like, gotcha." We start up the hill. It's hard to see in the deep night, and the crunch of dried leaves beneath our sneakers feels loud. As we get near the top, I can see the glow of a huge bonfire, and the sound of laughter and death metal rides on the cooling air.

"Do you hear that?" Zee whispers.

"Hear what, specifically?"

"The growling."

It takes a minute, but then I hear it. Among the voices there is the low rumble of growling. "Dogs?" I whisper.

"If it is, it sounds like a lot of them."

We crest the last rise in the hill, and the clearing opens up before us. There's a black velvet sky littered with glittering stars above and a perfect green lawn below. The bonfire in the center is huge, the flames reaching up to the sky like they're climbing. I look at the individual faces—there are so many—and try to find Sam, but I don't see him in the crowd. Zee points to a pair of nearby trees, and we duck behind them and park ourselves to watch and wait.

I peek around the side of my tree trunk. Circled around the bonfire are dozens of people. I peer closer and make out Rona, who is dirty dancing with some guy in a costume of some sort. A costume bonfire? Halloween was last month. He's supposed to be a goat maybe, but he's on his hind legs and is writhing against Rona like they're about to have sex right there. Must be an expensive costume, the backward bending legs are so real-looking, and his erect scruffy tail is twitching as if alive which is incredibly disturbing. He says something to Rona, and in answer she shoves him away and he flies through the air, hitting one of the surrounding trees and dropping unconscious to the ground.

"Did you see that?" Zee whispers.

"Yes. Guess I'm not the only one who can do that."

Rona turns away, laughing, and takes a long swig from the dark bottle in her hand.

I look around the circle again, but now there are creatures with horns and tails and snarling mouths mixed in among the faces of the people. There's no way they'd had time to change into costumes.

"Zee . . ."

"I see them."

"Is this a costume party?"

"Don't think so."

I focus in on one who has got to be seven or eight feet tall, its black lips curled in an evil smile that shows its long teeth; its hair and beard shot through with white. The ground seems to swell beneath me, and every cell in my body is telling me to run, to get as far away from here as I can. But I look over at Zee, her eyes wide but unflinching, and I thank God that she's here; that I'm not the only one witnessing this.

The group on the far side of the fire and closest to the huge mansion begins to part and hush. It's suddenly silent; the only sound the pop and hiss of the fire. Now the creatures are cowering, bending at the waist in supplication to whoever or whatever is coming from the house. I grasp the tree tighter, grateful for the scrape of the bark against my palm reminding me that something is real, solid.

"There he is," Zee whispers.

Sam looks so natural and unassuming, smiling, gliding through the crowd. He looks like a Hollywood actor who stumbled onto a horror movie set. The circle of creatures re-forms and closes in around him, still quiet. He stops in front of the fire, the warm orange light giving his face an unearthly glow, accentuating the angles of his sharp features.

He glances around at the assembled crowd, raises his arms up, and says in a booming voice, "I know we came up here for one task, and one task only." His voice sounds different, older, like from a different era. "The culmination of a quest we have been on for decades, and though we have not succeeded yet, we draw near. Right, Ronova?" He looks at his sister with a furious laser-like gaze, and Rona raises her bottle to him, flashing a catlike grin. "And when it is complete, it is not just me who my father, Satan, our one true king, will reward, but each and every one of you."

Shouts of evil cackling echo together, creating a demonic symphony.

My stomach drops. I would have fallen to my knees if I wasn't already crouched down in the dirt. Zee says something to me, but there's a ringing in my ears that seems to be momentarily blocking out every sound except for Sam's words.

Satan. One true king. *My father.*

There's a rumble through the crowd, and a high-pitched screaming sound. Zee jolts upright as a deer is led through the crowd by a rope around her neck. She's bucking and thrashing, but the creatures who are leading her have no trouble forcing her onto the platform Sam must be standing on.

They yank the doe right next to him, and he takes the rope in one hand and strokes her neck with the other. She calms slightly. Sam continues, as if talking to the deer. "Family, tonight, we celebrate, for soon we rule!" Sam thrusts his hand into the deer's chest, his muscles flex, and he pulls her still-beating heart from between her ribs, raising it up over the crowd, trails of blood dripping down his arm.

I hear Zee gasp beside me, but I can't look away.

With a massive force that blows back the fur of those that surround him, a huge pair of dark, leathery wings snap out from Sam's back, silhouetted against the blue and starry night sky.

"Vexilla, regis prodeunt inferni!" he yells, then brings the glistening heart to his lips and bites into it with large fangs.

I choke and cover my mouth as the roar of shouts and howls rises. Just then Sam looks up, his face covered in deer blood. He turns slightly in my direction, as if he can see me through the crowd, across the field, and into the trees.

"Oh my God, Mica! You're dating Satan's son. Mica?"

I jolt a bit and see Zee staring at me, grasping my upper arms.

"Mica, we have to go!"

With shaking hands, I shove off from the tree when the

sound of someone pushing through the brush a few yards away reaches us.

Zee and I crouch back behind the tree, and when I look in the direction of the sound, I see a quick flash of bright red hair.

Shit!

We inch around the trunk so that we're out of Rona's line of sight.

Then there are loud flapping sounds, gusts of wind, and a thump just outside the tree line. I peer around to see Sam pull his wings in. They just . . . disappear into his back. He heads into the trees toward Rona. Zee and I shift around a bit so we can still see him.

"Going somewhere, sis?"

"Yeah, I've had enough of your theatrics. I'm done."

Rona spits the words like venom.

"Aw, but you haven't completed the task Dad sent *you* to do for *me*."

"Then why are you here, Sam? I was supposed to do this alone. But no, you had to tag along and play your stupid games and frolic with the locals."

"No offense, Rona, but I'm not going to put my entire future in your hands. I'm not that stupid. And I like the locals. Particularly Mica." He's pacing a bit, as if in thought. "In fact, yesterday I decided I'm going to take her back with me."

Zee looks at me with big eyes.

Excuse me? I mouth.

Rona snorts. "I'd like to see you try, but you know Dad has a firm no-pet policy."

"She'd be my consort. You've seen this coming, though, right? That's why you're so threatened by her?"

I gasp and Zee throws her hand over my mouth to silence me, but it's too late.

"Did you hear that?" Rona whispers.

Shit! I'm fighting to stay as quiet as possible, but my chest is heaving with my panicked breaths.

"Don't try to distract me. I know what you're up to. You want it for yourself so you can have power over me." I can hear Sam's voice moving away.

Zee lets out a relieved breath and removes her hand.

Is he going back to the party? Oh, please, please, please!

"Guilty as charged," she replies. "You've never been a good leader, little brother. Someone else has to step up."

He whips around. "You always underestimate me. Did it ever occur to you that wooing Mica was a calculated choice?"

"Go on. I'm listening."

So am I.

"Tomorrow I'm going to seduce her—"

As if!

"—and then convince her to leave with me. She's desperate to get out of this place. I can't blame her. All that power, untapped and lying fallow. And you've seen what passes for the male species around here."

Rona cackles.

"Besides, once I've lured her in, we get what we want and turn our enemy into a strong ally at the same time."

She snorts again. Bitch snorts like a pig. "Strong? Have you seen her?"

Grrr.

"I've set the change in motion. It's only a matter of time until she's at full strength, and you know it. But when she is, she'll be on *our* side."

Rona stops and puts her hand to her chin. "Wow. Impressive. I should have known you weren't capable of *actual* romantic feelings. But this ruse? It's almost . . . well, Rona-like!"

"Glad you approve. Now, let's go finish off the sacrifice. I'm starving," he says.

And they both head back to the bonfire.

I stand there and try to breathe.

Zee comes over to me.

"Holy shit, Zee. Holy shit."

"Actually, I would say this classifies as '*un*holy shit.'"

As if on cue, we hear the sound of pounding hooves on packed dirt heading in our direction.

Zee grabs my hand, and without a word, we tear ass down the hill, stumbling over fallen branches and stones. I begin to understand why the women in vintage horror films trip while running away from the monster or axe-wielding lunatic. Hard to be sure-footed when you're scared for your life. As we run, I can hear the roar of the party behind us, and I pray no one saw us.

I start to slide, almost bringing Zee down with me, when my sneakers slip through mud, but she helps me to my feet and we scramble to the car. I hear Zee struggling with the keys. In this moment, I wish she'd listened to her parents and let them buy her a nice new car with a fob and a button you click to open. I finally hear the locks pop up—

And we both freeze at a sound.

"What was that?" Zee whispers.

"I don't know, but it's not from the party. Something closer."

I peer around in the shadows, but I don't see anything. But just as I'm about to open my door, I hear the unmistakable sound of wings flapping in the dark sky above us.

"Go!" Zee hisses.

We scramble into the car. Zee starts it up and slams it into drive with trembling hands.

She pulls into a driveway on the other side of the road, does a U-turn, and we race down the hill, stones spitting away from the tires.

My heart is pounding against my ribs, petrified that Sam or Rona is flying right above the roof of the car.

I breathe slightly easier when we reach Mountain Road, the pooling glow of streetlights like buoys bobbing in a black ocean. I'm still shaking as we take a left off Cottage Club Road, heading back toward town. As Zee drives, I consciously slow my breathing, reminding myself that we got away. We're going to be okay. But as I look toward the road illuminated by our headlights, smoke starts to bleed in from the sides, curling along the grass, onto the blacktop, until all I see is smoke.

I hear voices.

"Señora Angeles! Run!" The smoke clears, just a bit, and I'm standing, back in the courtyard from my vision. I look over and see a young girl, reaching for me as a teacher pulls at her arms, trying to lead her away.

Señora?

I look down at my chest and see a woman's body wrapped in a professional-looking pantsuit, bones no longer as cushioned, angles sharper, stronger.

I'm in someone else's body.

A nun bursts out of the doorway to my right, coughing into a handkerchief. She sees me and rushes over. "That's the last of them! They're all out. Joven, who was that creature you were fighting?" she asks, her eyes wide with fear.

I shake my head and say in a familiar but distant voice, "I don't know." And I don't.

Then she's pulling on my arms. "Alejandra! We must go! They're coming!"

Alejandra?

I freeze, staring at the woman's face. But I know I'm not going to go. I gently pull her fingers from my arm and point away from the building as she protests. Then she's gone, enveloped by the smoke that is coming from the building in waves. The heat is overwhelming, but there's something in that building I need to protect, to go in and get, but I can't quite think what it is.

In that exact moment, I feel a strong thrust into my back, but I don't fall forward from the impact. I'm held there by . . . something. My chest is on fire, and I look down and see the sharpened point of a carved wooden stick pushing its way through my chest wall, and out through my white shirt. I try to take a breath, but I just gasp through watery-sounding lungs, sticky blood soaking the front of my blouse. I feel pressure now, someone with their arm around me. I can feel their breath on my ear. . . .

When the smoke clears, I realize I'm slumped in the passenger seat of Zee's car, in a ditch on the side of the road. I look over and see my friend's head leaning against the steering wheel, a trail of blood running down her cheek.

I shake her by the shoulders. "Zee! Zee! Wake up!"

She groans and slowly opens her eyes.

I fall back into my seat, sighing with relief. "Thank God!"

Those words have way more meaning to me than they would have about an hour ago.

"Oh, my head hurts." She puts a hand to her forehead, then looks at her palm. "Blood. Great." She examines the wound in the mirror behind the visor. "It's just superficial. Could have been much worse."

"What happened? Why did we crash?"

"I was driving. Then I blinked and suddenly I was outside a school. There was fire everywhere, and something—" She looks down and runs her hand across her chest.

"You could see that too?" My voice is a whisper.

She looks over at me. "Was that your vision? From when you touched the altar?"

I nodded. "Well, a continuation of it. Zee, I think we just saw my mother's death."

We hear a car start in the distance, and we both jump a bit. "We better get out of here." I look over at Zee. "But should you even be driving?"

Zee laughs. "Oh, Mica. After what we just saw I think a mild head injury is the least of our problems!" Then she puts the car into drive, reverse, and drive, rocking us out of the grassy ditch.

As she guides the car out, she navigates around the store sign ahead of us, pulling into their parking lot and out onto the road. I notice the two parallel stripes of dirt on the formerly pristine store lawn. A few feet farther and we would have been wrapped around the telephone pole just ahead. I do the sign of the cross, and Zee does as well.

"Well, I guess we know now why our parents were so concerned we get a Catholic education that they built a freakin' school," I say, desperately trying to lighten the mood.

"I owe my parents an apology."

"You? *I* thought it was a good idea to date the devil's son! Brilliant, Mica."

She whips around in her seat a bit. "Oh, no, you don't. You are not going to blame yourself for that asshole being evil."

"But I sensed something was wrong. And so did Rage."

"Psh! Rage was just jealous cause he wanted you for himself."

"You knew he liked me?"

She chuckles. "Like, since we were six. You really never noticed?"

I sigh. "I don't know, maybe unconsciously. But he's always been such a close friend. And honestly? That meant more to me."

"Well, all relationships evolve."

I put my hand over hers on the steering wheel and give it a squeeze. "Speaking of which, thank you for being my sidekick tonight."

"There's nothing I'd rather be."

She wraps her hand around mine, and I feel a rush of gratitude for her. I have to admit, there's more than a flicker of doubt that I'll find ride-or-die friends like this at UCLA.

When I take my hand back, Zee says, "We should probably call another morning meeting for tomorrow."

"Ya think?"

And then I start to laugh. Loud. And then Zee is joining in, until we're both laughing so hard, we're crying. She actually has to pull over so we don't crash again. We laugh so hard we're having trouble breathing, and we sit there, on the sleeping main street of Stowe, until it passes, and we're calm—exhausted, but calm.

"Let's not text the guys until the morning. Somebody should get some sleep," Zee says, leaning against the headrest.

"Agreed. We need a plan, and I don't have a clue of where to start."

She smiles. "That's why you have the Host. We'll figure it out together."

XIV

These are the words of him who is holy and true,
who holds the key. . . . —Revelation 3:7

When Zee drops me off, I run to the house, hoping that tonight Abuela realized I was gone and is sitting sentry in her armchair, but the living room is empty and lifeless.

I go to her bedroom and gingerly open the door. From the light in the hall I see that she's sleeping soundly. I tiptoe over to her bed and gently sit on the edge. She looks so frail when she sleeps, her face slack. I put my hand on her upper arm and nudge her.

"Abuela?"

Nothing. My heart skips. She's never been a heavy sleeper. "Abuela." I nudge her again. She's not moving. A flood of desperation seizes my body, and I grab her by both shoulders. No. This can't be happening.

"Abuela!"

A small groan. A flicker of eyelids.

My breath returns in a rush.

Slowly, she rouses, though it looks like she's surfacing from being deep underwater. I'm so relieved that I sob in a way I haven't since I was little when a kid on the playground called me an orphan.

Abuela is fully awake now, and I can see I'm scaring her.

"Miguela! ¿Qué pasó? What happened? Are you hurt?" She's bolt upright now, her hands pressing my cheeks and examining my face.

I nod, but I'm so overcome with emotion that I drop my head into her lap and continue sobbing.

She strokes my hair, gently rocking us both.

Gradually, the crying slows, and I feel myself coming back, though my chest seems hollow, like my insides have been scraped out.

Abuela swipes my wet cheeks. "Miguela, everything is going to be okay."

"No, Abuela. Everything is falling apart."

"Why, m'ija?"

I sniff and sit up. "I know this is hard to believe. But Sam, the boy I've been dating, he's the son of the devil."

She deflates against her headboard, her hands shaking slightly. "Protégenos, Dios." She does the sign of the cross.

She seems to be taking this rather well.

"Zee and I went out looking for him tonight. We saw him and Rona, his sister, do an animal sacrifice in front of demons and other horrible creatures—"

A flash of panic in her eyes. "Did they see you?"

"No."

"Oh, thanks be to God."

"Abuela, I'm so sorry. I couldn't see who he really was until tonight. You tried to warn me, but I didn't listen. He just reeled me in, from the first time I saw him in church!"

Abuela furrows her brow. "He was inside the church?"

"No, he stood just outside."

She nods. "That is because he can't enter. He has no power on hallowed ground. In fact, if he crosses the threshold, he will burn."

"Something's telling me you didn't learn all this from Bible study."

She sighs. "Miguela, it's time I tell you who your mother was. Who *you* are."

I brace myself for what I'm about to hear. My whole life I've been waiting for this.

Abuela closes her eyes, gathers the saint medal that lies under her nightgown and takes a deep breath. Then she sits up straighter and takes both my hands in hers. "I was waiting for a sign from the Lord so I would know the right time to tell you. I believe that this is the sign."

What tipped you off? I keep the sarcasm to myself. No way I'm interrupting.

"Miguela. Your mother was, and you are . . . a descendent of Saint Michael the Archangel."

"Wait. You mean Lucifer's weaselly brother?"

She throws her hands up. "¡Ay, Dios mío! I hate the way that stupid show depicts him!"

I love that show, but I'm not saying a word.

"But this is why we wanted to ensure you went to a Catholic school."

"Well, I got news for you, Abuela. They haven't taught me anything that helps me deal with this!"

"Oh, m'ija, of course they did." She cups my chin. "They taught you to have faith."

"Yeah, but is that enough?"

In answer, Abuela pulls the medal on its chain from under her nightgown, lays it on her chest, and reaches behind her neck to unhook the clasp. "Michael was the leader of God's armies, the protector of us all." She pulls the chain free, then reaches over and places it around my neck. This feels like a ritual, a sacrament. She fastens it, moves the latch to behind my head, and admires it as it lays against my sweater.

I look down and run my fingers over the carved silver. It's an angel, triumphant, wielding a sword with his foot on the head of a devil. "This is him. Saint Michael." It's only then that I notice the key hanging behind the medal. "What's this for? Have you always had this key?"

"Only since your mother died. She gave it to me to hold for you, until you were old enough."

"Old enough for what?"

"To come into your powers."

I nod, feeling as if deep down, I already knew this part. "The speed and the strength."

"Yes, though not every descendent inherits them."

"Mom?"

"Yes. She was one of the strongest."

"But you don't . . . ?"

She shakes her head, her gray curls bouncing. "No, this is through your abuelo's line, not mine. When I saw you with that ladder, I wished your abuelo were here. He would have been able to prepare you for this, and your mother would have helped, but they both left us so early, and now no one remains to train you. But see, if a descendent inherits the powers, they don't come until they're needed. I was hoping you could have a normal and safe life, that you'd never have to use them, that maybe they passed over you, but I guess that was not meant to be."

I touch the medal, feeling the cool stillness of the silver. "Well, if I hadn't gone out with Sam, invited him into our home, endangering you, my friends—"

"No." Abuela grabs me by the arms, makes me look in her face. "You are not to blame, querida. Neither was your mother. Evil has powers beyond anything you can imagine. Your mother died trying to protect us, you, all the kids at the school."

My vision. "I think . . . I think I experienced her death. There was a building burning, and a wooden stick—"

She nods. "A staff. But no ordinary staff could have taken your mother's life. That one belonged to the Marquis of Hell."

I gape at her. "Marquis? There's royalty in hell? Of course there is." I remember the terrified faces at the school fire; how I could smell the smoke and feel the pain in my chest. I rub my hand there, where the staff pierced through my mother.

"I wanted to keep you both safe, to run, but Alejandra refused. She told me we can't deny who we are, and it was in her blood to stand and fight, not to run away."

"So why did we?"

She looks down at the blanket, her eyes so tired. "When Alejandra died, all I could think about was protecting you. I should have known that it was only a matter of time."

"And you've taken care of me, taught me right from wrong, kept me in line."

She chuckles. "Not lately, I'm afraid."

"Well, maybe it's my turn to take care of you."

She pats my cheek. "Maybe. I will get the other parents together tomorrow while you're at school—"

"No way! No more secrets! And if you think I'm going to school—"

"No! You must. You must act as if we still don't know who they are. We need to figure out what to do."

"Why are the other parents included in this, anyway?"

"Because, like you, your friends are also descended from very holy and ancient lines."

"Wait, what?"

A crash from the other room, the sound of shattering glass.

Abuela grabs my arm, tightly, and I whisper, "Stay here!"

As I pad to my room, I start to feel the rush of electricity to my limbs, the swell of power I had at the fair, tae kwon do, lifting the car off Zee. Now I understand *why* it's happening to me; I just don't know *how* to use it. Guess it's time for a test run. I get to the open door of my room and pause outside, listening. I just hear a wet fwapping sound.

I take a deep breath and whip around the corner and into the room, landing in full fighting stance, ready to take on whoever or whatever has violated our house.

Wait, the window's not broken, and . . . why is the rug wet? I look down and see that Sharknado's glass bowl is on the rug, shattered into a million pieces, and he is halfway across the room, almost to the door, madly flapping his body, his round mouth gasping for air. I call out, "Everything's okay, Abuela! I'll be right back in!"

I look down at him. "You little shit. You *were* gonna try to murder me, weren't you? You work for Sam? That whole game at the fair, fixed, huh?" I go to the kitchen and get the dustpan and brush and a glass bowl that I fill with warm water. When I get back to my room, I crouch next to him. "I should let you stay there, demon fish from hell." Instead, I use the dustpan to flip him into the bowl with a splash and place him on the desk.

It takes me about twenty minutes to clean up the glass and sop up the rug. After I'm done, the rug is still wet and it smells like a fish's asshole, but it's the best I can do.

I go back into Abuela's room and find her sound asleep sitting up, her chin on her chest. I gently shift her until she's lying comfortably and re-cover her with the blanket. Then I lie down, my arm draped across her middle, and fall asleep next to her.

XV

And the four angels who had been kept ready for this very hour and day and month and year were released. —Revelation 9:15

Oh my God! A shrill ringing sound jolts me awake. I look around and see Abuela's old-school windup alarm clock rattling on the nightstand. I smack it off and look around. She's gone, I'm still wearing my muddy jeans, and there's drool on the pillow. I shuffle to the kitchen and find a note with a small white book underneath.

I went to the church to prepare for the meeting.
We will talk later, there are more things to tell you.

This Bible was your mother's, and she put it aside for you.
Keep it with you, be careful today, and may God bless you, m'ija.

I pick up the leather-bound book with gold hinges and an ornate latch. I open it up and flip the thin, parchment-like pages.

It's in Spanish; the edges of each page kissed with bright yellow gold.

An heirloom.

An honest-to-God heirloom of my mother's. Was this what Sam was asking about?

I open the front cover and see handwriting on the inside, and my heart pounds. Her handwriting. That's my mother's handwriting. It has her name, then below:

Miguela, confía en tu poder.

Trust your power.

Fuego es la llave.

"Fire is the key?" I whisper. "What does that mean?"

I hold the book to my chest, salty tears reaching the edges of my smile. I go to my room, get my backpack, and tuck the Bible carefully inside. When that's safely stowed, I start gathering my uniform. I notice Sharknado giving me the stink eye from his mixing bowl, and I stick my tongue out at him. As I'm pulling off my sweatshirt, the chain around my neck lifts, then drops to my chest with a gentle clink.

Zee picks me up, and I don't update her in the car about my conversation with Abuela. I'd rather just do it once when Barry and Rage are there too. Besides, Zee's clearly as distracted as I am. When I finally look at my phone, there are a dozen texts from Sam asking to see me today. I turn it off.

We arrive at McCarthy's, the breakfast place near the movie theater, and I'm relieved to see it's quiet this morning. The guys are already at our usual booth, and we all look ragged at the edges, rings under our eyes. Rage and Barry are staring into their coffees as if the milky surface held answers.

I drop into the booth next to Rage. "You two okay?"

Barry runs his hand over his face. "I think our last conversation in the barn got into my brain. Zee's visions seem to be invading my dreams."

Rage looks up. "Mine too."

They both look at me. "Mica, what's going on?"

I gesture for them to lean in, and then with no pretense, no avoidance, I just come out with it. "Zee and I found out last night that Sam and his sister are offspring of Satan, and as you found out, Barry, they came here to find me 'cause . . . I'm a descendent of Saint Michael and pose some kind of threat to them." I say that last piece really quickly, like I had to get it out.

Zee sits back. "What? When did you learn that?"

"Last night when I got home, I confronted Abuela and she passed on that little tidbit. I mean, *before* the goldfish tried to kill me."

They're just looking at me, all three of them, mouths open.

Rage clears his throat and speaks first. "You mean Archangel Michael, who leads the army of angels? That Saint Michael?"

I nod, slowly. "And . . . it seems I inherited the family business of fighting evil. That's why I've been getting faster and stronger."

"Yes!" Barry reaches over for a high five. "Need a partner?"

"Actually, Barry, yes I do." I take another breath. "And

apparently, you three are also descendants of 'ancient lines,' whatever that means."

Six wide eyes stare at me.

"But Abuela isn't sure you've inherited their power. See, sometimes it skips genera—"

"Yes! I knew it!" Barry pumps his fist in the air.

"—tions . . . Wait, what?" I look around at my friends. "Why don't any of you look surprised?"

"Are you kidding me? I was born for this shit, girl!" Barry flexes his muscles. "I always knew I was destined for great things."

I look at Rage and Zee. "You too?" Was I the only one in the dark?

Rage gives his one-sided smile. "Kind of explains a lot, don't you think?"

Zee puts her arm around me. "Makes me want to tell that elementary school counselor who said my visions were 'a sign of delusions' a thing or two."

I put my arm around her as well, as always, grateful for my friends.

Barry impatiently waves his hand. "Go on! Did she say who we're descended from? And what powers we get? And—"

I hold up my hand. "No, sorry. We got interrupted by my fish trying to kill me."

"Yeah, about that. Can you elaborate?" Zee asks.

Rage puts his hand up. "Wait a minute, back up. What was that about the son of Satan?"

"Yeah, seems our suspicions about Sam were on the money."

"What do they want with you? Get revenge for what Michael did to their father or something? Like some celestial Hatfields and McCoys?" Barry's enjoying this.

"I don't think so." I swallow. "In fact, Sam wants to take me with him when they go . . . back."

Barry continues that thought. "You mean, back to hell."

I nod.

Rage is starting to look pissed. "He told you that?"

"Not exactly." I look at Zee, and she fills them in about the bonfire, the overheard conversation between Sam and Rona, the evil partygoers.

"Back up again, back up," Barry injects. "You mean to tell me that you two went to confront a whole party of Satan's minions *without* us?"

Rage adds, "He's right, you shouldn't have gone alone. Safety in numbers. The Host stick together."

"And that sounded like a party not to be missed!" Barry snorts.

Rage punches him in the arm.

"Look, we didn't expect to stumble into the devil's bonfire in the middle of Stowe! I was going to confront Sam and asked Zee to go with me . . . for moral support."

"What's our next move? We gonna fight them? We need a plan of attack! They picked the wrong town to infest!" Barry *is* enjoying this; he's gesturing big as he talks. Sitting back is not his forte.

I put my hand on his arm in what I hope is a calming gesture. The restaurant is getting more crowded, and I don't want him tweaking out, even if I'm grateful for his enthusiasm. "Abuela says the best thing we can do is go to school today as if everything is normal. There's going to be a meeting with our parents—"

"Oh, great. So, we're supposed to sit back while the"—Barry does air quotes—"'grown-ups' decide what to do?" He folds his muscly arms across his chest. "Because they've done *such* a good job of protecting us from this so far."

"Well, I wouldn't say . . ." But I would say, wouldn't I? I can't argue with that.

Rage cuts in. "Mica, does Sam know you found out who he is?"

I shake my head. "He didn't see us." I look to Zee for confirmation.

She nods but adds, "Though we heard wings overhead when we left."

Rage sits back, looking pale. "Wings. Jesus Christ, this is really happening, isn't it?"

"I'm afraid so."

"I think Abuela's right." We all look at Zee.

These days she's agreeing with Abuela way too often for my taste. But maybe I should rethink all that.

She continues. "We have to go ahead as if we don't know, particularly you, Mica. As if you think he's a regular guy."

"Maybe just for today." Now we gape at Barry. He shrugs. "We need time to formulate a plan. Strategy, people! Plus, I want to do some research."

Rage snorts at this. "'Cause you're such a research kinda guy."

As they banter back and forth, I stare off into the parking lot, and realization dawns as I notice my friends' faces reflected in the front window. Barry's got a point. We're not kids anymore. I break in: "Guys, we've spent our whole lives waiting for the adults to take care of things, fix things, resolve them." I pause, the revelation coming to me in fits and starts. "But Barry's right. I think we're the ones who have to get rid of Sam and his creepy minions."

"Yes!" Barry high-fives me again.

Zee leans forward. "The first step is to figure out what he wants. Why they're here."

"It's gotta be a weapon, right?" Of course Barry thinks it's a weapon.

"Maybe," Zee replies. "If we figure that out, I bet it's the key to how we defeat them."

Key.

"Wait!" I pull the chain out from under my uniform shirt and hold it up. "Abuela gave me this last night. She's never without it."

Barry leans over. "Cool medal. Love the sword and the grimace of pain on the devil's face."

"Not that!" I push it to the side. "The key!"

Rage picks it up and examines it. "But key to what?"

I deflate. "I don't know. Abuela was gone already when I woke up. I can ask her when I see her this afternoon."

"Wait!" Barry nearly yells. "There's a key and an angel in Revelation! 'I saw an angel coming down out of heaven, having the key to the Abyss.'"

Mute staring.

"What?"

Rage shakes his head. "B-Man, you just quoted scripture."

"Yeah? So? Revelation is cool, man! Action-packed."

"That's impressive, Barry, but what does that have to do with our situation?" Zee asks.

He throws his hands up. "I can't do *all* the thinking for this group!"

"Thanks, Barry, but I need to go to the source. I need to see Sam again." I realize this is what I've been planning in the back of my mind since last night.

"No, absolutely not," Rage says with macho certainty.

I look at him with a tilted head. "Excuse me?" Best way to get me to do something is to tell me *not* to do it, and he knows that better than anyone.

He sputters, "That didn't come out right. I just mean it's totally not safe, Mica. Especially not after what you guys found out last night."

"I'll back you up at this meet, M," Barry offers, cracking his knuckles in a totally cliché move.

"No, I have to do this alone."

"What, you're just going to pretend you're still his girlfriend?" Rage's voice has this up-and-down mocking tone, and it's really pissing me off. He actually looks jealous. Of Satan's son.

Boys.

I don't answer, so he keeps going.

"It's not like this is a leaky faucet or an overgrown lawn, Mica. The stakes could not possibly be any higher. How could you fight this alone?" Rage asks, his voice getting louder.

I throw up my hands. "I'm not talking about fighting him! I just want to get some answers! He owes me that. And you want to lecture *me* about stakes? I watched Sam eat a still-beating heart! He has leathery wings, for Christ's sake!"

"I know, I know, sorry. It's just . . ."

I hold up my now-glowing phone. "I've gotten twenty texts from him this morning alone asking when he's going to see me. I can't keep putting him off forever."

"I think she should meet him after school." Zee's voice is quiet but sure. "Mica's right—he owes her answers."

Barry puts his hand on the table. "Okay, but you meet him somewhere public, and we have to be nearby, just in case."

Rage looks at Barry like he's lost his mind.

Zee takes Rage's hand. "You're totally underestimating Mica. Do you know anyone who is more of a badass?"

Rage sinks back in his seat. "You think I don't know that?" He looks over at me and says in a quiet voice, "I just don't want you to get hurt."

I smile at him. "I can handle myself, Rager."

"And we have our own tasks to do," Zee says as she pushes away her untouched coffee. She points to Barry. "You do some more digging into Revelation; I have a feeling about that. I'll go talk to Abuela after school. Maybe I can get some more answers. And Rage? You need to drive Mica to this meeting."

"Fine." Rage sounds unhappy but resigned. "Where are you going to meet him?"

My phone buzzes with another text. "He just asked me to

meet him where he's staying."

"Yeah, so not gonna happen," Barry scoffs.

"The Depot Malt Shoppe," Rage blurts out. "Meet him there after school."

I look at him. "You hate that place."

"Exactly, so it won't ruin it forever."

"I'm going to text him now, suggest the Malt Shoppe."

The answer comes right away.

I wouldn't miss it for the world.

Zee looks at her phone. "And we all better get going. We have just enough time to get to class."

Barry throws up his hands. "Are we really just going to school? I mean, who can give the slightest shit about chemistry when demons are in town?"

Rage puts his hand on Barry's shoulder. "Bro, think about it as going undercover."

Zee turns my face so I'm looking at her. "But remember, don't let on that you know who he is or who you are. That would escalate things way faster than any of us want."

"And most important, Mica . . ." Rage waits until all our attention turns to him. "Don't do anything to piss him off."

"I won't." I smile. "You know me."

"That's what I'm worried about."

XVI

He is filled with fury, because he knows that his time is short.
—Revelation 12:12

After school, I find Rage waiting outside, pacing next to his already-running car. I weave through a sea of students around me who are teasing, laughing, flirting, with no idea of what's descended into our quiet town. Good, let them stay unaware. Ignorance is, in fact, bliss. I give Rage a quiet hug in greeting.

"Where are Zee and Barry?"

He gives a small smile. "The library, if you can believe it. Though right as I was leaving, Barry said he was going to check out the altar. He's actually excited. I'm scared shitless, and it's like he's found his freaking calling."

I give a strained laugh, and Rage opens the passenger door for me. I climb in, and the air feels heavy, solemn. Why do I feel like I'm going to my own funeral?

We drive in silence, the weight of our situation making conversation frivolous. My brain is hamster wheeling, spinning with the unbridled fear of what's to come, and, I'm sad to say, the excitement of seeing Sam again. Leather wings and all. I have no real excuse, but I think it's because since I've met him, I feel so much more . . . myself. Like he was the catalyst for me becoming me, which, according to Abuela, is pretty accurate.

When we're getting closer to the center of town, I say, "You better drop me off a few blocks away."

Rage's head snaps toward me.

"Just in case Sam sees us."

"What, a friend can't give you a ride to town?"

"Not if I'm going to get him to open up to me. He kept bringing you up, like he was threatened by you, or something."

He gives a bitter snort. "Satan's son, threatened by me. That's a hoot."

"Why? You're a badass, Raguel! And apparently you also have exceptional lineage. Maybe we should get our DNA tested, huh? 23andMe ain't ready for our celestial spit!"

He smiles, but there's fear in his eyes.

"I don't like this, Mica."

"I don't either, but I don't have much choice, do I?"

"This is more—way more—than any of us have ever dealt with."

"Yeah, but like Barry said, we were clearly 'born for this shit.'" I pat him on the shoulder, but he doesn't seem comforted at all.

"Why are you so worried about me, all of a sudden?"

"I always worry about you. I care about you."

"I care about you too, but you have to trust me." Of course, I have no idea how I'm going to handle this either, but I don't need to make us both uncomfortable, and I sure as hell don't want Rage bursting in when I'm trying to talk to Sam.

He signals a right turn before we get to town and pulls into the supermarket parking lot.

"Rage, what are you doing?"

He parks in a space at the edge of the lot and turns his body to face me. "No, Mica. I mean I *really* care about you."

Rage takes my hand, the sound of rattling shopping carts like a chorus around us.

"Mica . . . I love you. I always have. And not just as a friend."

His blue eyes are huge and open. He looks like he did that time when we were seven and seeing who could swing the highest. I flew off and hit my head on the gravel. He was so scared, but he took care of me. Wait, was love there even back then? Words just pile up in my throat, but I can't seem to say any of them. My mouth opens and closes like a fish's.

"You don't have to say it back, Mica. But I needed you to know. Just in case."

Just in case? Jesus, we've hit that point in this adventure, haven't we?

A wave of feelings floods my body. I launch forward and hug him, tight, like if I let go, I'll float off and be lost forever. When we finally pull apart, he gives me a sad smile and kisses me gently on the forehead. I watch him start the car, back out of the space, look in the rearview mirror, and I wonder if my heart is going to explode.

When we turn the corner into town, we see police cruisers parked around the church, blue and red lights flashing off the white clapboards of the building.

"What now?" Rage says under his breath. He parks in front of the real estate office a few doors down, and we walk back to the church. "I assume this has something to do with Sam?"

I shake my head. "It can't. He and his 'people' can't go on sacred ground." I shudder from the chill in my stomach.

We see Officer McHugh standing along the perimeter of the property.

"Afternoon, Officer. What's going on?" Rage nods toward the hive of activity.

"Hey, Rage." He nods to me and continues. "Allegedly the Benoit brothers broke into the church. Allegedly."

"What?" I exclaim. No surprise that those two broke the law, both are meth-heads from way back and are in the newspaper's police blotter weekly, but I figured whatever was going on was related somehow to Sam and Rona.

The officer looks at me. "Oh, it gets better. Your grandmother was the one who caught them, and she beat them over the head with the bronze processional cross."

I laugh. Loud. Can't help it, but then I grab his sleeve. "She's okay, right?"

He smiles. "You kidding? That woman is tiny but fierce as a bobcat."

Now I can hear her accented voice talking loudly from inside the church.

Just then, we see officers pulling the two guys toward a waiting state trooper SUV in cuffs. We can hear them yelling at the cops, pulling away half-heartedly as they walk. "Nah, man! That chick, that hot redheaded bitch! She told us if we did this, she'd give us whatever we wished for! You gotta find her—she's the one who told us to break in. It's not our fault we didn't find anything but a crazy old Mexican lady!"

Rage and I look at each other for a moment.

McHugh shakes his head. "Well, Mica—I mean Ms. Angeles, you're welcome to go in and check on your grandmother if you like."

"No! I mean no, I'll let her finish her statement. This is important." I pull on Rage's sleeve.

Rage puts his hand on the police officer's shoulder. "Thanks, Chris—I mean, Officer McHugh." Then we walk over in front of the candy store and out of earshot.

I whisper to Rage, "I can't let her see me. She won't let me leave if she does."

"Yep. She'll take the cop's handcuffs and lock you to a pew."

"Exactly."

"So what did Rona hire them to steal from the church?"

"Damned if I know." I sigh. "But we're not going to get answers standing here. Guess I better get this over with."

Rage puts his hands on the sides of my face, so gently. "I still don't like you going alone. Especially with all . . . this." He waves back toward the church.

"What could possibly happen with you and all of Vermont's finest just a few blocks away?" My voice sounds more confident than I feel. "Will you go check on Abuela?"

He smiles. "Of course."

I look at him for a heartbeat, then kiss him gently on the cheek and walk off to meet Sam without looking back.

I can't allow Rage's confession or the chaotic mess at the church to distract me. I must focus on the task at hand. I take a deep breath, try to clear my head.

Though the days are getting shorter, it's still light out, but I notice shadows where there shouldn't be any. When I pass the first store, I hear small whispering even over the traffic and people chatting. As I walk, I glance over to the bushes next to the general store and see something scurry. As I'm crossing the road, a feeling comes, that there are things crawling all over me, and my whole body shudders. I'm so distracted that when I arrive at the other side, I bump head-on into a man walking in front of me. "Oh, sorry, I—" He turns around, and I see it's Mr. Thomas, who runs the bakery in town. I've known him since I was two, so I try to smile and say, "Sorry, Mr. T, I wasn't—"

"You better be sorry!" His face is red and crumpled like a balled-up piece of paper.

"Mr. Thomas, it's me, Mica." I try to catch his gaze as he's basically growling. Then the edges of his lips slowly rise into a parody of a smile, his eyes leering and all black.

"You best get home, little girl, before something gets ya!" And then he throws back his head and laughs, and I stumble, right myself, and start to walk faster.

A woman's voice joins his: "Run away, little girl!" And they cackle together. I look at the faces I pass, and it seems as though they're all leering, spit on their chins, hatred in their gazes. And they're leaning toward me, narrowing the space I have to walk. Is this because of what's going on at the church?

I glance into the window of the coffee shop and see Rona sitting at a table, staring at me, bringing a cup of coffee to her bright red smiling lips. I'm sure she wanted a clear view of the plot she set in motion at the church. But is she also controlling Mr. Thomas and the people in town? After I get past the window, I take off in a full run, my school shoes hitting the sidewalk in rhythmic clops as the whispering follows me.

I turn the corner past Shaw's store, the Malt Shoppe in sight, and already it feels different. Like the air is clearer. I slow my pace and take a deep breath, trying to calm myself before going into the restaurant. I hate walking around in my uniform, but I wanted to be there already when Sam arrives, so there was no time to go home and change.

It's a ridiculously warm day—I'm sure it will only get hotter the longer that Sam is in town—and the walk goes by too quickly. Funny how time speeds up when you don't want it to. As I enter through the swinging door of the Malt Shoppe, I see the staff is setting up for the after-school rush, but it's still early. The smell of cheap coffee and frying potatoes greets me like an old friend. As I walk by, I pat the wigged head of Darlene for luck, the old-style mannequin dressed in 1950s clothes, poodle skirt and all, that welcomes diners as they enter.

And today I need all the luck I can get.

Sam isn't here yet; in fact the restaurant is empty, so I slide into the booth with all the James Dean pictures under the glass table-top. It's my favorite booth 'cause Dean was the original rebel. Rage can't understand why I like this place, bitching about how the '50s were eons ago, and all the food is fried. But there's something comforting about it, like being transported into a historical novel or a black-and-white movie.

A text comes in.

Abuela: I am at home. Come here and we will go to the meeting together. Abuela.

I stare at it. There must be a mistake.

Abuela? Is that you? You're TEXTING?

The owner, Joanne, places my usual, a tall, cold glass of root beer in front of me. "Thanks," I say with a sad smile, and take a sip. She puts a napkin and utensils down in front of me.

"Hey, did you hear about the museum?" Joanne prides herself on being up on all the local news, and at this point, all news is important.

"No, what happened?"

"Got broke into last night."

Interesting. "There's nothing in there but some antique skis and a printing press!"

"Well, that's the thing! They didn't take anything. Rumor has it, they were looking for something. Tore the place apart and left. Could have been those Benoit boys. I hear they were up to something at the church just today. Thieving at a church, yet! Can you imagine? I'm telling you; the world is going to hell."

Oh, Joanne, if you only knew . . .

She pats my arm. "Let me know if you need anything, hon."

"Salvation?" I blurt out.

Joanne gives a dismissive wave. "Oh, honey, don't we all?"

Then she's walking toward the back of the restaurant, and I feel so . . . alone. That's when the door swings open, bringing with it a whoosh of the unnaturally warm air from outside and . . . there he is.

Sam.

Speak of the devil.

It's as if all the oxygen is sucked from the room with his entrance.

Against my will, my heart jolts at the sight of him. He's wearing a bloodred sweater under a soft leather motorcycle jacket and black jeans. The contrast of the dark clothes makes his eyes stand out even more than usual. They're the color of my glass of root beer, earthy but with frost around the edges. Good Lord, he's dazzling.

Actually, scratch that, since we now know the Lord had nothing to do with it.

I'm so angry that he fooled me into thinking he was something he wasn't. But like the Host agreed this morning, I have to pretend I don't know any of that and act like we're just two teenagers having relationship issues. Well, one teenager and one probably thousand-year-old demon from hell. Ew.

He strides through the restaurant, and slides into the booth across from me. He leans over the table and tries to kiss me, but I'm able to turn my head just in time for his lips to land on my cheek.

Unfortunately, from his confused expression, it appears I've tipped him off that something is up.

Way to go, Mica.

"Where have you been lately? I've been trying to get ahold of you. I need to talk with you about something important."

"I've just been busy."

He arches an eyebrow. "Busy, huh?"

Shit. I'm terrible at this.

"I've got some things to ask you," I reply.

"Okay, but let me go first." He clears his throat. "I have to leave soon. I'm going to be traveling for a bit, and I was wondering if . . . well—"

My blood boils as the word "consort" plays over and over in my head.

"I was wondering if you might, possibly—"

Wait, is he . . . nervous? I stare at him, amazed. Either he's the best con artist in the world or maybe he really does have feelings for me. Was I the job he didn't want to do for his father? Not that it matters, but I've got a right to know.

"—leave with us?" he finally says.

"Us?"

"Yeah, me, Rona, the whole group of us. You'd get to see the world, meet important people." He's getting excited now, really trying to sell it. "I'd give you everything you want."

"Everything I want, huh?"

I stare at him, his face open and smiling. I promised my friends I'd pretend I don't know the truth about Sam and that I'd just . . . talk to him. And carefully.

But then I start thinking about my mother, her running through a burning building, and dying with a stake in her chest. I know Sam wasn't the one who killed her—according to Abuela, it was the Marquis, whoever he is—but Sam *is* connected. I just can't play dumb with him.

I must honor my mother and everything she did to fight for this world. "Why don't you cut the crap, Sam?" I blurt it out before I can stop myself.

He tilts his head, like he's innocent of all the crimes he's committed. "I don't know what you mean. I—"

"You lied to me about who you are."

He narrows his eyes. "And who am I, Mica? Tell me."

"The son of Satan."

"I never mentioned that?" Sam says. "My bad."

I snort. "Very funny. So, are you really nineteen? I'm guessing that was the first lie you made to my face and you're much older than that."

"Fine, I left a few zeros off the end."

"And Dante Vulgate? Why was he so scared of you?"

He throws his hands up in a defensive position. "Not because of anything *I* did. *He* made a deal with my father, and he thought I was coming to collect. As if I would do my father's dirty work." He scowls at the thought.

"A deal?"

"Yeah, without Dad, Melvin Smith would have been stuck writing death notices in that local rag in Weehawken for the rest of his sad life."

"Melvin Smith?"

"You didn't think his parents named him Dante Vulgate, did you?"

I can hear the sound of my childhood hero dissolving into a steaming pile of mediocrity.

"Listen, I had no choice but to keep certain details of my life to myself. If you knew who my father was on that first day in the bookstore, would you have gone out with me?"

"Ha!"

He throws his hands up. "Exactly. Look, I am not my family, Mica. I thought you of all people understood that."

He tries to take my hands, but I yank them away. He flinches like he's been slapped, but he takes a deep breath and presses on.

"That night on the mountain, and every time I've seen you since, I felt like we really had a connection. I just asked you to run away with me. Doesn't that show how much I care about you?"

"Yeah, sorry, don't buy it. I heard you tell Rona that you were faking your feelings to get close to me." Okay, so I didn't plan to spill that, but since the tea's already on the floor . . .

He narrows his eyes, realizing I was there, somewhere, at the party. But his gaze softens after a moment. "Can you blame me? Would *you* trust Rona with your true feelings?"

"I wouldn't trust Rona with my locker combination."

"So, you get it. I tell her what she wants to hear so she doesn't skewer me when my back is turned."

"Speaking of Rona, ever since I shook her hand at the fair, I've been having visions, of fire and death."

He shrugs. "Yeah, that's kind of her calling card. Screwing with people's minds is Rona's hobby. I told you, she's an evil shrew."

"Can *you* screw with people's minds like that?"

He leans back and crosses his arms, like he's waiting for me to get pissed. "Well, yeah."

I glare at him. "Were you screwing with mine? Is that why I liked you?"

He gapes at me. "No! Just because I *can* do it doesn't mean I do. And wait a minute, 'liked'? As in past tense?"

"What do you think?"

He reaches for my hand again, and I try to pull it away but this time I can't seem to make it move.

"Mica, I never used my powers to coerce you. Well . . . okay, maybe at first, but when I started to develop . . . feelings for you, I stopped." He gives me a half smile.

Ah, so that's why the tunnel vision started to wane. "I thought we had a connection too, Sam. But I still think what you said to Rona is true. You were just using me to get to something." I put my face close to his. "Tell me I'm wrong."

He squirms a bit in his seat but doesn't drop my gaze. "In the beginning, yes. I thought I could charm you, get some information, and beat Rona. But the truth is, I was drawn to you and I started to question what I came here to do. That's why I fought with my father that day. I didn't plan on falling for you." He means it; I can see it in his eyes. "Not much surprises me anymore, and you . . . surprised me."

"Yeah, you surprised me too," I say. The biggest understatement of my life.

I finally manage to pull away from his grip. "What was it you came here to get?"

He doesn't hesitate this time. "A weapon."

"A weapon?" I laugh. Barry was right. Wonder if he's right a lot more often than I give him credit for. "Why on earth would I have a weapon? In Stowe, Vermont, of all places!" Then I remember the vision. "Is it a staff?"

His turn to laugh. "A staff? No."

"Are you going to tell me what it is?"

"No." He looks right at me.

"Guess it wasn't at the museum or the church. Or my house, huh?"

"I would never do anything to hurt you, Miguela, you must know that."

"No, I don't know that." My phone skitters on the table. I look over and see a short text from Rage.

You can do this.

I silently thank him.

Sam points at the phone. "That from Raguel? He wants to hold you back, Miguela, keep you the way you are, from becoming who you are meant to be. Rage, your friends"—he gestures out the window and around the restaurant—"this place, all of it, is holding you back." Twin flames flare in the center of his eyes as he talks, and then they're gone, winked out of existence like the Sam I thought I knew.

"No, they're not. And yes, I understand now that you being here has helped me become who I am meant to be, but they've had my back for sixteen years."

Sam sniffs, his patience clearly waning. "Well, you're just going to have to choose, Mica. We take what we need, and you go off to UCLA, and after you get your meaningless piece of paper, you can come back to your little life here and marry your ginger farm boy and breed a bunch of crotch goblins—"

"Crotch goblins? That's what you call human babies? Jesus, Sam."

He ignores me. "Or, come with me, see worlds you can't even imagine, have unlimited power, and sit by my side."

"As your consort . . ."

"Yeah, rule together."

"In hell? Ha! Last I checked, your dad was ruler and he doesn't share power."

The flames flicker back into his eyes. "And that's why I'm here, why I need—" He stops talking and freezes.

"Why you need what?"

Sam adjusts his jacket, straightens his shoulders, and takes a breath. "Never mind."

I hear Rage's voice in my head: *Whatever you do, Mica, don't do anything to piss him off.*

To hell with that.

"Actually, Sam, I don't think we should see each other anymore."

He stares at me.

I glare back, trying to be tough, but I feel my lip twitch. Maybe he didn't hear me.

We look at each other, neither blinking, neither moving. It starts to feel like the staring contests my friends and I used to do when we were little. But if he expects me to blink, he'll be sorely disappointed. I was the champion three years in a—

Wait . . . what's that feeling?

It's coming from him, but it's not like anything I've felt before . . . it feels like . . . he's drawing out my free will like a straw at the bottom of an almost-empty glass.

I'm about to ask what he's doing when I notice his mouth slowly turn into a wicked smile, the edges of his lips rising like a cartoon villain's. It's the smile that a snake gives you before it swallows you whole. It's the smile that's on Rona's face 24-7.

"So . . ." I begin to say as I feel sweat pouring down my forehead, into my eyes, between my boobs. "Are you making it really hot in here?" I fan myself with the front of my uniform jacket. I look around for the staff, the other patrons. Where is everybody?

Sam bends his head, just a bit, and stares into me. I can sense him laying bare every fear I've felt my entire life. I want to run, but I'm not sure I could get my legs to move. Instead, I pick up my soda to take a sip while I figure out what to do next, when I notice a weird sound. It's coming from my drink. I look into the glass and see the brown liquid start to bubble, the ice rapidly disappearing, the clear glass getting so hot that it shatters in my hand, glass flying, the boiling liquid scalding my fingers, spraying across the tabletop and onto Sam's face. But no burns appear on his skin: it's still smooth and perfect.

My heart begins to gallop in my chest, but I try to keep it pulled together. *C'mon, you can do this!* "We can still be friends." Even I cringe at that line. Now rage is coming off him in a torrent, and he won't stop staring at me. I've never been so petrified in my entire life.

"I've been patient, Mica. So very patient." His voice is like ice, ironic given how freaking hot it is in here. "I could have just gotten the job done, but when Vulgate found you, I lost sight of what really matters."

"Hold on, when Vulgate found me?" I hear the writer's voice again: *You're her.*

He waves his hand dismissively. "Yeah. I've had bait planted in thousands of books, movies, websites over the years hoping one day we might get a bite."

"You've been influencing literature, film, just to find me?"

"Yeah, what's the big deal? If you'd ever worked in Hollywood or in publishing, you'd totally understand it wasn't hard to do. But once I met you, I realized you were the key to my future."

I jolt a bit, remembering the key beneath my uniform shirt, and I have an overwhelming desire to hold it, but I know I can't bring it to his attention. I'm about to ask him why I'm so important to his quest, but he just keeps monologuing.

"See, since I met you, I've realized that if I'm going to take over and rule, I need someone I can trust by my side. You've met Rona—that's my family!" He takes my hands in his again. "You never even lie, always saying what you really think. You're the first person I've ever trusted."

I don't doubt that.

"In return I can give you whatever you desire, Mica." He looks at me as if he's seeing all of me, as if my soul is once again laid bare. "What do you want?"

I stare at him, my eyes beginning to fill. I remember the vision, the violent thrust, the wood pushing through my mother's ribs. The time that was robbed from her. From us. From me. And then I say five words; five words for the only thing I've ever wanted. "I want my mother back."

He looks disappointed. "I mean, anything other than that."

I don't even try to hold back the tears now; I feel them running down my face in streaks. "You said anything. That's all I want."

He throws his free hand up, the one not gripping mine like a vise. "Well, she's in a place where I don't have much influence."

Oh my God.

I stare at him, not really seeing.

So . . . my mother's in heaven?

I had no reason to assume she wasn't, but with how little I know about her . . . My breath starts to come in easier. "Did your father kill her?"

"My father doesn't directly kill anyone."

"But you know who did?"

"Mica, I—"

"Do you know why?"

He sighs. "She was a threat."

"What kind of threat?"

"Enough!"

His voice comes from everywhere at once, and I have to fight the urge to cower from the sheer volume of it, and it begins to dawn on me that I'm in over my head. I guess I should have listened to Rage. Maybe I can still salvage the situation. "If you can't bring my mother back, then what I want is for you to leave this town and everyone in it in peace, including me."

For a millisecond, I swear I see hurt run through him like a brush fire. But then it's gone and a smile spreads across his face again, but this time his teeth are suddenly sharp and pointed, like they were when he ate the deer's heart. Is mine next? I'm aware of its fast beating in my chest and hope against hope it can stay there, tucked beneath my ribs. He tightens his grip on my hand, and his warm skin becomes burning hot. I can feel my flesh sizzle under his touch, the pain setting my teeth on edge while terror stirs in my stomach.

"I don't think you understand, Miguela." His voice is calm and smooth, which only makes what follows scarier. "You don't have a choice. You're going to hell one way or another."

I scoff, but my voice is shaking. "I always have a choice!" I try to pull my hand back, but his grip is like iron. I feel that rush of adrenaline that seems to come when my powers kick in, and I start to twist my hand away, bending his back in the process.

I catch him by surprise, and for a split second, I see his real face beneath the handsome one. It's still human, barely, the surface of his skin still pale but scaly, his eyes sunken into black sockets, and, yes, horns on his head. "Wow. I thought your horns would be bigger. Don't worry, maybe one day they'll grow in."

I feel him regain control over my hand, twisting it back despite my increased strength. The pain shoots through my upper arm, into my shoulders, and I'm terrified he's going to rip my arm from its socket. Tears trail down my cheeks, but I keep my face neutral, not willing to show how much he's hurting me.

"I'm going to destroy this town, and all its quaint little residents, including your friends, your abuela, everything and everyone you love." He pauses, letting the horror of that sink in. "Unless you tell me where your grandmother keeps your mother's things."

"I don't know, and even if I did, I wouldn't tell you."

He yanks my hand closer, and as he stares into me, his pupils burst into flames, and I feel as if my internal organs are melting. "Where does she keep your mother's things?"

It's as if I no longer have control of what I'm saying. It's like Sam is riffling through my brain and forcing me to tell him the truth. "She doesn't have many things. A Bible—" I try to stop talking, but words come unbidden. "The photo . . . that's it."

Somehow, I'm able to keep the key a secret. Maybe that's because as far as I know, it's Abuela's. She never did say directly that it was my mother's, just that she was holding it for me.

The flames die down. "You really don't have it."

"Have what? Let me go!" I look into his eyes and try one more time to pull away from him, willing my new strength into my hands, my arms, but it's no use. He's so much stronger than me.

What made me think I could do this? Rage would remind me that I've never lost a fight, but to say this one is out of my league is the understatement of the millennium. Maybe the safest option is to feed his ego.

"Sam, you can literally have anyone you want. Me breaking up with you isn't the end of the world," I say, trying to reason with him.

Suddenly he releases me. I pull my hand back and rub it. The skin looks fine, no burns, but I swear it was as if he were holding it over an open flame. I slowly shuffle out of the booth, keeping my gaze trained on him.

The air inside the diner begins to move, hot and dry like a desert wind, my lungs barely able to steal a breath. In my mind I picture an escape route—the side door right near the bathrooms—and slowly back up.

I'm inching away, the heat so bad I wonder if the water in my eye sockets is starting to boil, but when I go to step up onto the counter level, I hit something. Or someone. I turn around and see Joanne. She's leering at me, her eyes orange like Sam's, her hands reaching for me.

The front door it is, then.

I whip around and find myself face-to-face with Darlene the mannequin, her painted, empty eyes staring at me, wig hanging half off her pale, bald head. The faded red scarf that was jauntily tied around her neck now looks like a bloody gash. I gape at her as her thin plastic arms rise and she reaches for me with molded fingers.

I step back, and she lurches with a squealing of her unbending legs. My martial arts training kicks in, and I grab the mannequin around the waist, turn around, and hurl her at Joanne. As the restaurant owner turned evil minion falls to the floor, I take off toward the side exit, afraid to turn around and even look at Sam.

In that moment, the ice cream machine, the industrial coffee station, and the dishwasher all explode, boiling water spewing everywhere, electricity arcing and sputtering like indoor lightning. The stools at the counter begin to spin, faster and faster, the tops unscrewing and flying toward me as I bob and weave, knocking the first two away. The third one clips me on the side of the head, and I'm almost knocked off my feet. I feel blood begin to trail down beneath my hair, but right now that's the least of my worries.

I make it to the side exit just as the glass front of the old-fashioned jukebox shatters. The machine begins to shoot vinyl records at my head, my neck. I have to get out of here. I grab the doorknob even though the hot metal singes my hand. Then I hear Sam's voice. Not yelling over the loud hissing and crackling; he's talking calmly but very loudly, like from a speaker on the ceiling. Or from inside my own head.

"Actually, it *is* the end of the world, Mica. And it's. All. Your. Fault!"

XVII

*But woe to the earth and the sea, because the devil has gone
down to you! —Revelation 12:12*

When I bolt out the door and barrel into the side yard of the
restaurant, I'm shocked to discover that not only is it still daytime,
but it's sunny with blue skies. People are walking around eating
ice-cream cones and chattering like it's any old day.

I run full out, heading toward home, but just a block later, I see
movement in front of the Stowe Gems jewelry store, and I stumble
to a stop, ducking behind a fence. I peer through the slats to see a
creature dart out from its hiding place, stand on its hind legs, its
pointy nose in the air, sniffing. I can't see any detail on its features;
it's almost as if it is cut from the background. A shadow of a being,
the thin tail whipping around its body, ending in a sharp point.

When it looks in my direction, it's the eyes that undo me.
Sickly yellow with reptilian pupils. It's unlike anything I've ever

seen. I feel terror coil at the bottom of my stomach. Its pointy ears twist as it hears something around the corner, and I watch it skitter off in that direction.

Is it really gone? Are there more? No way to know, but I can't wait. Besides, I'm more worried about their boss back in the restaurant. I've broken up with boys before, but none of them made my root beer boil and tried to kill me with a flying stool top.

I start running again toward home, careening around our corner, and don't stop running until I reach—

The front door is flung wide open.

I burst into the house. It's not torn apart like during the break-in, but things are knocked off the coffee table, a mug cowering on its side under the couch.

"Abuela!" I scream as I rush to her bedroom. Nothing.

One by one, I check each room of our tiny house, but they're empty.

I grab my phone and call her. It just rings and rings. I see the text she sent earlier and realize there is no way she sent it. I should have known, but I was too focused on seeing Sam.

"No, no, no, no!"

I throw my phone on the kitchen counter. My head is throbbing, and I feel as if my entire life has been torn out from underneath me. I glance up to see if her keys are still hanging there and notice the memo board. It's been messily erased, and a new quote added in a shaky hand.

Never forget your mother's words or Matthew 7:7!

My mother's words? When have I ever heard my mother's wor—

I grab my bag and with shaking hands retrieve the Bible. I yank the cover back and look again at Mom's note:

To Mica, trust your power. Fuego es la llave.

I still don't know what that means! And Matthew 7:7. What—

I brush through the first few pages until I get to the table of contents. I flip to the book of Matthew, verse seven, and near the spine I see Abuela's tiny careful handwriting.

Fuego es en la capilla.

Fuego is in the chapel.

My mother and my grandmother left me messages in this book. The pieces begin to fall into place.

The chapel at school.

The altar is in the chapel.

Fuego is in the chapel.

Fuego is the relic that's in the altar!

I still don't know exactly what Fuego is, but I know it's what my mother wanted to go back into the burning building to get in my vision. What if I can't find it? And what if I do and I can't figure out what to do with it? What if I don't have my mother's strength to fight Sam? I can't do this without Abuela, without my friends.

Without my mother.

I grasp the Bible next to my heart and begin to sob. Then I do something I haven't done since I was five.

I cry out for my mother.

"Mom!" My voice is cracked and tired, so tired. "I don't know how to do this!" Maybe it would be easier to just give in, tell Sam where to get what he wants, the heirloom he's clearly after, and maybe he'll go away.

Then I feel it.

The key around my neck is . . . pulsing. I look down at it, lying against my chest, radiating a golden light. The key . . . is glowing.

Tears spring to my eyes, and I wrap my hand around the key and the medal. "Mom! It's you! You heard me!"

As if in response, the light in the room shifts, and I look toward the front windows. I glance out and up. In that moment, the sun disappears and the town is cast into darkness, as if the world was a birdcage and someone just threw a towel over the top.

I rush out the front door and stand on the walkway as thunder shakes the air around me. The ground beneath the house heaves, and I watch a great split run across the front lawn, moving like a snake, cracking Mr. Pembly's house next door right down the middle as ashes rain down from the sky. It's all our visions come to life.

I guess Sam's patience has worn out.

And that means we're running out of time.

The house where I celebrated nearly every birthday, decorated every Halloween, and read my first book, shakes and rumbles; bricks falling from the walls. I cover my head when the front windows burst in showers of glass. Over the crashing and rumbling, I hear something. Music.

"'Red Solo Cup'! That stupid, beautiful song!"

I watch as Pegasus rounds the corner and careens to a stop in front of me. Rage throws open the passenger door and leaps onto the sidewalk.

He grabs me by the arms and looks into my face. "Mica!" He pulls me into a hug. "Thank God you're all right!" Then he holds me at arm's length again and asks, "*Are* you all right?"

Barry comes up beside him and puts his arm around me. Kissing the top of my head, he says, "Damn, girl. You sure have some shitty taste in guys."

"You're telling me! Where's Zee?"

"She went to the hospital to get supplies."

"I think they've taken Abuela!"

Barry's speaking quickly. "That's why we're here. Our families are all at the church in town, and Dad said your grandmother got a text from you and headed home to meet you, but she never came back."

"A text from me? I didn't send her a text! I got one too. It was a trap." I think of my grandmother, how they used me to lure her to them. My knees give way, but Barry is right there holding me up.

Rage starts guiding us toward Pegasus. "We need to go look for her."

I stop short. "No."

"No?"

"She left me clues; I think she knew. She wants us to go get Fuego." I feel burning in my stomach as I say it, abandoning her is the last thing I want to do, but I also know it's the right thing. The tears flow anyway.

"Are you sure?" Rage asks, and I just nod. My throat's too tight to speak.

"What's Fuego?" Barry asks.

"A weapon," I croak out. "What kind I don't know, but it's in the altar at the chapel at school and this is the key." I pull it out from under my shirt.

"Let's hit it, then!" Barry steps toward his truck.

Suddenly, we hear a crashing sound and the chimney from Mr. Pembly's house tumbles off the roof. Bricks fly everywhere. A large chunk is hurtling toward the windshield of Abuela's car like an asteroid, and the next thing I know, I'm yanking the car out of the way and onto the lawn as the bricks scatter in the driveway.

I wipe my hands on my skirt and rush back to my friends. Their jaws are practically on the ground.

"Mica, that was just about the sickest thing I've ever seen!" Rage marvels.

"When do *I* get superpowers?" Barry whines.

Sections of the roof are starting to shake off and fly in a typhoon around us. Rage runs to the truck and opens the door.

I look back at our trembling house, then leap in.

The truck rocks as the ground swells and cracks beneath us. The second I pull the door closed, I turn to Barry and yell, "Go! Drive!"

The asphalt is lifting and buckling ahead of us, but the truck scales it easily. Barry makes a U-turn over Mr. Hansen's lawn and roars toward the main road.

"Suddenly this monster truck makes total sense," I say to Barry, and he smiles wide.

"See? I told you! I knew I needed Pegasus." He pats the dashboard. "I don't know why I knew, but I did."

I point out the window. "I think it's obvious now."

Barry tilts his head. "Huh?"

"You were preparing. For this."

The rescue squad receiver mounted on the dashboard squawks to life. "We are initiating evacuation protocol for all residents and businesses within five miles of downtown Stowe. This is not a drill—"

Barry switches off the radio. "Drill this, Skippy."

Rage pulls out his phone and begins to text. "I'm telling Zee to meet us at the school. We need to be together when this . . . whatever it is goes down."

"We absolutely do." I agree.

"I have to admit, the idea of going back to school in the middle of the apocalypse would not be my first choice, or even my last, as a location to ride out the end of the world," Barry says while navigating around a ball of flame that just landed in the middle of the street.

"Oh, we're not riding out anything," I say, and am surprised by the total conviction in my voice. "That thing, Fuego, whatever it is, that's hidden in the altar at school, will help in this fight; will get my grandmother back."

"I take it the conversation with Sam didn't go well?" Barry says while dodging a skidding mailbox.

"You could say that."

"Mica, what happened?" Rage asks from beside me.

"So, I kind of . . . broke up with him."

A chorus of groans and yells of "No!" from the two of them.

"I thought we agreed you wouldn't piss him off?" Rage asks.

I shrug. "I know." They're both staring at me. "What? He pissed *me* off first!"

Barry gestures out at the power lines that are falling along the road like dominoes. "And how did that work for you?"

I fold my arms across my chest. "Fine."

Barry seems awfully adept at talking while dodging flying debris. "I mean, you've pissed off a lot of guys in your day, present company included, but this is the first time it brought on the end of the world. Personally, I think the dude is overreacting a bit."

"Ya think?" Rage responds.

They're chuckling. Both of them. Chuckling.

I'm about to give them a piece of my mind, when a voice booms out from the center of town, so loud it makes the branches of the trees bend, shakes the truck with its timbre.

"MIGUELA! YOU CANNOT ESCAPE ME!"

I look over, and Barry and Rage are frozen, mid-laugh, staring at me with open mouths.

"Not laughing anymore, huh?"

The truck is barreling out of town, and I look back through the guns on Barry's rack at Main Street falling away, dropping into the abyss, clouds of steam rising and twisting in the air. I turn around and close my eyes and think about my responsibility in all this. Sam's here because of who I am and what my mother left me. As we near Barry's farm and Mount Mansfield comes into view, I look up and see that running down each of the ski trails is a river of glowing orange lava. Yep. Right on time.

Barry's gesturing big as he talks. Why is he so f-ing calm? "One thing I don't get . . ."

"Just one, huh?" Rage interjects.

"Why did he wait? He had you right there—why not torture you until you told him where the weapon is?"

"At that point, I didn't know where it was. Abuela and my mom left me notes."

"Your mom?" Rage's voice is gentle.

I nod. "Besides, he knew who I was and what I was capable of, even if I didn't."

Rage adds, "And he knew that Abuela was fully human. She's the key to getting to you."

"Wait, hold up. We're not fully human?" Barry's eyes light up. "We're not fully human! Yes!" He pumps his fist, ignoring the traffic light at the highway connector where the road to the school is, and I give him a look. "I think the apocalypse is a justifiable reason to run lights, no?"

Can't argue with that.

As we turn down the short drive that leads to the school, I see Zee's car sitting in the empty parking lot, her small figure leaning on it.

Thank God she's safe. For now, anyway.

We pull next to her, and the three of us jump down from the truck and join her. Zee rushes to hug each of us in turn.

We find ourselves standing in a circle.

Zee's the first to speak. "What the hell is going on back there, guys? I was at the hospital, and my mother was trying to convince me to head to the Catholic church in Morrisville, not even go back to Stowe. . . ."

I take a deep breath, but before I can say anything, Barry breaks in with "Mica here called Sam out on his son-of-Satan-ness *and* broke up with him, so he's bringing on the end of the world."

Zee looks at me. "Good for you, girl."

"What's good about it?" Barry asks, pointing back toward town.

"He's a gaslighting asshole, Barry!"

I grab her arm. "Zee, he has Abuela!"

"So, let's get her back. What's the plan?"

"We need to break into the school, use this key to open the altar, get whatever weapon is in there, then go back and fight Sam." I list each ridiculous step on my fingers.

Barry leans into the truck and starts rustling behind the seat. "I should have a sledgehammer in here somewhere to break the glass doors. Oh, this is going to be fun. . . ."

"We won't need that, bud. Why should we break in"—Rage is

grinning as he shakes a ring of keys at us—"when we have keys?"

"Where did you get those?" I ask.

"Coach has me put the equipment back after every game."

We run toward the front doors.

After he unlocks the school, Rage flips each of the switches by the door, and the line of fluorescent bulbs flick on down the long hallway. I take a deep breath, then push open the doors to the chapel and find that every candle is lit along the walls, behind the altar, giving the room a warm glow.

"Somebody knew we were coming," Barry says behind me. "You sure this isn't another trap?"

"Yeah. They can't come onto sacred ground. That's why they had to have those crackheads break into the Stowe church."

My eyes lock on the altar, and I make my way up the side aisle with the others following. I take a step up onto the dais and run my hands along the carvings as I have so many school days over the years.

"You've always been fascinated with those carvings. I guess now we know why," Zee whispers.

"I think on some level I always knew."

"So, what do we do?" she whispers beside me.

"We find the keyhole." I pull the necklace from beneath my blouse. The chain and key are glowing again.

"Is it supposed to be doing that?" Rage asks.

"I think so." But the truth is, I don't have a clue.

"Found it!" Barry exclaims, pointing to a hidden hole under a particularly ornate carving.

We all shuffle to the priest's side of the altar.

"See, I read in Revelation 7:2 that 'I saw another angel coming up from the east, having the seal of the living God.' I noticed this weird seal carved right under the lip. Pretty cool, huh?"

He's beaming he's so proud, and I get on my tiptoes and kiss his cheek.

"Nice job, B-Man!" Rage gives him a fist bump.

I step over and hold out the glowing key. We're all hushed, as if witnessing a holy ritual, which I guess we are. I don't have time to feel reverence, though; I just want to find out what this is, get it, and go get Abuela. I slide the key in and turn until a mechanical clicking echoes around the high ceiling of the chapel. I pull the key out and look at my friends.

"What, do we lift up the top, or something?" Rage asks, putting the tips of his fingers under the lip.

Barry grabs the other end, and Zee and I take either side of the middle. "One, two, three!" We all hoist, and it shifts but doesn't rise.

Rage cracks his neck left and right. "Let's give this everything we got. Ready?"

We count again and heave. This time the four of us lift the entire altar off the stone, and I look at the three of them and they're all stunned into silence. Guess everyone's strength is coming in.

When it's clear the top isn't going to budge, we place the altar back down on its dais again.

"Damn, bro! Superpowers activated!" Barry and Rage high-five each other, strutting around, flexing their muscles. Zee is just examining the altar, looking for a way in.

"You guys can pat yourselves on the back later. Right now, we have to get this damn thing open."

After a few more heaves and hoes, it's clear this method is not working. We're leaning against the altar, breathing heavy.

"So, your abuela didn't give you any hints about how to open the box *after* you use the key?"

"No, I—" In my mind, I see Abuela's scrawl on the message board, in the spine of the Bible. I spin around. "Wait, does anyone know what Matthew 7:7 says?"

Barry snorts. Zee shakes her head sadly.

Rage turns around and looks at the altar with me. "'Ask and it will be given to you; seek and you will find; knock and the door will be opened to you.'"

I feel a buzzing in the medal around my neck.

"That's it!"

I grab Rage and plant a kiss on his lips. "Thank you!"

I walk up to the front of the altar, take a deep breath, and knock twice. A rumbling comes from deep within, getting louder and louder until it sounds like the building is coming apart. Just when I think I can't stand it anymore, the rumbling slows. A beat of quiet, then a cracking sound like thunder follows, and the wooden walls of the altar fall outward at once. We each jump back to avoid getting hit. When the walls finish their clatter to the stone floor and the dust settles, we see a silver box with similar carvings sitting in its place on a raised platform.

"You're kidding me," Barry says.

"It's like a Russian nesting doll," Zee offers.

I go to lift the mirrored cover, but it won't move. "It's locked too. Do you see another keyhole?"

Rage runs his hand under the lip of the top. "There has to be a button or latch here somewhere." He crouches down next to me and examines the back while Zee and Barry start circling the box, staring at the surface. I knock again, but nothing happens. It feels like forever that we poke and prod, taking turns yanking on the top as if attempting to loosen Excalibur from the rock.

Nothing.

I bang my hand on the top in frustration. "Damn it! How can we get this far and be stopped by a stupid box?"

Zee puts her hand on my shoulder. "You can't force it, Mica."

"He's got Abuela!" I cry. I see Rage still crouching down and examining the carvings, and I get impatient. "Rage, what's the point? Even if we manage to get it open, I can pretty much guarantee that I have no clue how to use whatever weapon is in there, and there's no one left to teach me how."

"You have to have some faith, M," he says, still running his fingers along the carvings.

I wave my arms in frustration. "Faith? Abuela was going on about faith too, but I had no idea who I even was until last night! If I'd had time to prepare, maybe." I'm pacing now. "Time to train at least. You know that takes years." I stop short and throw my hands up. "I'm going in totally blind here! I can't save anyone! I don't even want this legacy!"

"Why the hell not?" Barry demands. "It's pretty much the most important job in the universe!"

I scoff. "No pressure or anything. Thanks, B."

"What *exactly* did your mother's note say about the weapon?" Zee asks.

"It said 'Fuego is the key.'"

"But what is fuego?" Barry asks.

"I told you! Some kind of weapon!"

"I know that, Señora Cranky Pants. I mean what does the word mean in English?"

Rage is still crouching at the very front of the box. "Fuego . . . that means 'fire,' right?"

"Yes! But why does that matter?"

Rage presses a carving—the one of a flame dancing at the end of Michael's sword—there's a loud metallic click, and the top of the box slowly rises as if alive. A collective gasp sounds around me, and it seems as if the inside of the box is lit as it reveals a glowing silver sword nestled in a bed of red velvet.

"Well, there's something you don't see every day," Zee says with awe in her voice.

"Fuego is a sword," I whisper.

Rage leans closer, examining the carvings in the glistening silver. "Guys, I don't think it's just any sword, I think this is Saint Michael's actual sword."

"Whoa," Barry breathes, staring reverently.

The sword has intricate carvings etched into the blade's surface, twisty flames that reach up from the hilt toward the sharp tip. The hilt is shining silver, an ornate cross at its heart, bookended by shields, and the handle is wood the color of flames.

I'm still just staring at it when Barry elbows me. "Well? Go ahead. You were the one it was left to."

I don't have a clue how to even hold a sword.

Rage says not helpfully, "You could start by picking it up, M."

I glare at him. "Yeah, it's not like they teach sword fighting in Phys Ed, Rager."

Zee whispers nearby, "Do it, Mica. It's in your blood, after all."

Trust your power, Miguela.

I don't remember my mother's voice, yet I know it's hers that I'm hearing in my head. I hold my hand out toward it and pause before grazing my fingertips over its surface. When I touch it and fail to be struck by lightning, I wrap my fingers around the handle and lift it from its velvet bed. It's way heavier than I thought it would be, but still manageable. I hold it out in front of me, admiring the reflection of the candles on its surface.

"It's beautiful," Zee says, and the others nod in agreement.

I Skywalker it over my head with both hands, while imagining the music crescendoing. . . .

Nothing happens.

"Hmm. I don't know what I expected, but that wasn't it." Barry clasps his hands together with a slap. "Now, let's talk strategy as we head back downtown." He steps off the dais, and the others join him. But I'm still staring at Fuego.

Rage realizes I'm not following and turns around. "Mica, you coming?"

"Yeah, I just wish I knew what to do." Then I remember the first half of the Matthew quote, "Ask and it will be given to you." I hold the sword up again. "Mom, please teach me how to use this sword."

The minute the words are out of my mouth, I'm hit with a wall of energy. I gasp when I look around to see I'm no longer in the chapel, but on a hillside . . . somewhere desertlike . . . sword still in my hand but moving, slicing at a pale man in front of me. His blade is swishing by me, but I'm too fast and Fuego is moving like it's a natural extension of my arm, the sharp edge slicing and cutting through the man's velvet jacket with a high whistle. The style of his clothes is old-fashioned, and when my hand comes into view, I'm surprised to find ropes of muscles along the back and hair across my knuckles. I'm a man, a big one from the looks of it. It's still Fuego in my hand, but it's longer, heavier. In the split seconds between moves, I thrust the sword toward my attacker's chest and feel it pierce between the ribs. I push it in farther and watch as realization of impending death dawns in the man's eyes. But before he falls, I'm somewhere else.

And I'm someone else. My body is thin and lithe, and though the sword is shorter, it's still heavy, but I wield it like its nothing. I'm someone young, younger than I am now, and I'm fighting a demon-like creature; its tongue forked and flicking in and out of its twisted lips, the cold black water of an ocean at night lapping at my ankles. I hear the shriek and call of other creatures all around me, the sound of other swords clashing. . . .

Then I'm bouncing up and down, my thighs gripping the wide

back of a dappled horse, the smell of sweat, blood, and fear heavy in the air. I'm swinging Fuego at something flying above, and as I tilt back my head, I see the scale-covered snout of a dragon peer back at me, and I swipe over and over at its claws dangling just above me as it flies overhead. I give one final swing with the entire weight of my body and lop off the creature's foot. The screeching sound is almost unbearable.

Different battle scenarios come faster and faster. I fight creatures and humans, all with the same sword, but its length adjusts depending on the body. Until I find myself back in school. But not my school; I think it's the one from the vision. There are rows and rows of empty desks around me, and as I glance out the classroom door I see the entrance to another in-school chapel, the candle glow inviting. I look down at my clothes and see that I'm my mother again. I don't have time to process this, though, as a low growling begins to vibrate the very floor beneath me. I look up and see a satyr, like the one at the bonfire, blocking the classroom doorway with its massive bulk. Then it's leaping toward me, scaling the rows of desks like a mountain goat. His red eyes are huge and reptilian, and there's saliva dripping from his snout and into his stained white beard.

I shift into fighting stance, Fuego at my side, and wait . . . a heartbeat . . . two, until he hurdles the final row and is flying toward me, cloven hooves spread wide, his scream cutting through the air. At the very last second, I pull Fuego up and skewer him just as he reaches me. Lifting my arms out straight, I throw his body to the side and through the huge plate-glass window next to me, a shower of glass joining the growing smoke outside.

I lean through the empty window frame and see him writhing and sputtering on the sidewalk below, black blood seeping across the gray concrete, when something flies at me through the broken window. Used to the bats in Vermont, I duck, then look up to see a winged creature, its hair flaming like in Zee's vision, closing in. It throws itself at me from the ceiling as I run toward the hallway, swiping Fuego over my head. But in that moment, there are dozens of those shadow creatures pulling at my ankles from beneath the desks, scraping and biting, and I lose my balance right when I get to the open door. I fall face-first and the sword goes clattering across the darkened hallway floor. Then I'm scrambling on my hands and knees, kicking off pointy-eared little demons as I try to reach the sword. My fingertips just touch it through the haze of smoke that covers the floor as I'm grabbed by the back of my jacket and lifted up by the winged creature. It's then that I notice the trio of nuns peeking over the last pew in the chapel across the hallway. I point to the hidden sword, and they nod. As I'm carried out of the school, I see the nuns pull Fuego into the chapel and close the door. Then I'm dropped in the center of the courtyard. As I scramble to my feet, I whip around, wanting to avoid the staff, wishing for a way to prevent my mother's death from ever happening, but as I spin, the smoke thickens, and . . .

I'm back in the present, standing on the dais. I nearly fall from the force of the visions. I stumble and find my balance, still staring at the sword, now hot to the touch, gripped in my hand. Grief pours in as I realize I no longer share my mother's body, but I feel as if each of the ancestors whose bodies I just inhabited are standing behind me in a long row. . . .

"Mica?"

I look toward the voice, and there are my three friends, standing in the same place, looking at me as if no time has passed. As I take them in and think about all who came before, it hits me: I was never alone. I smile to reassure them. "I'm okay." I feel as though I've lived a year or more in the space of those few seconds. I lift Fuego and slice it through the air with practiced technique, the clean swishing sound loud in the empty room.

Barry gapes at me. "She got a download from the Matrix. Did you just get a download from the Matrix?"

I smile down at him. "You know, I think I did, Barry. Old-school style." I look at my friends. "It's time to go get Abuela."

We turn to head out of the chapel. Rage looks back and stops. "Um, is that wood supposed to be glowing like that?" He points to the fallen side of the wooden altar that lies against the far wall.

"What in fresh hell now?" I mumble as I backtrack to the front of the chapel and walk over to the far side of the dais. Barry lifts the piece of wood.

"There!" Zee points, and I see that it's the list of names that ends with my mother.

"Is it burning up?" Rage asks.

"No, it's carving another name." They all lean in closer, but I don't need to. I know what name is being carved there.

When the "a" in "Miguela" appears, they all look up at me.

I shrug, Fuego in one hand. "Guess there's no turning back

now," and I stride toward the chapel door.

"We have to figure out what we're going to do when we get back into town," Rage says as we step into the hallway. He turns to me. "Do we know where Sam is?"

"No, but I know he's got Abuela, just to make sure I go to him. He'll want to make a show of this, I imagine."

Barry hoots. "Well, let's go find him, people!"

Rage whispers back, "B-Man, you could enjoy this just a little less."

I look around at my tribe. I love these people. They're ridiculous and motley, but they're mine. And I'm not sure I ever want to leave them.

We get to the glass doors, and I smash into Barry's back. He and Rage are rattling the long metal handles, but the doors aren't opening. "What's going on?"

Rage takes out his keys and tries to put them in, then crouches down to examine the locks. "They're melted." He stands, putting the useless keys back into his pockets. "Fused closed."

I hear something down the hall behind us and turn around just in time to see a small, pointy shadow scuttle away. "What the hell? I thought they couldn't step on hallowed ground?"

"Only the chapel is blessed," Zee says behind me. "Should we try the gym doors? I think—"

"Make a hole!" Barry yells, and when we look back, I see him raising the heavy porcelain bust that's been sitting over our lockers for almost twelve years.

"B! What are you doing with Beat—"

Barry hurls the sculpture at the glass doors, and they shatter spectacularly across the asphalt along with shards of the bust of Beatrice.

We stare at him, open-mouthed.

"What? I always hated that statue. I mean, who the hell was Beatrice, anyway?"

"Dante's love?" I say.

He shrugs.

"*The Divine Comedy*?" Zee adds.

Nothing.

"We read it sophomore year, Barry," Rage says.

"Maybe *you* did." He laughs, then steps through the now-empty metal doorframe.

"That was a priceless piece of art, you idiot," Zee says as she steps through.

"Well, the way I look at it, ol' Bea just earned her keep," he replies.

"Um, Mica? You might want to see this," Rage says behind me. I look over, and he's pointing at the baseball diamond beyond.

The night is dark, but under the lights around the baseball field, I can see movement, low to the ground. "What *is* that?"

Barry moves closer, squinting in the near dark. "Well, shit."

And then I see. Hundreds and thousands of snakes, slithering across the neatly trimmed grass. "Snakes. Why do there always have to be snakes?"

Zee squints. "And are those . . . spiders?"

A communal shudder comes over us as we see spiders of all sizes delicately picking their way along the edge of the school grounds, skittering over each other in their drive to reach their master. The fields are filled with slithering and crawling creatures and skulking rodents, like a carpet made from nightmares, all heading toward the center of town.

I sigh, loudly. "Well, I think I know how to find Sam." I point in the direction the crawlies are heading. "Just follow his minions."

"We better book it to Pegasus if we want to avoid getting over-run," Rage suggests, and without another word, we're off, all four of us sprinting to the truck at speeds only superheroes are capable of. Zee and Barry jump in the cab, but Rage and I are sidelined by a lawn-mower-size scorpion. We leap into the back of the truck, the vehicle shaking side to side as we land. Luckily—if anything can be called lucky today—the creatures appear more interested in answering Sam's call than attacking us.

Barry slides open the back window from the truck cab to the bed and yells, "We need more weapons, and fast."

"More?" I gesture to his full gun rack between us.

"Oh, I believe in nonviolent resistance," Zee offers from the passenger seat.

Barry pats her arm. "Zee, honey, you know I respect that"—he points to the grotesque army crawling and slithering nearby—"but I don't think they do."

"Dude, we need to get out of here fast!" Rage shouts over the rising hum of skittering creatures.

"On it!" Barry yells to us. "I have backup artillery on the farm."

We all turn around and look toward the road to town. In that moment, the highway begins to bubble and steam, melting into a sticky black river.

But Barry's still grinning. "No problem! We'll just take it off-road!"

He slams Pegasus into gear, and in response, she rears up and takes off toward the trees as if she really does have wings.

XVIII

*The sound of their wings was like the thundering of many horses
and chariots rushing into battle.* —Revelation 9:9

Pegasus, true to her name, is flying over the fields and through the
grove of trees on the snowmobile trail like she was born for it. And
seeing how much Barry is enjoying it, she surely was.

"Now I get why riding in the back of a truck is illegal!" I yell,
holding on for dear life to the ridiculous decorative piping that
frames the back of the truck cab.

Rage is looking ahead, beyond the part of forest we're driving
through. "Coming up on Paine's Christmas Tree Farm." He looks
over at me. "That should be a little less bumpy."

I picture the field of trees. "Yeah, but lots of obstacles."

"This is gonna be fun!" Barry shouts back over his shoulder.

As we approach Lawrence Farm Road, which separates the
land we're on from Paine's, I think about how, every December,
Rage's family takes me with them to get their Christmas tree and

they always buy one for me and my grandmother. Abuela never goes but gives me money to buy one ornament from the gift shop. "Walking around in the deep snow for an hour to saw down a tree in the freezing cold? No. This Caribbean lady would rather have a root canal. You go and have fun, m'ija." And we do, tromping through the snow with Rage and his brothers and sister in our oversized winter boots, throwing snowballs at each other, the smell of pine sap thick in the air, hunting for the perfectly shaped tree.

I'm smiling at the thought when we hit the dirt road with a thump. "This hasn't been that bad so far," I say just as the tires reach the ground of the farm.

Then every tree around us bursts into flames.

"Goddamn it!" Barry exclaims, looking out the window at the cones of orange fire.

"This is insane!" Rage shouts.

"No lies detected!" Zee yells back.

I flinch as flaming pieces of bark pop from the trees, travel on the hot air, and drop onto our clothing. I look over and see the back of Rage's shirt is on fire, so I take off my uniform jacket and pat his back with it until the flames die.

Barry's a good driver, but the burning branches brush against the truck, and the heat is unbelievable.

"Oh, c'mon. Christmas trees? That's just not cool! They're Christian symbols!" Barry yells.

Zee breaks in with, "Actually, they're not. They're pagan

symbols used as early as the fourth century to celebrate midwinter festiv—"

"Zee!" We all yell at the same time.

Rage points ahead. "We're halfway across!"

There's a clearer path through this half of the farm, and it starts to feel like we're going to make it.

"Hey, what's that?" Zee's peering deeper into the farm property, where the fields go back for acres. "There are . . . things, moving between the trees."

After my eyes adjust to the growing darkness, I see the tall grass between the trees bending down in swirling lines, all heading for us. I'm grasping the side of the truck so hard I'm losing the feeling in my fingers. "I bet it's those pointy-eared little bastards!"

Rage turns to me. "What?"

That's when the first little shadow demon leaps for the side of the truck.

"Holy shit!" Rage screams as a half dozen reach the vehicle and scramble up the sides with their pointy fingers.

"I don't think there's anything holy about these little shits!" Barry yells back as a demon appears at his window and reaches through to grab his arm. The truck lurches violently as Barry tries to throw it off, slowing down as he does. Zee rolls up her window just as a demon strikes it, scratching at the glass with its claws.

We veer violently the other way and see that another demon has climbed onto the one that has Barry's arm. The truck is totally out of control now, throngs of creatures breaching the sides of the bed and grabbing for our clothes as the high-pitched sound of their squealing rises higher and higher.

Barry can't see at all now, and the first demon is about to drag its claw across his neck when there's an explosion. The creature's head flies off, and the body disappears out the window. We all look in the cab and see Zee holding one of the rifles from the rack, smoke coming from the barrel.

"So much for being the pacifist!" Rage yells with a huge grin. "Give one here, Zee!"

She tosses one of the rifles to him. He cocks it and aims with one hand, blowing the other demons off Barry's door. Barry grabs one of the rifles as he steers with his knees. Zee hands the other back to me, and then we're all shooting the demons until they fly off in clouds of dark liquid.

"The farm! We're almost there!" Zee yells, but there seems to be a limitless wave of demons coming from all around us, one behind the next like shark teeth. But with Barry shooting too, the truck is slow and hard to control. Plus, they're multiplying.

"There's just too many of them!" Rage shouts as he runs out of bullets and is beating the creatures with the empty rifle. He looks around wildly, sees something, then yells up to Barry, "Bring the truck up to the gift shop!" He points at the small wooden building adorned with a faded Santa and reindeer sign.

"You want some ornaments?" Zee asks, bewildered.

Barry swerves the truck, running over half a dozen demons whose dying screeches tear through the night. When we're almost to the building, Rage puts one leg over the side. "Slow her down, B!"

I grab his sleeve. "What are you doing? You can't go down there!"

He ignores me and leans out, grabbing an armful of the hand saws they keep for patrons, dropping them to the bottom of the truck bed.

"Nice!" I say, snatching a red one and slicing off a demon's head in one swoop. I have Fuego in one hand and the saw in the other, like a demon-killing machine. But I look over at Rage and see him grabbing the tailgate; he's up to something. "What are you doing?"

He winks at me, then leaps off the back of the moving truck.

"No!" I scream as he disappears behind the building. I try to climb out of the truck after him, but there are demons scuttling up right next to me. I stop and hack off limbs with a wave of the rusted saw.

I look up and see several demons changing directions as they run, following Rage. Damn him!

I'm whacking at a pair that are crawling over the floor toward me, when they stop, pointy ears perking up. A mechanical roar rises from behind us as we cross the utility road, and when I look back, I see the arms and legs of demons flying through the air in a spray of black blood. I rush to the liftgate and see Rage driving a huge green-and-yellow John Deere tractor, pulling a massive, spiky hay thresher behind it. The demons are getting pulled into the whirling blades of the thresher and thrown back out, cut to pieces.

"Go, Rager!" Barry hoots from the front.

I look back at Rage, his red hair flying in the wind, his one-sided smile ever present, his strong arms whipping the steering wheel back and forth. He's a total badass, not afraid of anything, mowing down demons like grass.

Has he always been this hot?

Catching up to the truck, Rage smiles at me, then pulls the tractor around the side, overtaking Pegasus. Pretty soon he's driving in front of us, clearing the way of demons as we pass out of the tree farm and onto Barry's family's property.

Barry looks out over the black-spattered hood, turns on the windshield wipers—smearing demon blood and guts across the glass—and coos, "Don't worry, darlin', I'll give you a good wash and wax as soon as this is over."

We approach the large barn, and I can see the outlines of the cows, standing and chewing calmly, as hell literally breaks out around them, shadow demons moving toward the herd like locusts.

"No!" Barry yells, losing his cool for the first time. "We have to get them out of here and into the barn before those . . . things get to them!" He slams on the brakes and is out of the truck before we can stop him.

He yells back at us, "You have to help me get them inside!"

But right then, the nearest cow looks up at Barry, and its eyes begin to glow orange. I look over at the other cows in the field.

One by one, they look up with glowing orange eyes and begin to turn toward us, bowing their heads in ramming position. Suddenly those gentle creatures are fifteen-hundred-pound weapons.

"Barry! Get out of there!" Rage jumps off the tractor before it even comes to a stop. Barry turns around slowly and sees the possessed cows moving toward him.

He puts his hands up. "Good girls! You remember me, right? I feed you—"

By now we're all climbing out of the truck, me holding Fuego tight in my fist. Rage and Zee grab an arm each and start pulling Barry toward the barn while I open the huge doors.

Barry tries to pull free. "No, really! I've known all these girls since they were born—they'd never hurt me!"

But the entire herd is moving closer, stamping their hooves, and staring at us with those glowing Terminator eyes.

The placid cud-chewing bovines are now officially demons from hell.

The front one snorts, and they all take off galloping toward us, the sound of their hooves like thunder I can feel through the soles of my shoes. We rush through the barn doors and barely close and secure them behind us before the creatures hit the barn, their huge bodies like battering rams on the old wooden doors. We step back slowly as a group, farther into the barn.

We stand there, frozen.

The ramming stops.

Silence. Only the snuffling of the pigs in their pen.

We let out a collective breath.

"Yup. We need more weapons," Rage says.

"Speaking of which, nice job with that thresher, bro!" Barry says, and gives him a high five.

Testosterone. Sigh.

Barry continues. "But these are what I brought us here for!" And he proudly points to the wall of farm implements: rakes, pitchforks, scythes. Most of them antiques, all of them deadly.

"Jackpot!" I yell, and rush over to start pulling them off the wall. Soon everyone is there, unhooking, yanking down, piling up rusty implements in a scary, tetanus-threatening pile on the hay-strewn dirt floor.

"Now, we're not going to use these on any of my animals, right? Just the little devil dudes?" Barry asks as he throws a particularly sharp scythe on the pile.

Zee pats his shoulder like he's in kindergarten. "Of course, Barry. We'd never hurt your children."

After the pegs on the wall are empty, Rage puts his hands on his hips in satisfaction. "Now that's what I'm talking about!"

Barry starts back toward the barn doors. "I'll just get Pegasus and bring her in here."

"Wait!" we all yell in a chorus. Barry freezes.

"The possessed cows," Zee whispers. "They're still out there!"

Barry tiptoes over to the door and peeks through. "It looks okay." As he walks quietly toward the truck, we all line up and look out. The cows have dispersed again and are passively chewing their cud, occasionally looking up with their velvet-brown eyes.

The demons seem to have moved on, probably hearing the silent whistle of their master. I shudder.

We open the doors as quietly as we can given their rusted hinges and squealing two-hundred-year-old wood, and Barry eases the truck into the barn. Rage closes the door and bolts it. "Just in case."

We immediately get to the job of loading the farm implements into the truck bed. We work silently, the sound of metal hitting the hard plastic liner like weird, postmodern music. After the last one settles on the pile, it's only silent for a second when we hear a loud snort.

Facing us is Penelope, her tiny pig eyes glowing bright orange, her Buick-size body quivering with fury. She starts to move on her dainty cloven-hooved feet, when Rage yells, "In the truck! Now!"

We scramble wildly; then three of us hurtle into the truck cab. But Barry stops, holding his hands out to the sow. "It's okay, girl. It's me . . . remember me? Good Penny . . ."

I scream out the open door, "Barry! Are you out of your damn mind? Get in here!" All I can think about is *bitten-off kneecaps*. And in that second, as if she read my mind, Penelope charges.

"No!!" We all scream and watch that sedan-size pig ram into Barry right at the knees. He bends backward with a yowl, and as Penelope sets up for another run, Rage and Zee leap out of the truck and drag a nearly unconscious Barry into the cab and I slam the passenger door, tucking Fuego carefully next to me.

Barry's body is lying over our knees when he lifts his head and looks around. "Why are you all in here?" he whines.

I point back to the truck bed full of sharp implements and yell, "You go back there if you want, but I have no desire to be impaled on your rusty pitchfork!"

Rage adds, "And a thank-you would be nice!"

Zee is already examining his leg.

"Ouch!"

"Sorry."

A snorting sound rises from the direction of the pen, and an earth-shaking banging resumes against the barn door, where the cows are.

I look at Zee, who ended up in the driver's seat. "What are you waiting for? We have to get out of here!" I yell.

Zee's looking at the floor. "Yeah, one problem. Who's going to drive?"

We stare at her.

She points. "Stick shift."

A communal groan.

"I don't really know how to drive one of these," Zee says. "Rage?"

He scoffs. "Don't look at me! Gen Z'er!" He puts his hand up. "No one drives them anymore but farm boy here."

Barry yells, "No one is going to drive Pegasus but me!" He tries to sit up and ends up yowling again.

"It's okay! Eleanor Roosevelt said we should do one thing every day that scares us," Zee says brightly.

Barry gapes at her as she smiles back from the driver's seat.

"Besides, you gave me lessons once, remember?"

He grimaces. "Yeah, and I remember how those went."

As if in response, she tries to start the already-running car and a horrible grinding noise echoes in the barn. She turns around, smiles, and says sweetly, "Sorry!"

Barry gets more and more agitated. "Oh, no, no, no, no. This is *not* happening."

"What's this little switch do?"

"Don't touch anything!"

At that, the barn fills with the earsplitting wail of a siren, and a blinding red light flashes in a circle around the rough wood walls and ceiling.

"Zee? What the hell did you do?" I yell over the swelling noise, made even louder by the cavernousness of the barn.

"I'm trying to turn it off, but it's not working. . . ." Zee mumbles.

"Why do you have a siren and light anyway, Barry?" I scoff.

He jerks up to sitting and moans. "Volunteer firefighter? Remember?"

I glance out the side window over Barry's booted feet and see Penelope rear up, her orange eyes ablaze. And then I see dozens and dozens of smaller orange eyes, an army of cannibalistic baby pigs surrounding her. "Zee! You're pissing off the pigs!"

A loud rumbling sound rises from outside, and the barn door behind us shatters. I look back and see cows with glowing eyes barreling through, more shadow demons crawling over their backs, like a hellish rodeo.

We're just pissing everybody off today.

I scream, "Go, Zee, go!"

Zee looks over with a smile, throws the truck into gear, revs the engine, and blasts through the side of the barn, wood splintering and flying everywhere. She pops a wheelie, and the truck careens onto the dirt cow path that runs throughout the farm and eventually ends behind the church.

"This is fun!" she squeals.

That's when I see Barry cry for the first time.

XIX

Its tail swept a third of the stars out of the sky and flung them to the earth. —Revelation 12:4

As we near the center of town, I see the tiny demons rushing from shadow to shadow. It's now the full dark of deep night, even though it's not even five o'clock. The smell of sulfur and ash is thick in the air, and pieces of land have just collapsed inward, leaving behind dark, gaping maws of nothingness. I sit holding Barry's torso as we bump over fields and roads, all of us silently looking out the windows, and I'm grateful to have my chosen family close. Barry jolts with pain and elbows me in the chest. Well, maybe not *this* close.

"It's those things from the tree farm," Rage whispers next to me, his breath tickling across my skin.

I nod, but I'm suddenly very aware of the warmth of his arm around the back of my neck. I can't help but remember the feel of his lips that night at my house. *Not a helpful line of thinking right now, Mica.*

Rage looks out the window. "The church is the only building that still has power."

Barry points several buildings down. "And town hall."

And then I know. "That's where he's holding Abuela."

"How can you be sure?" Rage asks, gnawing on his lip.

"I can feel him now."

"Well, that's not creepy at all." Barry snorts.

"The church is right ahead," Zee says.

"Get us as close as you can," I tell her.

In the distance, the lava makes its way down Mountain Road, exactly like my dream. I look back at the church and see it is almost completely cut off, the land caving in around it. But not the church itself. Warm light beams from its windows like a beacon.

Hallowed ground.

Zee pulls Pegasus up alongside the church—rather smoothly I must say—on a stretch of the only connecting ground left, and we start to pile out.

We help Barry down, and Rage and Zee try to put one of his arms over each of their shoulders, but he snaps, "I'm fine, really! I can fight!"

"Well, let's go out front and see what we're dealing with." I pat Fuego's hilt affectionately and close the truck door behind me.

Rage goes around the rear, grabs a pile of farm equipment, and carries them behind us. For a split second, I worry about him getting tetanus, but then I remember that we're about to take on the devil's children and an army of hell's minions. Tetanus would be the least of our problems.

We make our way to the front, careful to stay close to the building since the ground is iffy. Surprisingly the front lawn is intact, but there's a thin channel of darkness growing around it. The street is a moat of melted asphalt, and evacuees are running down what's left of the sidewalk toward the church. Rage goes to help them over the chasm as Barry hands out weapons to those who want them, and the skiing priest stands in the doorway to the church, herding them inside, constant prayer tumbling from his lips.

I turn to Zee. "Now we have to figure out how we're going to face Sam. Maybe we should divide Barry's . . . Wait, what's that noise?"

Over the shouting of the people and the roar of flames, there's a sound I've heard before. . . .

Beating wings.

"I thought he was in town hall?" I look up, my heart taking off at a gallop, and a massive shape blocks out what little light there is in the sky over the church, huge, leathery wings flapping.

"What the hell is that?" Rage asks, running up beside me.

Then there are seven gusts of flames at once, and heat blasts down over us, scorching the grass on the side lawn. Through a wall of smoke, I see the outline of the creature, which seems to have seven heads.

"It's the dragon from my vision," Zee says.

Barry's voice rises from behind me. "'Then another sign appeared in heaven: an enormous red dragon with seven heads and ten horns and seven crowns on its heads. Its tail swept a third of the stars out of the sky and flung them to the earth.'"

I look back at him. "Revelation again, Barry?"

He nods, his mouth open in awe. "12:3–4."

"Great. Helpful. Thanks."

He seems to break from his spell. "I need to get my crossbow."

Rage puts an arm out to stop him. "I'll get it. You still got a box of ammo in the lock box?"

Barry nods, tosses him the keys, and Rage takes off.

"Grab some—"

"Mica! Look out!" Zee yells, and then shoves me to the ground.

I'm flat on the lawn, Zee lying over me. "What—"

A scream cuts through my words.

I get to my knees just in time to see Zee's feet leave the ground, her torso solidly in the grips of the seven-headed dragon.

"No!" I shriek, and jump up, trying to grasp Zee's feet, but my hands just miss reaching her, as the beast ascends into the air.

Rage comes back from the truck, careening around the corner, rifle in hand, blasting away in the dragon's direction, but he can't get a clear shot without risking hitting Zee.

The creature clears the spire of the church, then heads down toward the river, along the recreation path. "No! Bring her back!" I yell up at the dragon helplessly. I drop to the ground, my mother's sword landing with a clatter. "This is all my fault!"

Rage offers me his hand. "You can feel sorry for yourself later,

Mica!" He lifts me to my feet with barely an effort. "I'll go get Zee."

"No, no, it should be me. I—"

Rage is shaking his head. "I wanted to stand with you, but I think Sam is your fight. My fight is to go and get Zee." He pulls out a box of ammo from his pocket and starts to reload the rifle.

I scream at him, "With what? One rifle? Did you see that thing?"

Barry hobbles up next to him. "And me, the best shot in New England, if not the world." He's wrapping duct tape around his leg, crossbow slung over his shoulder.

"No! I need to come with you! I can't have you taken too!" I shriek.

Rage puts his hands on my arms. "Mica, it's okay, you don't have to do this alone. We're a team; we've always been."

"No! I'm coming—"

Then Rage stands to his full height, his freckled face red and angry, and there's a loud whooshing sound that comes from everywhere at once. With a crisp snap, a massive pair of bright white feather-covered wings explode from Rage's back. They're so large they block my view of the church, but I can hear the gasps of everyone inside.

I stagger back with shock, and my vision gets blurry as I look upon my lifelong friend, my Rage, in all his angelic glory. My mouth opens and closes, but I can't think what to say. I'm stunned, but also, something about it makes sense, like I've always known this was his destiny.

Barry ducks around a wing and gapes at our friend. "Jesus, Rage. *That* is now the sickest thing I have ever seen! That is an entirely new category of sick!" He turns to me. "When do I get my wings?"

Rage looks just as shocked as we do, but anger quickly bleeds back into his face. "I'm going after Zee."

"Take me with you, bro."

I look over at Barry, his injured leg stiff, the silver duct tape securing a rifle as a splint. "What? It's not loaded." He smiles.

My shoulders sink; I know they're right. I look up at Rage, tears clouding my vision. "I have to go get my grandmother. She's all I have."

Rage takes me by the shoulders, his wings bent slightly and enclosing me in their bright white glow. "She's not all you have, Mica. You have us. Just because you're going to face him by yourself doesn't mean you're alone. We're all with you."

Rage tilts up my chin.

I look into his beautiful pale blue eyes, pull him to me, and press my lips to his. His wings curl and wrap around us in a feathery hug.

I let him go and his wings part, raising up high. I grin at the dazed look on his face, turn, start to run full out, and leap over the growing chasm to hell.

XX

Give back to her as she has given; pay her back double for what
she has done. Pour her a double portion from her own cup.
—*Revelation 18:6*

As I jump over the crack in my world, I make the mistake of looking down in that split second. I expect nothingness, oblivion, but
a fire is building and rising from the bottom and its flames are
reaching for me. I land on the other side with a thump that I feel
but don't hear. The roar from the chasm and the screams around
me are so loud I can barely think.

As I go, I hold up my mother's sword, the silver shining as if lit
from within. My reflection burns in the flat of the blade among
the etched flames. My mother's reflection is there too, as she was
in her high school photograph.

I whisper to it, "I swear, Mom. I will find a way to get her back.
Even if I have to go to hell with Sam to do it."

Fuego in hand, I continue toward the town hall as people run past me, heading toward the church. Mrs. Lauzon from the art center grabs my arm.

"Miguela! Where are you going? We're heading to the church—come with us!"

I smile and pat her shoulder. "I'll be right behind you. Keep going."

"But . . . what are you doing with that sword?" Luckily her husband pulls her away, though she looks around just in time to see me turn in the other direction.

As I jog past the burning visitor center, it feels like déjà vu from the vision of my mother outside the school, but this time I'm in my body, not hers. I make my way, thoughts spinning in my mind, grasping at anything resembling strategy. But I'm afraid they don't cover combat with the devil's son in my Christian Culture in a Changing World class. If they did, I would have paid more attention.

And maybe, after this, they should start.

The sidewalk is shaking beneath my feet. Main Street a roiling mass of steam and melted asphalt, the ground broken away and half the buildings swallowed on the other side. As I look up the path that leads to town hall, I know he kept it intact for me, for this very walk. How thoughtful of him.

I arrive in front of the building and face the steps leading up to the columned front, the carefully manicured garden now scorched on either side, black spikes reaching up to the sky for mercy. I hear a chorus of screams coming from up Mountain Road, and I know the lava is almost here, the vision almost complete. My town is about to be turned into a hellmouth taking everything and everyone I've ever known with it. Each nerve ending and molecule in my body is vibrating, telling me to run. But alongside the human fear is the electricity, my inherited power, that's pushing me forward.

It's time to end this.

I take a deep breath and head up the stairs.

It's dark under the portico as I reach for the large wooden doors. I press my hand on the brass push plate, but it's so hot it singes my skin. I pull my hand back, shake it, and push the door open with my shoulder on the warm but not yet burning wood. The lobby is dark and silent, the creak of the door shockingly loud after the hellish cacophony outside. The air inside is tight and stale, like it's been closed off for a hundred years. The door slowly clicks shut behind me, and the lobby descends to near darkness. There's just a slight orange glow coming through the front windows from the fires outside.

I hear a thump from upstairs and the thrum of hip-hop bass coming from speakers, but I don't need those clues to know that Sam is in the theater on the second floor, holding my abuela. The blood is vibrating in my veins in a way I now recognize as a warning of the presence of evil. Fury heats up my limbs, displacing some of the fear, and I start toward the stairs. Seems appropriate that he would set up camp in the theater since everything he's done since arriving has been a performance. Including his relationship with me, apparently. I'm about to step onto the staircase when something slams into me from behind.

I smash into the steps, chest first, pain radiating through my body; then my forehead hits, and I feel my teeth clatter. The sword flies from my hand and clanks across the floor, just like it did for Mom in her last fight. I've barely gotten in the building, and already I've lost Fuego. I scramble for a minute, but then my martial arts training kicks in. I throw my attacker off and launch to my feet, landing in fighting stance.

Rona steps into the low firelight from the windows.

Great. Not enough that I have to take on Sam, but also his creepy Goth-ho sister?

"Well, if it isn't my brother's little pet." Rona's circling me in her own fighting stance, her smile threatening to split her face.

Oh, she wants to talk smack? *I'm* his pet? I'm not the one who jumps whenever he snaps his clawed fingers! I thought you were the *older* sibling. But I bet that's why he's the heir to hell and you're not."

She rears up a bit, and her eyes flame. "Is that what he told you? Father is never leaving his throne, and if he did? It would be me he chooses." Her voice gets louder with each word, and her nostrils flare.

I hit a nerve. Good.

"I'm just here to stop my little brother from starting something he shouldn't."

"Ah, I see."

Rona looks satisfied as she continues to circle me with a renewed smile.

I point at her. "Then you're his babysitter!"

At that, Rona lets out a low growl that I can feel in my chest, and launches at me. I manage to evade her and attempt to sweep my leg under hers, but she merely jumps it, turns around, and gives me a right hook to the face. The impact sends me flying across the room, and when I hit the wall next to the stairs, I reach for my jaw, which feels like it's been loosened from its hinges. Then she's on me again, so I ignore the pain and give it all I can while Sam's playlist blasts a new song from upstairs like a soundtrack.

She goes for another punch to my head that I block, so the punch lands on my arm. It hurts like hell, but at least it's not my skull. I kick at her torso, but she manages to grab my ankle and flip me onto the floor. Normally I would have seen that coming, but Rona is so fast I almost can't see her movements. The impact shudders through my body. I groan as she hovers over me and pins me down.

My newfound powers can kick in anytime now. I use the only weapon available to me in the moment: distraction. My voice comes out as a croak. "What's your beef with me, anyway? Am I not good enough for your baby brother?"

She recoils. "Oh, please. I don't give a shit who he screws. Still, I have to admit, I've been looking forward to this for a long time."

"A long time? How long have you known about me, two weeks?"

She puts her hands around my neck, and I try to work my fingers underneath hers to release the pressure on my trachea.

"I suppose my little brother is good for some things. I thought his book lure idea was ridiculous, but then when it actually worked, I knew I had to get here before he did. I couldn't let him take power when it is rightfully mine."

"Take power?" I manage to eke out. "From me?"

She laughs like a supervillain on steroids and then tightens her grip around my neck. If I don't find a way to stop this, she's going to strangle me to death and that prick will take my abuela. Sam! An idea forms. I look up toward the stairs above us and croak, "Sam!" moving my eyes as if watching someone coming down.

Rona lets go, lurches to her knees looking to the stairs, and I use that second to throw her on her back and get to my feet.

I smile. I can't believe she fell for that. I'd taunt her by pointing that out, but I'm too busy coughing and hacking through the burning in my throat.

When she flips to her feet, it's like something from *The Matrix*. Then she comes at me so fast I have no time to react before she hits me like a freight train.

The next few minutes stretch out into what feels like a lifetime, blows raining down all over my body; my eyeballs rattling in my head from the impact, my shoulders bashing against the floor in rapid succession. I guess she got tired of toying with me and decided to flex her supernatural skills, which isn't exactly fair, but then again, she *is* from hell.

I must lose consciousness for a minute, because when I wake up, I'm moving, or rather, being dragged, across the floor. My hand hits something as I slide, and I manage to wrap my fingers around Fuego and drag it with us. When we reach the wall, she smashes my hand against it, and I drop the sword again. Rona lifts me, sliding me up along the marble wall, holding me by the shirt. Guess she wants to make sure I stay awake for the kill.

As she stares into my eyes with her red rabbit ones, I think of my abuela upstairs, and my chest fills with a pain of a different kind. Will he torture her? Let her suffer in hell for all eternity? *I'm so sorry, Abuela*, I think, and a voice answers in my head, as loud as if she were standing next to me.

Trust your power, Miguela.

Mom?

"I have to say, I'm kind of disappointed. I expected more." Her breath smells like roadkill, and her bony fingers are digging into my chest.

"You disappoint the shit out of me too, hell ho." My voice is still raspy.

"*Hell ho?* I'll have you know, little girl, that I'm Ronova, the Marquis of Hell. And you will treat me with respect." Then she whips a weapon from behind her back, and I already know what it will be when the wooden staff comes into view.

I freeze.

Jesus.

"You . . . you're the Marquis? It was you . . ."

"Who killed your mother?" She smiles as if excited to be recognized. "Guilty as charged."

I stare at her, my mouth dry, tears blurring my vision.

I've clearly given her the reaction she wants, as the smile continues to spread across her face. Then she looks at me, tilting her head sideways, the way I used to find so attractive in Sam. "You look like her, you know? Your mother. I have to admit, she gave me the fight of my life."

Anger burns in my stomach.

"She did well, without her precious weapon. But I couldn't let her retrieve it, and time was a-wasting. All she had to do was give us what we wanted. But those sneaky nuns took off with it. Then your grandmother thought she could hide you from us?" A cackling laugh escapes from her red lips. "I mean, she must have had some help 'cause it took us a tic, but sixteen years for you is a blip for us."

Hatred doesn't even come close to describing what I'm feeling as I glare into this monster's face. "What's in it for you?" I croak.

"Everything. Absolutely everything. You see, if I succeed, I can kill Sam, my father, and rule hell myself."

"Why am I not surprised you'd kill your own family?"

"Speaking of family . . ." She leans in, putting her face right up to mine, and shoves the tip of her staff against my chest. I can feel the sharpened wood push against my ribs, the heat from her rancid breath as she says, "I'm going to kill you the same way I killed her."

"No. You stabbed *her* in the back. Like a coward," I say in a quiet, steady voice, and the anger in my stomach flares to life, spreading through my chest, into my arms, and down my legs. The pain recedes, and that electrical charge blasts through my veins, filling my body, awakening each of my pores. The energy comes up like a flood, and I easily shove Rona on the chest, tossing her across the room on her ass, a shocked look on her face, her staff clattering to the tiles.

Something's calling me. My eyes snap across the floor and see Fuego glowing, like Bilbo's sword but with white light instead of blue. I scrabble to pick it up. As I grasp it, it's as if invisible connective tissue is growing from my skin around the hilt, like it is completing my arm, extending it, just like it did for my ancestors in my fighting visions.

"That's it, isn't it?" Rona says, looking at Fuego like she's a starving person at a buffet. "That's my ticket out of here." Then she rushes toward me, but she looks slowed down this time. Her superfast movements are at normal speed. I leap to my feet in one smooth move and watch her come at me. As she gets within range, I wield the short sword the best I can. Rona manages to dodge the first few slashes, but the last one scratches across her chest, splitting her fitted leather jacket in two. She pulls a weapon from the holster around her waist and hits the blade with another of her own, the clashing of metal ringing up to the ceiling of the empty lobby.

I slice at her, spinning and parrying as if my feet knew only these steps, as if the next was engraved in my mind. I watch as Rona begins to tire, her movements getting heavier. But with one surprisingly strong lunge, she manages to catch the edge of my arm, and I stop, watching the blood trail down the cut sleeve of my jacket, waiting for the pain to hit. But nothing. Rona stands in front of me, breathing heavily.

"Aww! Is the Marquis of Hell tired?"

She growls an answer. "It's this ridiculous form in this shitty place. I can't believe I had to come to this stupid town."

"Well, this is *my* stupid town and I'm going to do what I have to do to protect it. Even if it means fighting a skank like you."

Rona's eyes flare red again, and she launches for me.

I hold the sword up and think of my mother, of what Rona took from me. I begin to trust my power as my mother told me to. Just as she's getting closer, I dodge to the right, duck under her arm, and plunge Fuego into the Marquis's side, slipping the blade between her ribs.

I yank it out and watch Rona look down and realize what I've done. She stares at Fuego by my side, and her face falls, literally, the human facade sloughing away like skin peeled off a chicken, leaving behind a skull with a long, pointed nose, the human cover pooling at her feet as her huge, bent, rodent-like skeleton stands for one second, its empty eyes turned toward me, and then collapses into a pile of black ashes.

I look at what remains of the Marquis of Hell for a moment, then step over and spit into the ashy black pile.

"See you in hell, bitch!" I say, then turn around and head for the stairs . . . and the main event.

XXI

Holding in his hand a great chain. —Revelation 20:1

I feel his presence the minute I turn the staircase corner. I inhale deeply and take the last steps purposefully, back straight, my sword at the ready by my side. Just then, "Soy El Diablo" remix by Bad Bunny starts blaring from the speakers as if it's my entrance song, the vibration from the acoustic guitar track thrumming through the entire building.

Oh no, he's not going to ruin my favorite Puerto Rican artist for me.

That's just taking it too far.

When I reach the top, I see the performance hall is dark in the back, the rows of chairs outlined in faint orange light from the front windows. At first, the audience appears empty, but as I look closer, I see the outline of hundreds of pairs of spiked ears over the back of each and every seat. Just to add insult to injury, they're rocking side to side with the music, like a Disney movie scene from hell. So that's where the shadow demons went. They're all facing the stage, which is lit up, Sam sitting in the center on the big throne left over from the Stowe Theatre Guild's fall production of *Hamlet*.

The real Sam is *so* subtle.

He's slumped down, one leg slung over an arm of the throne, looking bored and tapping away on his phone. The whole scene, complete with demon audience, would be funny except for what is to the right of him.

Or who.

Abuela is two yards away. There's a chair right nearby, but she's standing straight and proud, hands folded in front of her, a resigned but angry look on her face. I let out a long breath. She doesn't look hurt, thank God. But there's a wide golden metal band around her neck, and from it, trailing across the floor and ending wrapped around Sam's chair, is a massively thick gold chain.

I start striding down the center aisle as the hundreds of shadowy eyes follow me.

"Took you long enough," Sam says idly from his perch, swinging his leg off the arm and putting his elbows on his knees so he can watch me walk toward him.

"Let. Her. Go." My voice is loud and steady.

He puts his finger up. "Hold up a sec. Gotta turn down the music." He grins at me. "Like my song choice?"

"A little too on the nose for my taste."

He shrugs. "Sometimes I can't help myself. Where were we again?"

"Let her go, Sam."

"Yeah, not gonna happen. At least not until you and I have a little talk." He looks me up and down as I step into the overflow light from the stage. "I meant to tell you earlier at the diner, but you distracted me. I love the warrior Catholic school girl outfit. Very Buffy and *very* sexy!"

Damn uniform.

He's staring at me with concentration. "And there's something else different about you. You look . . . older than when I saw you a few hours ago. You connected with your ancestors, didn't you?"

I say nothing, not willing to play his game. I get to the last row of chairs and stop. I ignore the turned faces of the demons to either side waiting to see what I do like I'm part of the show. Sadly, I think I am. But not by choice.

His gaze flicks down to Fuego lying against my thigh. "And there it is." Sam's eyes have that same thirsty gleam as his sister's.

I lift it up a bit so the light catches and shines off its surface. "What, this old thing?" I taunt him a little with it, and his gaze follows.

"See? So simple. All you had to do is bring it to me." Then he looks at me. "And here you are."

"Oh, I'm not bringing it to you." I look toward my grand-mother. "¿Abuela, estás bien?"

"Sí, m'ija, pero esto malcriado es loco." She gestures toward Sam.

Sam turns to Abuela like he's affronted. "You assume I don't understand? I assure you, Abuela, puedo hablar *todos* los idiomas," he says with an elegant Castilian accent, then bows.

"Well, aren't you talented." I glare at Sam. "So? Pick a language and talk."

He straightens up. "Oh, so *now* you want to talk? When we were in the diner, you didn't have time for me, but now you do?"

Wow. This is almost word for word every breakup I've ever had. (Well, except for the hell-on-earth part and that he's holding my grandmother hostage.) "Yes. You got my attention and now I'm willing to talk. But only if you let her go."

He looks over at Abuela with a pouty face. "Oh, but Father never lets me have pets, and this one is so . . . feisty." He yanks the chain, just a bit, and my abuela stumbles, the sound of clanging metal ringing in the rafters.

I can't help it, I lurch forward, ready to kill him. But my abuela gives me a look, and I can almost hear her voice in my head. *He's trying to bait you.*

Two can play that game. "Sorry I'm late. I would have been here sooner, but I ran into your sister Ronova, the Marquis of Hell, in the lobby."

A smile spreads across Sam's face. "And you're still alive! Shocking given how hotheaded she is."

"Was."

"What?"

"Ronova *was* hotheaded." I pause, for dramatic effect. Sam isn't the only one who can be theatrical.

He's still grinning, until I see the realization of what I just said land. He gets to his feet, his face no longer disguised by that false smile. "That's not possible."

"Oh, it's possible all right. Your sister is a pile of ashes near the front door if you want to go visit her." I point toward the stairs. "But you might want to bring a dustpan and a broom."

Sam rearranges his face to his default amused but judgy smirk. "Nice try, but fake news. Ronova *does* the destroying. No one can destroy her but my father. Certainly not a weak human like you."

"Well, I had a little help." I hold Fuego up, the lights from the stage glinting off it like the sun. "I mean, you at least suspected it could, or you wouldn't have made this trip." I put the sword down against my leg again. "So really, isn't her death kind of *your* fault?"

Sam lets out a roar that starts from the earth itself, travels through the foundation of the building, the floorboards beneath me, until it vibrates up my legs and through my body. The sound stops, and Sam shakes out his shoulders and bends his head to the left and right. Then he begins to pace back and forth across the stage, his gestures large and exaggerated. "You merely saved me the trouble. I was going to kill her before we went home anyway."

"Wow. The tenderness of your family just warms the heart."

He points at me. "She got what has been coming to her for thousands of years, and because you did it, Father can't blame me for it. But I want to talk about me now!" He pounds on his chest in a cartoon show of masculinity.

"That seems to be your favorite subject lately," I say to buy some time to figure out my next move.

"And why wouldn't it be? See, I'm the one with all the power here." He waves his arms around at me and my grandmother and across the audience of little demon theatergoers. "Is anyone else here an heir to an entire realm?"

Abuela coughs. "Well, actually, Miguela is—"

He cuts her off. "Yes! I know who Miguela is, old woman!"

I point Fuego at him. "You call her 'old woman' one more time and I'm going to slice your pretty little head off."

He stops pacing and looks at me with a big smile. "Mica, always the warrior. It's one of the many things I find so attractive about you."

"There used to be many things I found attractive about you too, until you turned out to be a lava-filled douchebag from hell!"

His eyes flash deep orange and narrow as he looks at me. "Give. Me. The sword."

I look at it, tauntingly, then smile at him and shake my head. "I inherited it. No take-backs."

"Ha! As if you have any idea what to do with it."

"I think Rona would argue. I mean, if she *could* still argue." I grin. "But in her last minutes, she told me she was planning to use it to kill you and your father and take the throne."

He stops, looks at me, then lets out a theatrical laugh. "Classic Rona. Of course, we beat her to it, didn't we?"

"We?"

"Yes, we, Miguela. I had plans for us. Of course, I hadn't planned to fall in love with you, but then I'm like, why not offer her a seat at my side? A literal kingdom! Yet you have the nerve to turn me down? No one has ever turned me down." The last sentence is said in that God voice thing that sounds like it's coming from everywhere all at once.

"Wow. Entitled much?" My expression grows serious. "You lied to me about who you were." I'm surprised to still feel a kernel of hurt in my chest at that. Then I get an idea. "I was falling for you too." It isn't a lie.

Seems Sam can tell it isn't. His eyes soften.

"But I bet you don't actually even look like that. I feel kind of like I've been catfished, 'cause the truth is, I don't know *who* you really are." I'm laying it on thick, but so is he.

"You couldn't handle my true magnificence."

"Try me."

As I look at him, the image shifts like Rona's Instagram posts, and Sam takes on what I assume is his true form. He grows and stretches in front of me, his body covered with iridescent scales the same color as his skin that glisten as he moves. His head is a flesh-covered skull topped by the smallish golden horns I saw for a second in the diner and framed by pointed ears. His legs bend backward like the goat man and end in cloven hooves. And to complete the horrifying ensemble, he sports a fur-tipped tail that whips back and forth behind him like an angry cat.

"I'm going to take the sword as planned, and as a bonus, I'm going to destroy your stupid little hick town, and"—he yanks on Abuela's chain—"take everyone you care about back to hell with me."

My grandmother winces for a moment when the metal collar yanks her head toward Sam, but then she smiles at me.

"Abuela?"

"You look just like your mother."

I smile back at her.

Sam's voice rumbles through the cavernous theater. "Say goodbye to your abuela, Mica."

Sam yanks the chain hard, pulling Abuela to the floor, and I rush the stage, leaping six feet as if they were one.

XXII

Hold on to what you have, so that no one will take your crown.
—Revelation 3:11

I land smoothly on the stage and move right into fighting stance.

"Whoa!" Sam's grinning at me with his freaky skull head and pointy teeth. "Little Mica's fully come into her powers! I'm sure I helped with that." He turns his head. "Oh, Abuela, our girl is all grown up!"

I use Sam's mocking distraction to take a swing at him, but my blade is met by something long, thin, and covered with scales. When the fur tip appears, I realize it's his tail, and it's hard as iron.

Ew.

The tail wraps around my hand, trying to flip Fuego from my grip, but I hold tight, regain control, and wield a heavy blow at his upper arm, which is now a good foot over my head. His true form is way taller than his human one. But the blade glances off the shiny scales.

He leans down and spits fire at me. Nice trick, totally unexpected, but I manage to block my face with the sword, and the fire is reflected off its surface and back at Sam.

No wonder they all want this thing. What else can it do?

I look from Fuego over to the long, thick chain leading to my abuela and get an idea. I see his phone sitting on the arm of the throne. Devil's son or not, I know something he can't do without. I take Fuego and sweep the phone to the floor, where it hits with a shattering sound.

"Oh, shit! Not my phone!" And he rushes over to pick it up in his clawed hand.

I turn, raise the sword, and bring it down on the golden metal like an ax, and the whole length of chain shatters like glass, then disappears along with the collar around her neck.

Abuela gets to her feet, her eyes wide with shock.

I yell at her, "Run!"

Then I'm being yanked backward by the head, my scalp on fire. I flail with my arms and look back to see Sam is dragging me by my hair. I try to hit him with my weapon, but I can't connect; my hair's just too long and Fuego too short.

"Tsk, tsk. You really should listen to your grandmother and keep this wild mane in check, Mica."

He drags me down the stairs leading from the stage, and I feel the thump of each step against my back as I try to swipe at him with Fuego, but I can't reach him from this angle. Then we're moving across the worn wooden floorboards of the theater. I have to do something to stop this caveman bullshit.

I take the sword, swing it around my head, and slice my hair through, just above my skull. Then I'm flipping over and onto my feet before he's even realized what's happened.

Sam's standing there, looking at the bouquet of my dismembered hair in his hands, and I can't help but laugh. He throws the hair to the ground, looks up, and hurls himself at me with a growl. I duck, knocking down two chairs as I catch my balance, sending shadow demons skittering to the floor. He comes roaring at me again, and I swipe the blade around and aim for his neck, but he blocks the blow with his tail. Immediately, I whip Fuego around again, and before he can recover, I cut the end of his tail off, the severed tip with its fur end twitching on the floor. Again, ew.

He looks at it forlornly, then at me with rage.

I shrug. "You made me cut *my* hair."

There's a rustling sound echoing through the theater, and I look around and see that the hundreds of little demons have stood up and are all glaring at me. "Oh, letting minion hordes do your fighting for you is *so* not fair!" I whine, aiming at his ego.

"Do not touch her!" Sam roars in his rumbling voice. "She's mine!"

They sit back down all at once, like a little army.

He throws himself at me again, and then we're tumbling backward, demons screeching and wooden chairs flying around like straw as his blows rain down on me, his claws scratching across my skin until my blood is splattering around like paint. I keep whaling on him with the sword, but the weapon doesn't appear able to penetrate his scaly, armored skin. With each swing I feel my strength decreasing, exhaustion making my limbs heavier and heavier. WTF? What good is supernatural strength and a magic sword if I can't beat Sam?

I manage to get to my feet, stumble, and turn toward him again, but the room seems to be tilting.

He stops and smiles down at me.

We stand there, facing each other, in the center of a circle of ruined wood and disemboweled seat cushions splattered with blood, in front of a rapt audience of his followers, like some kind of improv class gone terribly wrong.

"Sam, there's something I can't figure out." I'm buying time again, but I also want to know. "Why didn't Rona take the sword after she killed my mother?"

He lets out a breath and rolls his eyes. "Your mother had help. All those damn nuns at the school. They took it while she and Rona fought. My stupid sister's ego got in the way of the true mission, and then it was too late. They brought it into the chapel, then snuck it out somehow."

I pictured the trio of nuns I spied while Rona flew me out of the school. I'll never make fun of the sisters again.

"So, what, you're just going to destroy my town and leave?"

His voice deepens with anger. "Be grateful I'm not taking all of humanity with me!"

"Oh, no, you wouldn't do that. Whose lives and hearts would be left to toy with?" I'm breathing heavily, I can feel warm blood pouring down the side of my face, and I'm pretty sure my ankle's broken. "But I agree with you. It's time for you to go, but you're not taking any of my people with you."

He grabs me faster than I can see, and lifts me up so I'm staring into his soulless eyes. I want to look away, to raise Fuego, but I find I can't move. I feel my free will spiraling, all hope leaving my body in a whoosh. I'm falling . . . spinning . . .

A voice comes booming from above.

"Ángel de la Guarda." Abuela's voice.

Sam glances away, and the feeling breaks.

"Dulce compañía." Her voice booming like God's.

I'm able to move my fingers, my eyes.

"No me desampares ni de noche ni de día."

I look at the ceiling as I still hang from Sam's claws. Where is her voice coming from? I look up at the tech booth in the balcony in the back and see Abuela holding a microphone.

"No me dejes sola que me perdería."

The words to my grandmother's favorite prayer fill the room, a prayer to her guardian angel. I finally understand why it means so much to her. I guess we've both always had Mom as our guardian angel. I feel some of my strength return. I look back at Sam, and he's also noticed Abuela. He drops me to the floor, and his face twists with mockery.

"That's the best you can do?" he yells up at her, then looks back down at me with a twisted smile. "Do you really think your ridiculous, pious old grandmother can hurt me with her empty words?" At this point, he bends his huge frame and holds his stomach as laughter racks his body.

"Ni vivir, ni morir en pecado mortal." Abuela's voice hasn't faltered.

I look at Fuego, then back at Sam. I have to end this. But the sword isn't penetrating his scales. . . .

"Jesús en la vida."

He wipes the tears of laughter from his glowing orange eyes and sighs, standing to his full height. "You guys sure are good for a few laughs, but I really have to get going. You know, places to destroy, father to kill." He looks down at me. "I'm going to ask one more time: Are you going to give me that sword, or am I going to have to take it from you?"

"Jesús en la muerte."

"You can try."

"Have it your way," he growls. Then he points up to the booth with his long-clawed finger. "First, I'm going to take care of your abuela since that will hurt you most of all; then I'm coming for you."

I move between him and the stairs to the balcony and hold Fuego up in front of me; I can at least try to take him with me when I go. I will do whatever is necessary to keep him from getting to Abuela. "You'll have to get through me first."

"No, actually. I won't."

The massive gray wings rise from his back with a snap. They begin to flap, wind currents rising from either side of him.

His cloven hooves leave the floor, but he stops for a moment, hovering, and looks down at me. "In payment for your disloyalty, I'm going to rip her head from her body as you watch."

"Jesús para siempre."

I look up into his flame eyes, the wind from his wings blowing my newly sheared hair back.

Trust your power, Miguela.

The fury builds in my stomach, pushing out my chest, along my arms, and then I feel it.

A bursting from my back, a cool wind swirls around me, and I'm lifting. I feel the muscles in my back coming alive to keep my wings beating.

Sam misses this as he's busy looking toward the balcony as he rises. But now I can follow. As I reach him, Abuela and I say the final word together—

"Amén."

—and my sword bursts into blue and red flames in my hand. I pull it back, then thrust the burning sword into Sam's stomach as we rise above the floor. It breaches his scales easily, pushes through his stomach, and out his back, the flames lighting up his body from inside.

He looks down, surprised, and together we slowly sink back toward the floor. He gapes at me, shock widening his eyes.

When his hooves hit the planks, in one swift move, I pull Fuego from Sam's body and hold it in front of me, still flaming.

He bellows, a horrifying sound, like an animal's dying cry. His hands cradle his stomach, the flaming hole growing, spreading to his chest, his leathery wings wrapping around his torso. He stumbles toward the windows, trying to fly out them as the glass explodes outward with the impact of his massive body.

He's teetering on the window ledge when he looks at me one last time . . . then bursts into flames as he falls out backward, like diving off a boat.

I hear running footsteps, and about a dozen demons join me at the window as we watch Sam fall. He gives one last cry before he reaches the ground calling, "Dad?" With that he is swallowed by the fiery chasm in the road, the flames blending in with his, obliterating even his outline. The demons surrounding me disappear with a *pop* sound, then the road knits together and heals up behind him as if he had never existed.

I step back from the window and let out a huge breath, then feel my wings pull into my body and they're gone. I spin around and around, until my swollen ankle starts to hurt.

"Mica, what are you doing, amor?" Abuela appears next to me.

"Damn it! I didn't even get to see them!" I scrunch up my face and try to make the wings burst out, but nothing. I look over at Abuela. "Were they pretty?"

She laughs. "M'ija, they were heavenly."

XXIII

Then I saw a new heaven and a new earth. . . .
—*Revelation 21:1*

Abuela and I are making our way down the stairs from the theater to the first floor, slowly on my swollen ankle, when the whir of electricity coming to life runs through the building and the lights flicker on. When we get to the bottom, I slide my sword into the sheath on my hip. "Fuego, huh? Guess now we know why it's called that."

"Your mother gave it that name. I think she meant it facetiously."

I smile and hobble through the lobby. I stand for a moment next to the ashes of Rona. "She killed my mother." My words echo in the empty room, and my grandmother stops, turns, and comes to stand beside me.

I feel Abuela's arm around me, and I lay my head on her shoulder, never taking my gaze off the ashes, afraid they might reconstitute and start this all over again, but nothing happens.

"Why me, Abuela? I'm nothing special."

She turns me around to face her. "If you thought you were special, you wouldn't be much better than him!" She points up to the ceiling, to the room where Sam had held court. "Proverbs 16:18: 'Pride goes before destruction, a haughty spirit before a fall.'"

I'm about to roll my eyes; then I realize that perhaps from now on I should pay more attention to Abuela's Bible quotes.

"You come from a long line of warriors, Miguela. Your mother could have been the best, but even she couldn't beat this evil."

I look down at the ashes and think of Zee, Barry, and Rage. "But I had help." I kiss her on the forehead, then reach for the front door. When it opens, the ashes of Rona rise from the floor in a cyclone shape, then fly over our heads and out the door, riding the wind, then dispersing to the four directions. I look up and down the street and see the lava is gone, the road repaired and whole as if it had never been any other way, though a slight smell of sulfur still hangs in the air.

Then I ask my grandmother a question that I had asked her many times when I was little. But this time, I'm thinking, she can finally answer. "Abuela, what about my dad? Did he leave because of what my mother was? Because of what I might be?"

Her eyes soften. "When he found your mother outside the school and then found out what she was . . . what our family was, he couldn't grasp it. It happens sometimes; people's minds just can't make the leap to comprehend the divine." She takes my face in her hands. "He loved you; they both did. Never forget that."

"But in the end, he left. And I'm his child."

She sweeps a shortened strand of hair out of my eyes. Even a hell battle can't stop my grandmother from grooming me. "Ay, Miguela. You must forgive him. Not all of us are strong enough to play the hand we are dealt."

"But you are."

"No, m'ija. I told you, I have no pow—"

I cut her off. "You're the one who stayed. The one who fed me, housed me, made sure Fuego was hidden. Made sure that I was safe."

She sighs. "Yes, but I must say, I'm very, very tired. My job was to make sure you grew up and became the woman you were meant to be, whether you inherited the legacy or not. And I could not be prouder of who you've become."

My throat tightens. "Thank you, Abuela. For everything."

She gives me a big smile, something I don't see on her often, but it's like the sun coming out after a storm. "It is my honor, Miguela." She takes my hand. "M'ija, there is something else I want to say. If you wish to go to Los Angeles for college, you have my blessing." She pats my cheek. "You deserve to make your own choices, and no matter what, I will always be so proud of you."

She embraces me, her warm smell of home so comforting. Then we head down the town hall stairs, arm in arm. I look around into the falling dusk's shadows, but I don't see any scurrying demons, no creatures crawling along the ground. The people who had been running from the lava down Mountain Road look confused and lost, the river of red-hot magma dried up to ash and, like Rona, blown off on the wind.

"Mica!"

My head whips around at the familiar voice, and my heart sparks when I see Rage running toward us.

I hobble the best I can with my bum ankle, throw myself at him, and pull him into a hug, blurting questions at him the whole time. "Are you okay? How's Zee? Did you kill the dragon?"

But he just pulls away and stares at my forehead and at the slices in my jacket. "Mica, what's wrong with your leg? And you're bleeding! Are you okay?" Then he looks closer. "And you got a haircut." He picks up a piece of my shorn locks. "Very punk rock." His grin is infectious.

"Yeah, you know. A friend told me it was time to let out the real me." I look around him, and my heart tightens. "Where's Zee?"

He smiles big. "Barry and I followed that dragon across the whole valley, up into the lower mountains until we found it circling that field near Mayo Road. We could hear Zee yelling from the clutches of the dragon's claws. I put Barry on the ground, and he hit it with his arrows over and over, and the dragon was lagging, but we had to be careful so Zee didn't get hurt. I flew alongside it, trying to grab Zee from its claws, but it was too quick. It was about to fly up and over the mountain, and Barry shot one last arrow, when . . ."

I gesture impatiently. "When what??"

"I can't explain it, but the dragon burst into flames."

Abuela and I look at each other.

Rage shrugs. "Must have been some kind of exploding-tip arrow Barry discovered. Anyway, the fire from the arrow spread in the dragon's chest, and then it just . . . combusted. It turned to ash and blew away, so Zee was let go, plummeting through the air from so far up." His voice got tight, and I could almost picture it. "I could see her arms, flailing like a rag doll. She was falling into the river. But I swooped down and caught her right when she was about to hit, with these . . ." And he screws up his face, then stops and looks disappointed. Again.

"Are you trying to . . . ?"

"What the hell?"

"The wings?" I shrug. "Seems they don't come out unless they're needed."

He looks at me. "Wait, how do *you* know?"

I give him a sly smile, and he laughs and pulls me to him, and we hug with our entire bodies, and it feels unbelievably right. I smile at the familiar feel of him, but there's something else, a warm stirring, a heat I've felt before, but this time it's stronger, more urgent. I can tell he feels it too. I turn my face to his, look at his lips, and—

"Ahem."

Oh. My. God.

I feel warmth rush behind my face.

We pull apart and look over at Abuela standing there with her arms crossed. "Raguel, if you two are finished, where are Barakiel and Zerachiel?"

"Wait. Is this why we have such ridiculous names?" Rage asks.

"Ridiculous?" Abuela gapes at him in horror. "Those are ancient and sacred names that have been passed down for generations!"

"Yeah, well, I need to have a long talk with my parents. I mean, lying about Santa Claus was one thing . . ."

She puts her hand on his arm. "It was for your own safety, joven. Now, where are our friends?"

"They're all at the church."

Rage walks ahead, giving us our space. Always so thoughtful, that guy.

I take Abuela's arm in mine. "So, I have wings. What else can I do?"

"Ay, Mica. I told you, I don't know. But I look forward to watching you find out."

As we walk, it hits me that finally, I know who I am, who my mother was. I notice the familiar touch of my grandmother's soft skin, the golden light coming from the church ahead, and I feel like the warmth in my chest is going to burst through my eyes, my mouth, shine like light over us all.

The moon is kissing the horizon near the mountains, the setting sun low against the skyline. For a moment, we just walk and admire the beauty of the town that is our home. Abuela gives a contented sigh. "This was the perfect place, surrounded by mountains, easy to defend, and cold enough during winter that even the

Devil avoids it." She gives me a wry smile. "Though on that point I cannot say I blame him!"

I hear a phone buzz, but I lost track of mine sometime between the flaming Christmas trees and the fight with the Marquis of Hell. Abuela takes hers out of her sweater pocket and peers at the screen over her glasses. I watch her until she puts it away again.

"Text from your boyfriend?" I tease.

"Ha!"

"Well, Abuela, what do we do now?"

"Very soon, the work begins."

"Excuse me? Work?" I gesture back toward the town hall. "Did you miss the Satan's son ass whooping I just dealt out?"

"Yes, but you have so much to learn, and I can't teach you. I wasn't sure you would even have powers, after all."

"But what difference does it make? The threat is over."

She stops and stares at me. "M'ija. You do not think you can kill one of Lucifer's children and not anger him, do you?"

I swallow. "*One* of his children?"

"Oh, yes, he has many. And he will not take this lightly; Sam was his favorite."

Well, isn't that a kick in the ass?

"Then I guess I better stay in Vermont for a while," I say, taking her hand in mine. "Since it sounds like there's going to be unsettled business."

Abuela squeezes my hand. "Then we can start preparing for your training. But now I would like some café con leche. Come along."

"Wait, I thought you said there was no one who could train me?"

"There wasn't, but word of your triumph immediately spread among the celestial realm, and it seems there is a distant uncle we have never met. We will get him here to train you."

"What? How do you know? Did you get some kind of psychic message or something?"

"No, dear." She takes her phone out of her pocket and waves it at me. "By text. It is the twenty-first century, joven. You must keep up."

I laugh and put my arm around her. We arrive on the front lawn of the church and find my friends waiting. They're weary but smiling. I have so many more questions for Abuela, but they can wait until later. For now, I just want to celebrate with my family. I thought they were a chosen family, but as it turns out? Our bonds go *way* back.

Barry limps up to Abuela. "Señora Angeles, may I treat you to some bad coffee and a ham sandwich?" He indicates the open door of the church and holds out his arm.

She pats his hand. "Why, Barakiel, I would be honored." Then for good measure she pinches his cheek. "Such a good boy. Now, let's go. I'm very hungry."

Barry turns around, looks at me, and mouths an *Ouch!*

I laugh.

Almost everyone disappears into the church, but I see Rage hanging back on the steps. I take his hand and pull him closer to me. I like the way he doesn't tower over me; that I can look up at him without straining my neck. That we fit together in so many ways.

He looks down at my hand in his. "So, you're not going to UCLA now?"

"I didn't say that. I'm just keeping my options open."

His raises his gaze and looks into my eyes. "I hope you know, no matter where you go, I'm yours."

My heart warms at how sweet he is. "You'll always have my back, won't you?"

He brushes a strand of hair away from my face. "Always."

I adjust the front of his shirt as if it weren't torn, covered with black demon blood, and smelling of smoke from the bowels of hell. "By the way, you look mighty hot when you're fighting evil, Raguel."

He delivers his sexy one-sided grin and leans toward me. "Right back at you, Devil Slayer."

"Oh, now that nickname I like! And the wings? Maybe there are other kinds of excitement that will bring them out. We can experiment later." I wink.

When our lips touch, it feels like climbing between crisp clean sheets in summer, or being warmed by a woodstove in the winter. A current of joy spreads throughout my body. In that moment, I realize that after all those long years of wishing I was somewhere else, there is no place in the world I'd rather be than right here, right now.

"Are you two done?" Barry is leaning against a column in front of the church, his rifle leg out straight, arms folded. Abuela hugging the priest behind him.

"Yeah! Being abducted by a dragon makes me hungry!" Zee adds from the other side.

"How long have they been standing there?" I ask Rage in a small voice.

"Long enough!" Barry yells. "Now get in here, you crazy kids! The boiled meat isn't going to eat itself!"

We head toward the church, arms around each other, but I stop for a second and look at the moon hanging over the far-off mountains, then glance back into the warm, glowing light inside the church. It is in this moment that I'm certain that this boy next to me, these friends, these people, are my true loves. And I can't think of a better future than protecting them all.

. . . the First and the Last, the Beginning and **the End**.
—Revelation 22:13

ACKNOWLEDGMENTS

It took one hell of a Host to bring this book to life! First and foremost, I am grateful to my wonderful editor, Claudia Gabel, and her team at HarperCollins for coming up with this brilliant concept and for midwifing this story. Special thanks to editorial assistant Sophie Schmidt for her never-waning help and for writing the best tagline EVER. Also, my eternal gratitude to managing editor Alexandra Rakaczki, and brilliant production team Annabelle Sinoff and Nicole Moulaison. Design angels Jessie Gang and Alison Klapthor, and artist Diana Novich, for bringing Mica and Sam to life on our cover and for the badass graphics inside. And as a former publicist I know how hard Lauren Levite works, and Shannon Cox in marketing, thank you! And finally, there couldn't be a finished product without copyeditor Jackie Hornberger and proofreader Jill Freshney; thank you for your attention to detail. All you HP people are DIVINE!

As always, I am SO grateful for Linda Camacho, who has believed in me from day one. She's the best agent, and I'm pleased to call her friend. To my dear friend, author Dawn Kurtagich, for reading the book chapter by chapter and giving me invaluable feedback, not to mention our biweekly Wales-Vermont sanity check-ins! To my mentor and honorary hijo, Cory McCarthy Rose, and August McCarthy Rose for feedback, brilliant advice, and emotional support. Gratitude to my husband, Doug Cardinal, for educating me on farming equipment, talking through plot points on dozens of three-mile walks, and for unerring general support. And to our son, Carlos Victor Cardinal, for plot and character consultation, and teaching me about the horrors of raising pigs.

And finally, to my fellow Michaelites from Saint Michael Academy, class of 1981, (with particular gratitude to class president, Jane Miskell Burns). You inspired the spirit behind Mica, and I hope you found the Easter egg I left you. 🌚